SCARRED: TREY AND AUTUMN

CLIFFSIDE BAY SERIES, BOOK 8

TESS THOMPSON

This book is dedicated to the memory of my uncle Robert Keith Thompson. Gone too soon.

May he rest in peace, making music with the angels.

A NOTE TO READERS

Dear Reader,

I'm so glad you've found your way to Cliffside Bay. What a journey it's been writing these love stories. I first imagined the town and characters at the end of 2017. Since then, I've spent a lot of days with my #ButtInSeat. I still love the Dogs and Wolves and the women they love as much as I did when I started the series with Traded: Brody and Kara. *I hope you do, too.*

If you're new to me or the series, I'm happy to "meet" you. I love to hear from readers, so drop me a note at tess@tthompsonwrites.com. If you haven't read the rest of the series, you can find them all on my website at https://tesswrites.com/. Finally, although each book can be read as a standalone, I think they're much more fun read in order. I hope you enjoy Trey and Autumn's story as much as I enjoyed writing it. Happy reading. Xo

Tess

1

T rey

THE FIRST EVENING of summer smelled of the sea and honey-suckle. A warm breeze kissed Trey Wattson's skin with a promise of the long, languid days to come. All memories of the sulky grey days of the northern California winter seemed only a dream under the clear night sky. Stars twinkled down at them, competing for attention with the white lights strung between the pool house and outdoor kitchen of the Mullens' stone patio. A half-dozen couples danced, silhouettes on the other end of the pool deck. Others mingled near the pizza oven and bar area, drinking beer from etched pint glasses or cham-pagne from skinny flutes. Their laughter combined with a country ballad that streamed through unseen speakers. Beyond the patio, a stretch of freshly mowed grass ended at the edge of a steep cliff, with the sea below. A steel fence kept intruders out and little children in while maintaining the integrity of the view.

Trey sat in a lounge chair just outside the open doors of the newly decorated pool house with his legs stretched out, watching as the party went on around him. Unlike the rest of the men, who were dressed in cargo shorts and T-shirts, he wore pressed khaki pants and a cotton shirt the color of the cobalt-tiled pool. His wavy brown hair, almost tamed by products and a meticulously styled cut, disobeyed by flopping over his forehead. These days, he spent too long deciding what to wear and how to comb his hair. Falling in love with a woman did that to a man.

Next to him, the object of his tortured heart, Autumn Hickman, shared an oversize lounge chair with her friend Sara. Their heads were together, chatting as women do about things men were not privy to and probably didn't want to be. If he'd strained, he might have heard what they whispered to each other, but it was of no interest to him. He was content to sit next to Autumn and occasionally catch a whiff of her perfume.

Kara and Brody Mullen's property was an oasis from noise, traffic, and tourists who would flood the stores and beach all summer. Here, it was as if the rest of the world didn't exist. Thick woods to the south and north hid a cottage and Brody's brother's house. Although not visible from here, the town of Cliffside Bay was five miles down the road, in the valley between two competing slopes.

His gaze fixed on the host and hostess. Kara and Brody, separated by her very pregnant belly, swayed to the music at arm's length like two kids at a Catholic school dance.

Tonight's party was to celebrate the redecoration of their pool house. Trey had spent the last few weeks transforming it from bland to bright and cheery. Kara had asked for citrus colors to brighten up the dried-grass and eggshell interiors of the pool house. He'd combined lemon-yellow walls with lime and orange accents but kept the eggshell cabinets and colors subtle. No one wanted a room that looked like a carton of Popsicles. The outside patio furniture mirrored the inside, including striped lime-and-orange umbrellas, which he'd had specially made.

To thank him for his work, Kara had invited him to the party. He didn't usually run in the same circle as the former professional quarterback turned color commentator and his stunning wife. The Mullens were good people, without a hint of pretention, but they were rich and like finely bred race-horses, stronger and smarter than the rest of the world. Brody was tall with a muscular body made for football and a chiseled face perfect for television. Kara was dark-haired and athletic. A nurse practitioner, she was as smart as she was compassionate. They hung with a group of four other couples, all rich and shiny and as close as family. They called themselves the Dogs and the Wags. Trey was simply their decorator. Not that he was complaining. He and the other four partners of their construction company, Wolf Enterprises, were grateful for their business.

On the poolside dance floor, Brody placed his hand on Kara's stomach. Darned if Trey's eyes didn't sting at the sight of them. What had happened to him over the last few months? As if he didn't know. Right. He knew. He knew exactly.

Autumn had happened. Like a strong riptide, she'd pulled him under and out to sea. Autumn and her ridiculously charming cottage. She'd hired him to remodel the 1940s beach bungalow. What should have been a simple job had turned into much more than that. The job and the woman had changed him. Before any of the walls had succumbed to his jackhammer, he'd fallen into Autumn's current, never to return to his bitter, disillusioned, cuckold self. Or was it former cuckold? Was that a temporary title, expunged after a divorce?

Autumn's presence in his life had turned back time to the

man he was before his heart had been shattered. He'd once been a romantic, a dreamer. A man who believed in marriage and loyalty and building a life with the woman he loved. His ex-wife had killed that man. Like the dish running away with the spoon, she'd run off with their intern. That had been that. He'd fallen from the moon, done with love. Ruined. Shattered. Scarred. His heart transformed into a bitter mass of humiliation and rage. He was no longer a romantic-comedy-loving fool. No, he was a cold, hard lone wolf who watched action films and drank scotch and felt nothing but disdain for his former self.

That had been his intent, anyway. He'd been determined to be a lone wolf, except for hanging out with the other mangy Wolves of Cliffside Bay. His friends were one thing. Sure, he could love the other Wolves and his mother and sister. His heart wasn't totally dead. Just dead to the idea of romance.

Or it *had* been. Past tense. He'd tried to retain the promise he'd made to himself. For months, he'd kept his lovesick feelings hidden first from himself, then from her and everyone else in their lives. He'd pushed his feckless thoughts aside time and again. Yet there they were. Like the honeysuckle's blooms and long summer days, love had come around again.

He loved Autumn Hickman. He wanted her to be his forever.

"Trey," Autumn said, startling him from his meandering thoughts. "You're quieter than usual. All good?"

He turned to look at her. "Yes, just watching."

"Nothing odd there." Her mouth curved into her gentle smile and his stomach fluttered. He'd not known a smile could do that to a person.

"How about you?" he asked. "You okay?"

"Yes, more than okay." Autumn's hair, a color somewhere between brown and red, shone under the lights. She smiled again, looking younger than her thirty years with her fair skin caressed into a pink blush by a few glasses of wine. "Thanks for bringing us tonight."

"Seriously," Sara said, poking her head around Autumn to look at him. "I haven't had a night out in ages." She sighed, seeming slightly tipsy. "If only I had what those two have." She pointed to the Mullens. "I most certainly do not have that, do I now?" Sara was raising her baby daughter alone, with the help of an au pair, after her husband's death.

"You will," Autumn said. "It's only been a year."

"Isn't one year supposed to be the magic number?" Sara asked. "The time I'm supposed to feel better?"

Autumn tilted her head to rest on Sara's shoulder and patted her friend's hand. "Give it a little more time."

"I've had too much wine and now I'm feeling sorry for myself." She said this with a lighthearted lilt to her voice, but Trey suspected the words were very true. There was no timeline for grief. He wished there were.

Sara glanced at her watch. "I should call my nanny and check on Harper. Mimi's old-school. She won't go to bed until I call and tell her I'm fine and what time I'll be home. It's like living with my mother." She rolled out of the chaise with a husky giggle. "This chair's way taller than it was a minute ago." She straightened her dress and patted the back of her auburn tresses. "I'll call her from the house. Too noisy out here."

As Sara walked toward the house, the first notes of an eighties rock ballad came from the speakers. A Journey song— one of Autumn's favorites.

"Would you like to dance?" he asked.

She hesitated, almost like a silent hiccup. Autumn had to ration her dances. Her damaged legs grew weak after a long day. After dinner he'd sensed she was fatigued and had suggested they sit by the pool instead of joining the dancing couples. Autumn had been in a car accident when she was fourteen, both her legs broken in multiple places. Her left leg had been so mangled they'd considered amputation. In the end, they did what they could, including taking skin from her hip to replace what had been torn from her legs. For the most part, through physical therapy and several surgeries, doctors had been able to restore the functionality of her legs. Still, she tired easily and she never, ever showed her bare legs to anyone.

"Do you feel up to dancing?" he asked.

She rested her fingertips on his wrist, smiling over at him. "Do you know you're the only one who's ever asked me to dance?"

"Really?"

"It's true. You, Trey Wattson, are the first man ever to ask me to dance. Men are too afraid I'll stumble and embarrass them or myself."

"I'd never let you stumble. It's my job to make sure you're safe." He would hold her tightly, make sure she didn't fall or trip.

She smacked his shoulder. "What're you talking about? I'm not your responsibility."

I want you to be. Out loud, he said, "Last time I checked, you were busy looking after me."

"How so?" Her finely shaped brows knit together.

"Sara told me what you did the other day. In the city." While shopping for furniture in San Francisco, the ladies had stumbled into the showroom of Wattson and Smith Design before realizing it was the former showroom he shared with his ex-wife. The name had once been Wattson and Wattson Design. Smith was the name of the intern. *River* Smith. A boy with hippie parents. He didn't actually know River Smith's background, but that didn't stop him from making assumptions. The twerp had slept with Malia in Trey's house. Gloves were off, knives sharpened. After all, the little upstart had taken Trey's whole life.

"Oh, that? That was nothing. Any friend would do it." The

lights from the pool threw shadows across Autumn's face. He couldn't be sure, but he thought he detected a hint of triumph in the set of her jaw.

After the divorce, he'd left San Francisco and moved to Cliffside Bay to start another business. A few years into his fledging interior design business, he'd met the other Wolves and agreed to join them in partnership. They were now gaining steady business, and Trey was finally starting to climb out of the financial hole he'd created when he let his ex-wife take everything he'd worked so hard to build.

He could have fought harder, spent more money on attorney fees, but his inner warrior was stuck in the trenches. The humiliation had been so intense, the betrayal so hurtful, that he'd walked away from the entire mess and entered survival mode. Even though he had to start again, it was the only thing he could do at the time.

He now found himself at the other end of his starting-over period. He was ready to live fully without the burden of his bitterness. The past was the past.

"What did you think of her?" he asked Autumn.

"Your ex-wife?" Autumn touched her fingertips to her temple and tilted her head, continuing to look out to the pool. "She's very beautiful."

"I used to think so."

She turned toward him. "You don't now?"

"No. Not when I know the inside doesn't match the outside."

She nodded, smiling as a slightly evil glint came to her eyes. "She was taken aback when we said we knew you. In fact, she went a little green."

He chuckled. "Is that when you told her off?"

"I didn't tell her off *exactly*. I simply told her we knew her former partner and pointed out how well you're doing in Cliffside Bay. I might have dropped Brody Mullen's name as an example of one of your new clients and said something about how you can't keep true talent down, even when someone without any steals his business." She laughed. "I don't know what came over me. When I saw her, I just wanted to make her hurt for what she'd done to you."

"I'm fine now." He lifted one shoulder in a shrug. "I don't care anymore. I'm glad it all happened. Now I have the Wolves and Cliffside Bay." *And you.* "But thanks for making her a little green."

With her face propped in her hand, she regarded him. "Careful now, Wattson, you're losing all your bitter edges."

"You didn't answer my question. Do you want to dance? I'll be there to catch you if you stumble."

She stared at him for a few seconds longer than she should have. Did she know his words covered more than just dancing? If so, she didn't let on. Instead, she held out her hand. "I'd love to dance. At least for a song or two."

He rose to his feet and helped her up with a gentle tug. Still holding her hand in his, he led her across the pool deck to the makeshift dance floor. When they reached where the other couples were dancing, she went easily into his embrace. Neither tall nor short, she came up to his shoulders. She almost never wore high heels; he supposed they were too unsteady. Tonight, she wore a white-and-yellow maxi dress that made him think of a fresh daisy.

He gazed down at her. The swoop of her long eyelashes reminded him of a cresting wave. She nestled against him, resting her cheek on his chest. Her hair smelled clean and sweet. He'd never known anyone to smell as good as Autumn. She shifted slightly in his arms, and a faint squeak came from her throat, as if she were settling against his body for a long nap. A feeling of bottomless tenderness washed through him. If it were possible to hold her with more care, he would. Yet she was as strong and tough as anyone he knew. The pain and rehabilitation from her accident would have taken most girls of fourteen down. Not Autumn. Under her delicate appearance lay level upon level of strength.

Next to them, Zane and Honor Shaw, in a rare night out without their two kids, danced with their bodies pressed so tightly against each other they might as well have been super-glued. Lance and Mary Mullen, having confessed earlier that this was their first night out after their second baby, a little boy, had arrived the last week of April, were currently staring into each other's eyes as they moved around the pool deck. No one looked at his wife with more adoration than Lance. Although a savvy hedge fund manager type, Lance had opened a bookstore to make his librarian wife happy. If that wasn't love, he didn't know what was. He'd had such a great time planning the interiors for the Cliffside Bay Bookstore with Lance. Like him and Autumn, the Mullens had started out as friends before they fell in love. This gave him hope that someday Autumn would look at him as a man instead of just a friend.

Autumn's oldest brother, Kyle, danced with his wife, Violet, near the edge of the pool. They had their arms around each other, almost propping each other up, like those old photos from the 1930s of couples in a dance contest. Violet yawned and buried her face in her husband's neck. They'd be headed home soon. Trey figured four kids under the age of seven made for early bedtimes.

What was it like to go home to a houseful of children with the love of your life? Trey had thought he'd have that with Malia. The bitterness rose in his throat, but not as strong as it used to be. Really only a twinge now. He'd let it go, moved on. Because of Autumn.

He wasn't even sure when his feelings had changed from platonic to love. One day he woke up and knew. *I love Autumn Hickman.*

That truth had frozen him in place. He didn't know what to

do with his feelings. Did he tell her and risk rejection? Was it possible she felt the same way? He doubted it, which kept him from saying the words out loud to her or anyone else. His tender heart, so recently hurt, seemed content to remain hidden.

One day she'd announced her desire to meet a man. *The* man. Then she joined an online dating site, and his nightmare began.

It was the frenzied pace of Autumn's coffee dates that woke him from his apathetic longings and made him want to take a sledgehammer to an abandoned building. The men were everywhere, raising their virtual hands from inside the online dating site. *Pick me, Autumn. Pick me.* This week alone, she'd met three different men for coffee. Men grew from trees on that godforsaken site. All a man had to do was see her pretty face and decide to click *yes, please match me,* as if that made them worthy of Autumn.

Trey wasn't a math guy, but he figured the odds of her meeting the wrong man disguised as the right man went up with every sip of iced latte. He had to do something. His passivity was getting him nowhere. He was disgusted with himself that he'd let his bitterness over his divorce keep him from making his move before she'd put him steadily in the friend category.

He was the one who knew exactly how Autumn liked her latte: two shots of espresso, nonfat milk, no foam, and one squirt of sugar-free caramel syrup. She asked for it over ice in the spring and summer and one hundred forty degrees in the fall and winter. Not that she would make a fuss if it wasn't exact. She wasn't like that. But he made sure, whenever they were together, that she got precisely what she wanted. *He* knew what she liked. Not some stranger. He ordered it for her every Saturday morning from the coffee shop in the Cliffside Bay Bookstore. Or he had, until she'd decided to explore online dating. Now her Saturday mornings were busy with other men. Unworthy men who drew her away from their comfortable Saturday morning stroll down to the coffee shop, where they'd spent hours reading together.

Comfortable. That was the very word that did him in. They were so darn comfortable together. He provided comfort instead of stirring her emotions. And he certainly hadn't awakened any feelings of desire. He was like a Labrador puppy, all soft and fuzzy and harmless. Women wanted a little danger, maybe some mystery, not good old comfortable Trey.

They saw movies together and shopped for antiques or had coffee at the bookstore. All activities that encouraged comfortable silences. These activities had contributed to his downfall. They kept the words stuck inside him.

She lifted her face to look into his eyes. "What is it? You stumbled."

"Did I?" The muscles in his left cheek twitched as they fought to keep his persona intact. He'd once been an amateur at hiding his feelings, but after his divorce, he'd become an expert at conveying a lighthearted stoicism. No one could know the depth of his wounds.

"You're supposed to hold me up," she said, smiling. "Wasn't that our agreement?"

"I'd like to. I want to." The words spilled out of him, pushing against their prison at the base of his throat to break free. "I mean, would you...would you ever consider me... Could I ever be one of the guys you'd let take you to coffee?"

She loosened her grip on his shoulder and punched him lightly on his upper arm. "We go to coffee all the time."

"A date type of coffee."

She went still in his arms and looked up at him with an amused expression in her eyes. Then she laughed. "Very funny. I know your stance on love and marriage. You've only been saying you're done with love and marriage every day since I met you. Anyway, even if you were serious, I would never risk what we have. Eventually, the whole thing would blow up, and I'd be without my best friend." She fluttered her eyelashes and spoke lightly, as if the next sentence was supposed to be funny. "Plus, you like pretty objects, not awful, damaged things like me."

He wanted to say a good many words in response, but now his throat had closed back up and they were trapped once more. If he'd been able to, he would have told her that whatever her scars and damage, it didn't matter. He didn't care what her legs looked like. He knew her heart. And it was as lovely as anything he'd ever seen.

She was right. He liked beautiful things, and she was one of them.

"Why would things blow up?" he asked.

"Because they do. You, of all people, know that."

"I suppose they do," he said as his throat constricted and his stomach lurched.

"And you and me—we're forever. Best friends never leave each other." The dancing couples swayed around them, but for him the world stopped. It was only Autumn's face that he saw. The fierce love in her eyes broke his heart and made it soar at the same time.

"Anyway, stop saying all these weird things," she said. "How much wine did you have?"

"Not much. I promise," he said, matching her teasing tone.

She laid her cheek on his chest. "I'm tired suddenly. Would you take us home now?"

"Sure. I'll get Sara and meet you at the car."

* * *

HE DROPPED Autumn off at her cottage by the beach, then drove Sara out to her place. She lived up a country road not far from Jackson and Maggie's place. They passed by the gate with the sign that read The Wallers and then shortly thereafter, another that read "The Hickses." Kyle was Autumn and Stone Hickman's brother, but he'd changed his name when he went into the commercial real estate business. "Long story," Autumn had told Trey when he first asked about the name change. Later, she'd explained that he'd wanted to separate from everything from his childhood. She and Stone had been estranged from Kyle for over a decade. Just two years ago, they'd reunited, and Stone and Autumn had decided to join their older brother in Cliffside Bay.

Trey had decorated both the Wallers' and Hickses' homes. The Waller place had been a remodel of a crumbling house built in the style of a French château. He'd enjoyed working with Maggie Waller to honor the ornate architectural aspects of the interiors while bringing in a modern feel at the same time. The Hicks house had been the first project he and Stone Hickman had done together and had cemented their friendship and their decision to become partners. The other members of Wolf Enterprises had been added later: David Perry, architect; Rafael Soto, business manager; and Nico Bentley, landscape architect.

Before they formed Wolf Enterprises, they'd jokingly named themselves the mangy Wolves of Cliffside Bay. When Rafael, Stone, Trey, and later Nico and David had decided to partner up, they were broke and broken. In the last year, things had changed drastically for Rafael and Stone. Rafael had married Lisa, a beautiful blonde, currently the "it" girl of Hollywood. Stone was engaged to Lisa's best friend, Pepper, also a rising star of stage and screen.

Sara didn't say much as he rounded a corner and then took a right turn into her long driveway. When he pulled up to her house, with its newly landscaped yard, thanks to Nico, she turned to him. "Did something happen at the party?" The tone of her voice had lifted from its usual husky tone to a slightly teasing intonation that said loud and clear—whatever it was that upset Autumn most likely had to do with him. "Autumn was strangely quiet on the way home."

"She was, yeah." Autumn's silence on the way home, as opposed to her happy chatter on the way there, had been starkly noticeable. He'd thought she'd dismissed his awkward advances as a joke. Her quietness indicated something else. "Maybe she was just tired."

"No, that wasn't it. I've been her friend since freshman year of college," Sara said. "We know each other well. She knew, for example, that moving here was just what I needed...after everything."

He nodded, unsure what to say. *Everything.* What a loaded word that was. Sara's daughter had been only a few weeks old when her husband was killed. Autumn had convinced her to move to Cliffside Bay. Here she could start over and heal. Trey and Nico had done the same after their disastrous breakups. Sara had bought a piece of property and subsequently hired Wolf Enterprises to build her a home. Currently, Trey was helping her decorate the interiors. As an heir to a massive fortune, money was no object, yet Sara was particular, wanting an eclectic combination of unique pieces found at antiques stores and boutique furniture sellers. All of which made an interesting but complex design experience.

He sighed as he gripped the steering wheel. "I kind of hinted that I'd like more than friendship."

Her mouth dropped as her even features stretched long in both directions. "You did? You do?"

"She thought I was joking and then shut me down fast." He placed his forehead on the steering wheel between his hands. "I made a complete idiot out of myself. Worse, I think I freaked her out."

Sara cleared her throat. The leather seat groaned as she shifted toward him. "Why would she think it was a joke?"

He lifted his head to look over at her. "I've been telling anyone who would listen that I have no intention of ever getting seriously involved with anyone. I meant it until I met Autumn."

She scratched behind her ear and narrowed her eyes, staring out the front window. "You *have* been vocal about your feelings on romance. Not that I can blame you. Having been cheated on myself, I know how hard it is to get past the betrayal." Sara Ness had a way of speaking that reminded him of a history professor he had in college. Well-spoken but a bit aloof, as though she was preparing for an eventual seat on the Supreme Court.

"I should've asked her out right away. Maybe everything would be different now."

Sara pressed the palms of her hands against the faux wood strip that ran along the dash, as if working out what to say next. "When thinking about Autumn, you must keep in mind everything she's been through. There's a reason Autumn and I are so close. At school, we were odd ducks in a lake of swans. She sees herself as unworthy of a man like you, so she never lets herself go there in her mind."

"A man like me?"

"Physically perfect."

"I'm hardly perfect," he said, thinking of his height and slight build compared to most of his friends.

She unfastened her seat belt and turned to face him. "I'll deny saying this if she ever asks, but I believe she has feelings for you, too. That said, she's never going to admit to them."

"Why?"

"She's terrified she'd lose you the moment you saw what she looks like without clothes."

"I don't care about her scars."

Sara ducked her head. Her copper-tinted hair covered her face for a moment before she looked back up at him. "It's happened to her before. Twice now. Men she cared for deeply rejected her when they saw all of her, so to speak." Her fists clenched in her lap. "They crushed her. Do you know how brave you have to be to put yourself out there like that when you've been through what she's been through?"

Kind of. Only his wounds were internal.

Sara tossed her hair behind her shoulder. "Men, especially young ones, can be so cruel. Any girl who's ever been called a fatty knows that."

He opened his mouth to agree when he realized she must be talking about herself. *Odd ducks in a lake of swans.* Maybe they'd felt they were ugly ducks instead of just odd. Had Sara been overweight? She wasn't now. Not super thin, but just right, with curves and muscles. He remembered, suddenly, the magnet she had on her refrigerator. *Nothing tastes as good as thin feels.*

"I'm sorry," he said. "Guys can be such idiots." His heart ached for Sara and Autumn. He knew how college had been—guys evaluating girls, rating them on a numbered scale. Jerks. He and Nico had not participated in that kind of thing, but they were witness to it more times than he cared to admit.

"Both of us spent a lot of nights in, watching movies and eating ice cream. Until I stopped eating ice cream. But my body issues could be dieted away. Autumn's can't. With that comes a feeling of hopelessness and a basic distrust of most men."

"I can understand, but I'm not that way," he said. "I adore her. No scarring or misshapen legs can change that." He paused, swallowing against the ache at the back of his throat. "Actually, I love her. I have for a while now. She's my favorite person. I could never get enough of her. *All* of her. But I have no idea how to win her heart."

She gave him a good, hard look. "If you truly love her, then you're going to have to get creative. She will never let you in if she thinks there's a chance you would reject her. If you break her heart, she'll never recover. There will be no more trying. No more coffee dates with these guys she finds online, hoping that one of them will be decent enough to look past her physical imperfections. She'll curl up on her couch with her books and movies and comfortable pajamas and that'll be it." She didn't have to add *like me* for Trey to hear it loud and clear.

He returned her stare, hoping his sincerity showed in his eyes. "I'm not going to break her heart. I had mine broken, so I know."

"Well, then, Trey Wattson, what're you going to do?"

"I'm not sure." His friends might be able to help. The Wolves had promised to always have one another's backs, in both work and their personal lives. Maybe they would help him come up with a plan, as they did for their construction and remodel projects. This would require asking for help and speaking his secret out loud. Not easy for a man like him, but these were desperate times. He must reach deep inside for courage. "I'm not going down without a fight."

Sara smiled at him and patted his hand. "All you need is patience and persistence and total honesty about your feelings. She loves you, which is why she's so terrified to lose you." With that, she was out of the car and bounding up her stone walkway to the double front doors. He waited until she was safely inside before pulling out of the curved driveway and onto the road that would take him back to town and his quiet, lonely apartment.

* * *

THE NEXT DAY, Trey met the other Wolves at their favorite local haunt, The Oar. They sat around a table by the window, sharing a pitcher of the local IPA and eating burgers. Trey pushed his turkey burger around his plate, his appetite suppressed by his lovesick heart. While the others talked about baseball, he looked out the window. Tourist season had wakened their slumbering town. Families carrying beach umbrellas and baskets headed toward the strip of sand at the end of town. Teenagers hung out in clumps in front of the grocery store, playing hacky sack or gossiping and flirting. Young women in bikinis tops and shorts strolled by the business windows, showing off their tans. Surfers, wearing wetsuits with the torsos hanging from their waists, carried boards tucked under muscular arms. Cars inched along Main Street. Drivers craned necks as they looked for parking. They wouldn't find anything downtown. Not on a warm summer day.

And summer had come to Cliffside Bay with a sudden urgency, as if the dormant flowers and trees were anxious to please the sun. Bright-colored flowers decorated the baskets that hung from the awnings of businesses. Red-leaved cherry trees, oaks, and maples dotted the hillside above town. Rhododendrons burst with lush, fat clusters of red and fuchsia flowers. Birds sang their happy tunes from the newly budded oaks that lined Main Street.

Between the lunch and dinner crowd, The Oar was surprisingly slow. The Wolves planned it this way on Saturdays during the summer, often meeting around two for a leisurely lunch during which they talked business. Because they were busy during the week working on the projects themselves, they weren't often all together, as the houses were in various stages.

"Hey, earth to Trey." Nico Bentley's light brown hair caught the sunlight coming in through the window as he set aside the remnants of his veggie burger. After a diagnosis a few years back of high cholesterol, the guy had totally changed his diet. Unlike their college days together, which consisted of burgers, fries, and beer, now it was all red wine, poultry, and vegetables. Looking at the guy, you'd never think he had cholesterol issues. He was a lean and muscular surfer type, tanned to a golden caramel from all his time outside.

"You okay, man?" Stone Hickman slipped an errant slice of jalapeno back into his beef burger. He liked everything spicy, including his fiancée, Pepper Griffin. And no joke, Pepper was aptly named. Stone placed one muscular arm on the table. "You've been super quiet." Stone, as steady as his Pepper was feisty, was also one heck of a general contractor. One only had to look at their completed houses to know the kind of work he did and the integrity with which he approached each endeavor. God didn't make them better than Stone Hickman.

"Yeah, you look a little rough today." Rafael's dark brown eyes focused on Trey for a split second before returning his attention to a steak fry and pool of ketchup.

"I'm good," Trey said. Lying about his feelings came as naturally as breathing. He could thank his father for that attribute. Talking about emotions had been forbidden in the Wattson house growing up. The few times Trey had made the mistake of showing weakness or fear, it had been sufficiently snuffed out by his father's ridicule. "Just a little tired."

"Late night?" David Perry lifted the top bun off his chicken burger and slid the onions off with a swift flick of one long finger.

Rafael's wedding ring flashed gold as he lifted a fry to his mouth, then chewed appreciatively. "God, this is a good fry. I love my wife, but Lisa's trying to starve me with all the salads and bean sprouts."

David, who happened to be Lisa's twin brother, laughed. "The price you pay for living with a famous actress."

Stone shook his head ruefully. "Pepper isn't *trying* to starve me, but given her sudden desire to learn to cook, I just might."

Trey, despite his bad mood, chuckled before taking a bite of his turkey burger. Just yesterday, the fire alarm in their apartment kitchen had sounded off, loud and obnoxious, followed by Pepper's wail of dismay, like two discordant creatures calling out to each other. Other than her mishaps in the kitchen and her natural inclination toward messiness, he would miss Pepper when she and Stone moved into their own house. He'd grown accustomed to her lively ways and curious mind. She was always quick to suggest a party or a game, drawing Trey out of his shell. The sounds of Pepper's and Stone's voices in the mornings made him feel as if he shared a home with a family. A home completely different from the cold, quiet one he'd grown up in, but that was another story.

While Wolf Enterprises had built Pepper and Stone's home on his brother's property, they continued to share a two-bedroom apartment with him in the old Victorian Rafael had renovated into six apartments. When the house was complete, they would move, and Trey would be alone. They were days away from completion. He sighed, feeling sorry for himself.

"Hey, seriously, bro, you all right?" Nico asked. "You're like on another planet."

He met his friend's gaze. Although opposite in personality, Nico was his oldest friend. He was talkative and outgoing; Trey was quiet and reserved. They'd met in college in San Diego and had bonded over their controlling fathers and the expectations that they would follow them into the family business. In Nico's case, he was supposed to join the family law firm like his older brother, Zander. Trey's family had assumed he would follow his dad into the pharmaceutical business. His father was CEO of the company that made drugs for people with autoimmune diseases. As the major shareholder, his father had gotten very rich.

On a beach in San Diego, he and Nico had decided together to rebel against their fathers' wishes. Trey changed his major to design; Nico changed his to botany. Their families both withdrew their tuition money, and the boys were on their own. They'd graduated and both gone on to graduate school, funded by loans and more loans. At the end, though, they'd chosen what they each felt was their calling.

When Nico's fiancée had decided she preferred her bridesmaid, he'd been devastated. At loose ends, he'd gladly accepted Trey and the other Wolves' offer to join the firm as their landscape architect.

Sophie, The Oar's co-owner, approached with a bottle of wine. "Hey, boys. Who wants to taste my latest find from my trip to Napa? Nico?" She held the bottle against her chest. Tall and tanned, with masses of blond hair, Sophie Woods was like a piece of lemon pie: sweet, zesty, and bright.

Nico smiled stiffly, then looked down at his plate. "Not today. Drinking beer with the guys."

Sophie's blue eyes flashed as she backed up a few inches from the table. "Is that how we're playing this?"

Everyone at the table seemed to freeze. Nico glanced up at her, his usual playful expression tense. "We talked about it. You know the deal."

Her eyes filled with tears. "You're an ass, you know that, Nico Bentley?"

"I'm trying not to be. That's the whole point," Nico said.

"Well, you're completely misguided." Sophie turned so quickly her tennis shoes squeaked against the wood floor. Seconds later, she stomped through the door to the back office.

"What just happened?" Stone asked.

"She was about to cry," Rafael said. "What did you do to her?"

"It's what I didn't do," Nico said before burying his face in his hands. He spoke through his fingers. "I had to put a stop to this thing. Before I did something we both regretted."

Everyone knew, including Nico, that Sophie had it bad for him. However, she was only twenty-two and a virgin. Nico was twelve years older and definitely *not* a virgin. Since his fiancée had left him for a woman, Nico seemed to be on a mission to prove that at least part of the female population of California found him attractive.

"What do you mean, put a stop to this thing?" Rafael asked. His dark eyes looked wary, as if afraid of what Nico was about to admit.

"Dude, I find her impossible to stay away from," Nico said. "It's like we're magnets or something. The attraction between us is off the charts. The other night I gave in and kissed her, even though we'd agreed to be just friends."

"She does *not* want to be just your friend," David said with his usual serious countenance. "That's been obvious for as long as I've been in town."

"I know, that's the problem," Nico said. "When she throws that luscious body at me, I'm powerless. Anyway, I told her after our kiss that I couldn't hang out with her anymore. It wasn't right, and she needs to find someone her own age. I mean, it's obscene."

"You're not *that* old," Stone said.

"It's not that I'm old; it's that she's so young," Nico said. "And innocent. It's not for me to take that from her. Plus, there's the problem of her brother."

"Zane?" Stone asked.

"Yeah. He pretty much told me he'd run me out of town if I so much as touched her." Nico took a long slug of beer from his pint and grimaced, as if he really wished he'd said yes to that glass of wine.

"Was he serious?" Rafael asked.

Nico nodded. "I think so. He's protective of her, as he should be."

Zane Shaw owned both The Oar and Dog's Brewery. Although they were half siblings and had discovered the other's existence only a few years ago, Zane had given Sophie part ownership in both businesses. As far as Trey could tell, the siblings were close. In fact, Sophie had been Zane and Honor's surrogate. You couldn't get closer than giving your brother a baby.

Nico ran a hand through his light brown hair. "Anyway, I guess she didn't take me seriously or she wouldn't have come over here all human-sunshine-like and offered me wine."

"You're right not to lead her on," Stone said. "But I don't see why the age difference should matter. Love is love."

"True. Look at Lisa and me," Rafael said. "Beauty and the beast."

"But you two are soul mates," Nico said. "Sophie's soul mate is out there probably working an entry-level job at some company and going clubbing at night. I'm home and in bed by ten after looking in on Mrs. Coventry. Just because there's a physical attraction between us doesn't mean we're right for each other. If she were older, she'd know that."

Before anyone could answer, Autumn walked into the restaurant and made a beeline toward them.

Trey sucked in his breath at the sight of her. She had her hair down and teased into waves around her shoulders and wore tight white jeans and a flowy, pale green blouse. She was without her cane. She must be feeling strong and rested. When she was fatigued, she sometimes used a cane for support, which she'd once confessed to him made her feel like a lonely old maid.

She flashed a smile around the table as she lowered herself carefully into the only empty chair. "Hey, guys."

"You look extra pretty," Stone said. "I don't know if I should let my little sister out of the house looking so good."

"I have a date," she said. "I'm meeting someone for a drink."

Trey's stomach clenched with a sudden rage. He blamed Nico for this. He was the one who had the bright idea about online dating. Then, in an attempt to squelch his jealousy, Trey had offered to help Autumn answer emails from these jerks. That hadn't lasted long. He'd had to recuse himself or risk giving himself away. What he'd really wanted to type as responses would not have been met with enthusiasm on the other end.

"Which one is this?" Nico asked.

"I haven't told you about him yet," Autumn said. "We exchanged an email just yesterday for the first time and he asked if I wanted to get a drink. He said he was trying to be more aggressive, rather than send a thousand emails back and forth."

"One email?" Trey asked. "Is that enough time to assess his character? He could be a total player."

"Player?" Autumn asked. "No. I didn't get that vibe. He seemed forthright."

She was so cute with her innocence and those wide-set green eyes and the way her brow furrowed in confusion when he said something stupid. "Well, goody for him," he muttered under his breath. "Just be careful. You're not letting him pick you up, are you?"

Her small mouth turned up in an indulgent smile. "No, of course not. I'm meeting him over at the Dog's Brewery."

"Is he local?" Stone asked.

"He lives up in Stowaway," Autumn said.

"That's almost an hour away," Trey said. "*Way* too far for him to be able to come see you much."

"It's only a drink." Rafael tilted his head, peering at him with a little too much curiosity. "Let's not get ahead of ourselves."

"Regardless, don't forget what I told you," Nico said. "No compromises. You find a guy willing to give up everything to be with you."

Autumn lowered her eyes. "He probably won't ask for a second date once I tell him how bad my scars are." She'd written into her profile a sentence about her legs being scarred and maimed from her accident. He and Nico had thought it best to leave it out, but she'd insisted. "It's a good way to weed out the guys who would care about something like that," she'd said at the time.

"Then he's not worthy of you," Nico said. "The right guy won't care."

Trey couldn't tear his eyes from her. The sage-green blouse really brought out her almond-shaped eyes. Her complexion reminded him of apple blossoms, white with a tinge of pink. The scattering of freckles over her nose made him want to count every one of them and give her the same number of kisses.

She touched the faint scar on her right cheekbone and looked up at Nico. "This might be a deterrent as well."

"You can't even see it," David said softly.

Trey turned to him, surprised. Other than to his sister, David rarely spoke to a woman unless spoken to directly. He had a shield a mile thick over his heart, which translated into a reserve that could be interpreted as aloofness. But Trey knew better. David was too fragile to put himself out there with most people, but especially women. Finding out your wife was dealing drugs from the back of her minivan with two little kids in the back seat could really mess with a man's mind. Betrayal ate away at you until your only desire was to hide behind whatever wall you could find.

"Maybe not in a dim room," Autumn said. "Which is why I suggested we meet at the brewery." In the right light, the scar on her right cheek *was* visible, even under her carefully applied makeup. He often saw her conceal the area with her fingers in what seemed like an unconscious habit. To him, her imperfections made her even more lovely. She was like a piece of artwork, imperfectly exquisite.

"Don't even think of it," David said. "Be yourself."

"He won't be able to stop himself from falling in love with you," Trey said. Had he said that out loud?

Other than Autumn, who looked back down at her lap, the

entire table turned to him. Well, that answered his question. He *had* spoken out loud. Four pairs of eyes scrutinized him. He went hot, embarrassed. Why had he said it with such emotion, so emphatic? God, he was an idiot. They knew. The knowing glimmer in Rafael's and Stone's eyes told him everything he needed to understand. They could all see he was in love with her now.

"Well, I should go." Autumn stood so abruptly she knocked a knife off the table. "I should just get this over with. You guys have a good afternoon." She waggled her fingers, then headed across the restaurant and out the door. Trey watched through the window as she walked with a slight hitch to her gait toward her car.

When he shifted his gaze back to the table, all four of the guys were watching him. Watching *him* watching Autumn.

He grabbed his beer and guzzled from the glass.

"What is going on here?" Nico asked. "I've missed something, obviously."

Trey shrugged and took another drink from his glass.

"Trey, do you have feelings for Autumn?" Stone asked.

He looked back out the window just as Autumn's car passed by, headed east toward the end of town. She was hunched over with both hands wrapped around the steering wheel. Even from this distance he recognized the tension in her shoulders and the way she clenched her mouth when she was nervous or upset. His heart broke in two at the sight of her, so vulnerable, so brave for putting herself out there, for hoping that love might be waiting at the other end of the day. If she only knew that it was right here. Right here with him.

Stone nudged him with one of his giant shoulders. "Did you hear what I said?"

Suddenly it was too much. Keeping his feelings bottled up inside himself all these months was like holding on to the stern of a boat in a storm. Any loosening and he'd fall right into the ocean. Tears pricked his eyes. Horrified, he brought his beer back to his mouth, but he couldn't drink. He set aside the glass and swallowed.

"Dude, you're in love with her, aren't you?" Nico asked.

Across from him, Rafael shifted slightly and leaned over the table to pat his shoulder. "It's all right. We've got your back. You can talk to us."

"Are you?" Stone asked, with a tone as soft and compassionate as Trey had always wished his father to be.

Trey looked at his hands, helpless to think of any way to explain other than to come right out with the truth. "I'm in love with her and have been for a long time now."

"Why didn't you tell me?" Stone asked.

"Because I'm scared that she doesn't feel the same," Trey said. "I've been humiliated enough by my ex-wife to last a lifetime. I don't think Autumn could ever feel the same way about me."

Stone muttered an expletive under his breath. "That's just her fear talking. It's about her legs." He cursed again. "I can't believe it. I hoped you felt this way, but I didn't think you did."

"I shouldn't," Trey said. "But I do."

"You were helping her with the online dating stuff." Nico was staring at him as if he'd never seen him before, despite their knowing each other for almost fifteen years. "Like a *buddy* does."

"I had to. I want her to be happy, even if it's not with me," Trey said. "Even though I feel like a truck is driving over my chest just thinking about her with anyone else."

"She's told me repeatedly that you guys are just friends," Stone said.

"I'm afraid that's all it will ever be between us," Trey said, feeling more miserable by the minute. "I wasn't ready when we first met. My feelings came slowly...and maybe I was in denial because I was afraid to get hurt again. But they're here now and not going away anytime soon."

"It's natural to feel reticent after having your heart broken," Nico said.

"And bitter," David said. "If only we could go back in time and make different choices, right?" He took a sorrowful drink from his beer glass.

"The ending of my marriage destroyed me," Trey said. "Autumn thinks she's the only one with scars."

David nodded. "It's like the person you used to be vanished with the betrayal, and now all you are is the pain and distrust."

"I keep thinking if I could just start over with Autumn, maybe I could be different, more open, less vocal about my vow to never marry again. That was so stupid. She took all that to heart."

"She doesn't want to get hurt," Rafael said. "That's clear as anything."

"And lose you as a friend *and* a boyfriend," Nico said. "It makes sense that she's kept a distance."

"A guy in Denver hurt her really bad," Stone said.

"I'd like to kill that guy," Trey said.

Stone raised his eyebrows, clearly surprised. Trey wasn't usually the type of man interested in violence. He spent his days figuring out how to arrange beautiful pieces into pleasing living spaces, not contemplating beating some guy's face in with his fists.

"Did she tell you about him?" Stone asked.

"She mentioned him just once," Trey said. "After a few glasses of wine one night." The story she'd told him had ripped a hole in his heart.

"What did he do to her?" Nico asked.

Trey winced, remembering how Autumn's voice had sounded when she told him the story. "She waited a long time to go to bed with him because of her scarring. When she finally did, he told her it was no problem, but he turned out the lights."

"Then bailed on her in the middle of the night," Stone said. "After...you know, with her first. I can't say that word in relation to my sister."

"What a total douche," David said.

No one spoke for a few seconds. Trey was vaguely aware of voices coming from the bar and the clatter of dishes and silverware, but they didn't penetrate the Wolves' vortex. Men rarely talked like this. Certainly not this group, anyway. It was as if they'd created a temporary space where they could put aside their male egos and talk, the way women did. They were so much smarter than men.

Stone bowed his head, then turned slowly to look at Trey. "I have an idea. It's probably a really bad one, but here goes. You said you wanted a chance to start over with her, right?"

"Yes, but that's impossible," Trey said.

"You guys ever see that chick flick, *You've Got Mail*?" Stone asked.

"Sure. Everyone's seen that one," Rafael said. "At least anyone raised by Mama."

"That's the one where they're writing to each other without realizing they know each other in real life, right?" David asked.

"That's right," Stone said. "What if we set up a fake profile on that dating site? You could start fresh. Show her you're ready for a relationship. Open up to her."

The conversation came to an abrupt halt, as if a time continuum glitch in the universe had skipped them forward without any idea of what just happened.

"A fake profile?" Rafael asked. "What good would that do? You'd just be lying to her and once she found out it was you—she'd be really mad."

"But what if they fell in love over letters like in the movie?" Stone asked. "I could totally see my sister doing that."

Nico was rocking back and forth the way he did when he was thinking through a problem. "But those two were both in the dark, weren't they? This isn't fair if Trey knows and she doesn't."

David picked up a knife and tapped the flat side against the palm of his hand. "Yes, but it's true what Stone says. It would be a great way to show her a different side. We all find it easier to express ourselves in almost any other way than verbally. I mean, we're all work-with-our-hands type of guys."

Rafael crossed his arms over his chest, a deep furrow between his brows. "Won't she guess it's him? I mean, if you're really going to get to know her and show her the true you, won't you have to tell her things about yourself? Things she probably already knows?"

Trey thought about the question for a moment before answering. "I'm kind of ashamed to say this, but as much time as we've spent together, I haven't told her much about my family or my childhood. She knows about what happened with Malia, but not how I felt about it. I could leave out the details of my job. I could just say I'm an artist."

"What about a photograph?" Rafael asked. "What will we do about a profile picture?"

That seemed to stump them. They were regular guys, after all, and not particularly smart when it came to deception.

David raised his eyes from where he'd been turning a cardboard coaster over and over between his fingers. "This might be a little out there...a lot out there."

"Go ahead," Stone said.

"She's afraid you can't love her because of her scars, right?" David asked. "What if you flip it around on her? What if you say you don't have a photo because your face is scarred?" He folded the coaster in half and set it on the table like a tent.

Nico's eyes blazed with excitement as he straightened in his chair. "As a way to get her to see how wrong she is—that physical imperfections don't make you unlovable. I like it."

Rafael tapped his fingers on the table. "No, I have a better idea. We're looking at this all wrong. She's a sensible girl. Very practical, right?"

"True," Trey said.

"We raised ourselves," Stone said. "There was no time or money for frills."

"Exactly my point," Rafael said. "I'm thinking you set up a correspondence with her as a friend. He...I mean, Trey, would tell her that her profile caught his attention because he too is scarred, only it's his face." He paused, obviously thinking through the rest. "He should live overseas, so there's no way they could meet. He'd propose an email correspondence to support each other in their romantic pursuits."

"Put him in Paris," Nico said. "It's romantic there."

Rafael shook his head, laughing. "What does that matter? It's not like she's there with him."

"It'll play in her mind," Nico said. "Girls love Paris." He snapped his fingers. "And he should have a woman he's in love with, but they're only friends. Like a parallel story that will open her mind to the possibility of Trey."

Rafael stroked his chin as he gazed up at the ceiling. "Yes, that's good. We want her to see that her thought process is all wrong. There's no better way to do that than see someone else making the same mistake you are."

"This is kind of twisted," Trey said as the anxiety slivered up from his gut to his throat. "I'm not a good liar."

Stone had been quiet during the last exchanges. Trey looked over at him. "Stone, what do you think? I'd be lying to your sister."

"It wouldn't be exactly lying," Stone said slowly. "You'd just be leaving out that Autumn's the woman you're in love with."

"And saying that you're scarred when you're not." Rafael grimaced as he picked up his beer. "That's a big lie."

"But I *am* scarred," Trey said. "They're just not visible."

Nods around the table told him they understood exactly what he meant.

"I painted an abstract self-portrait shortly after my marriage blew up," Trey said. "It's in the cubist style. I could use that for my profile picture."

"Cubist? Like Picasso?" Stone asked.

"Yes. My face is all fragmented to represent how shattered I was," Trey said.

"It's the perfect profile picture," David said. "And definitely not a lie."

"And something Autumn would respond to," Stone said.

Trey asked his friend once more, knowing how protective he was of his sister, "Are you sure you're okay with this? Autumn's your sister. You're the one person at this table who loves her as much as I do."

Stone was quiet for a moment as a myriad of emotions crossed his rugged features. When he spoke, his voice sounded hoarse. "Dude, you love her as much as I do? For real?"

"I'm hopelessly in love with her," Trey said. "She thinks her legs will repulse me, but she doesn't understand that I'm in love with who she is, not what she looks like. We fit together."

"*Everyone* can see that," Rafael said. "We've all been saying it for months."

"Except Autumn," Trey said.

"You love her." Stone slowly shook his head as a faint smile lifted his mouth. "And I believe in my heart she feels the same way about you. We have to do everything in our power to make her see what's right in front of her." He slapped the table. "If I could get Pepper to fall in love with me, then anything is possible."

"Same with Lisa and me," Rafael said.

"You have to go for it, even if the method's a little...what's the word?" Stone asked.

"Unorthodox," David said.

"All's fair in love and war," Nico said.

"Here's to Operation Autumn," Stone said as he raised his pint glass.

"We need a code word," Rafael said.

"Paris," Nico said. "Has to be Paris."

They raised their glasses.

"Polish up those writing skills," Nico said. "You're about to write one heck of a school essay."

"To Paris," Stone said.

"To Paris," they all repeated.

* * *

THE WOLVES GATHERED around Trey's desk in his bedroom at the apartment. He had his laptop open, with Rafael and Stone on one side of him and Nico and David on the other. The irony was not lost on him that five grown men were currently using their considerable creative and intellectual talents to come up with a profile they hoped would entice the site's algorithms to make a match of Trey Wattson and Autumn Hickman.

"Are you sure this is a good idea?" Trey asked for the twelfth time in as many minutes.

No one bothered to answer this time.

"How should I describe myself?" he asked.

Nico tapped him on the shoulder. "Move out of the way. I'll do it."

Trey let him have the chair and flopped onto his bed as Nico typed away. Rafael slid to the floor by the window. Dave sprawled over the armchair.

"Okay, read this." Nico handed the laptop to Trey.

Trey sat up and leaned against the pillows to read.

Nico had given him the handle Artyboy34 and written a short profile description.

"It's not bad," Trey said before reading out loud to the others. "'Artistic soul seeks same. The left side of my face was disfigured a few years ago. I'm looking for a woman who can see through my appearance to love me for who I am underneath the scars. I'm an artist living temporarily in Paris. Decent income by painting portraits of people with their dogs. It's a niche, but hey, who am I to judge?'"

Trey looked up from reading. "Pictures of people with their dogs? Isn't that a little weird?"

Nico shrugged. "It has to be believable. The truth is always stranger than fiction. Plus, I can totally see people paying for a portrait with their dogs."

"Or kids," Rafael said. "Maybe add that."

"No, it has to be dogs," Nico said. "It's quirky and kind of funny."

Trey scratched under his chin. "Is quirky what we're going for here?"

"You're quirky in real life," Stone said. "With all your cooking shows and antiquing."

"And glass ball collection," Rafael said.

"And obsession with textures," David said with a chuckle.

Trey shook his head, as if wounded. "You guys are hurtful, that's what you are. Anyway, here's the rest. 'I like art, music, sports, romantic comedies, cooking, and long walks on the beach.'" Trey laughed. "Long walks on the beach?"

Nico grinned. "I was just messing with you."

"You *do* like walks on the beach," Stone said.

"Yes, but it somehow sounds creepy in here," Trey said. "Like I'm the type who wants to lure unsuspecting young women onto the beach and then murder them." He deleted *long walks on the beach* and changed it to just *the beach* before reading the rest out loud. "The rest is good. 'I'm not perfect and

I'm not looking for a perfect woman, but the woman perfect for me.'"

"I thought that was a nice touch," Nico said.

Trey took in a deep breath before loading a photograph of his painting for his profile picture.

Stone sat next to him on the bed. "There's no way she's thinking that's you." He pointed to a smudge of peach paint near the middle. "What's that?"

"My nose. Isn't it obvious?"

"Not really," Stone said. "But maybe you better stick with your dog paintings."

"My *pretend* dog paintings," Trey said.

"And their masters," Rafael said. "Don't forget that part."

"All right. Here goes," Trey said. He hit the Go Live button. "What if we don't get matched up?"

"You will. This thing matches you by ages and superficial interests," Nico said. "Trust me, there's no complicated algorithm that detects soul mates. I met my Allie on this thing, for example."

"It didn't detect that she liked girls?" Stone asked.

"Unfortunately, no," Nico said.

David uncurled from the chair. "Let's get Artyboy a drink and wait for the response."

"It's not coming anytime soon," Trey said. "She's on her date, remember?"

His stomach twisted at the thought.

 utumn

AUTUMN SPOTTED Troy Billings the moment he walked through the door. He was dressed in tan slacks and a blue button-down shirt. She wondered, absently, how many men in America were wearing the exact same ensemble at this very moment. Trey had told her once that most men chose clothes that were safe, expected. Men didn't want to stand out or be different from their peers. They weren't like women, he said, who expressed their individuality through clothing choices. She'd never thought of it that way.

Trey's wealthy upbringing had afforded him the indulgence of analysis and observation of culture and human nature, whereas hers had been about one thing and one thing only. Survival. When you're poor, it's always the damn weather that decides how painful the day will be. Growing up in a tin can of a trailer with a leaky roof and stained walls and a woodstove for heat, she'd wake a dozen times from chill or, in the summer, suffocating heat.

She'd chosen clothes from Goodwill based on whatever season had to be endured. Food came in boxes priced ten for ten dollars, packed with salt and carbohydrates to fill empty stomachs between subsidized school lunches.

But Trey was of a different place. He came from a world where spaces were made beautiful. There were summer homes and flowers tended by gardeners and sprawling lawn parties. Clothes were about drape and cut and the perfect hue to flatter complexions. Food was arranged on a plate to please eyes and palate with the added benefit of a precise combination of carbs, fats, and protein. Good fats. Not the kind that came in a packet of ramen noodles.

He'd been the one to explain beauty to her. It was about symmetry, he'd said. Even the human face. Those with symmetrical sides to their faces were considered the most beautiful.

Which was why she could never show him her legs. One was scarred from surgeries. The other was scarred and dented. Part of the muscle had been destroyed in the accident, causing a dip near her calf, like someone had taken a chunk out of her. Someone had, of course. The Miller brothers, who'd caused the car accident that had almost killed her and had made her already hard life harder. No more cheerleading—her one joy, her one luxury not about survival. Until they took even that from her.

Never mind that. She must focus on her date. Troy. His name was Troy, not Trey. She must be careful to say the right name.

Troy must have caught sight of her because he waved. She returned the gesture as her stomach turned over, nervous. *God, just let him be the one so I never have to go on one of these again.*

He crossed the main floor of the restaurant. The brewery

buzzed with people. The wide room with its exposed beams and high ceilings felt cold and lonely in the winter, but today happy chatter and laughter filled the space. That was the thing with this town. Without the tourists around, everything took on a hazy, sleepy quality. She knew the old-time residents liked it that way, but she missed the visitors during the winter months. Maybe it was her abandonment issues. Most definitely her abandonment issues.

She stood when he made it to the booth she'd chosen. They shook hands. "Nice to meet you," Troy said.

"Thanks for making the trip." Her thoughts tumbled. Making the trip? Was that even the right word? He'd come an hour to see her, so yes, it was a trip. A commute of some distance.

"My pleasure." He gestured for her to sit before sliding into the booth on the opposite side of the table.

A young server wearing a name tag that read *Stephanie* brought menus and filled their water glasses. Before either of them could order a drink, Zane Shaw appeared at the table. "Thanks, Steph, but I'll take care of these two."

"Sounds good," Stephanie said with a look of adoration at her boss. All the young people who worked for him gazed at him like that, even the boys. Zane was blond, tanned, and muscular with a pair of turquoise-blue eyes. The girls all had crushes on him and the boys admired his physical strength. Fortunately for his wife, Honor Sullivan Shaw, Zane never seemed to notice anyone but her.

Zane smiled at Autumn, then looked over at Troy, then back again at her. He was too polite to say anything, but she knew he knew. This was a date.

She introduced them by explaining that Zane was the owner of Dog's Brewery as well as a good friend of her brother Kyle.

"Your brother and Violet were just in with the kids for lunch earlier today," Zane said.

"All four of them?" Autumn asked. Kyle and Violet had four children under the age of seven. Autumn adored her nieces and nephews. However, when all together, the children seemed to multiply like magnitudes on a Richter scale. One child alone was still one, but four together seemed like sixteen little hooligans. She didn't know how Violet did it every day. Whenever Autumn took care of them, she had to take a long nap afterward.

Zane smiled, shaking his head. "We had to bring out a mop and broom after they left. There was more food on the floor than they managed to get in their mouths. Anyway, what can I get you two? Sophie's got some good red open in the wine bar or I can bring you one of our handcrafted beers."

"How *is* the wine bar doing?" Autumn asked.

"It's taken off like crazy," Zane said. "Sophie was right. The women of this town love their wine."

Autumn laughed. "Yes, we do." Six months ago, Zane and Sophie, his sister, had opened a wine bar in what had been a room for private parties. Sophie had thought it would attract more female customers if they had a haven within the sprawling industrial-type building for book club meetings and wedding showers or even just girls' nights out. They served wine from California and Washington state, all carefully chosen by Sophie. Trey had done the interiors for them—burgundy accessories and dark varnish for the walls and furniture. The result was inviting with a hint of formality to pair with the fine wines.

"And everyone loves what Trey did with the interiors," Zane said. "The guy is so talented."

Trey *was* talented. More so than he realized. He could meet a person and after a short time understand the aesthetic that appealed to their soul. The whole thing was intangible but somehow, he knew. He created clients' happy places. What a gift. She couldn't imagine having a gift like that. As a pharmacist, her contributions to society were of the scientific variety.

What was the matter with her? Trey and more Trey. He so often occupied her thoughts. If he only knew, he'd be frightened by the intensity of her feelings for him.

She must not think of him while on a date. She'd forbidden herself to compare him to Troy or any of the others she'd accepted coffee dates with over the last few months. Because if she did, they would all fall short. No one could stack up to Trey Wattson with his good heart, quick mind, and absolutely symmetrical face.

She reminded herself of the rules. He was her friend. That was all. He would never be anything more than that. Not with her imperfections. He liked beautiful things.

He'd asked her last night at the Mullens' party if she'd ever thought about the two of them being anything more than friends. Although the wine she'd consumed made it now seem more like a dream, she recalled the panic that flooded her as she realized this was a crossroads. Whatever her answer, it would decide their fate. She'd felt this terrible longing to shout, *yes, please, take me home and love me.* But she couldn't. It would break her heart to have him see her without clothing and be repulsed. If that happened, she would never forgive him. And that would ruin their friendship. Anyway, she was pretty sure he was just joking around. If he liked her that way, he would have said so before now. He knew she wanted to get married and have children. He didn't. So they were better as friends. Simple.

While Troy perused the menu, she took the opportunity to examine her date more closely. Other than appearing slightly older than his headshot had suggested, he looked pretty much as she thought he would. Troy was good-looking in a buttered-white-toast kind of way. Not complex like a croissant, but a great addition to a good, wholesome American breakfast. He was tall and thin with sandy-colored hair and eyes that were neither blue nor green but a murky gray. On someone else, they might have seemed mysterious and moody, but peering out of his buttery-toast round face, they were nothing but earnest.

I should like this guy.

They chatted about his drive down from Stowaway. The weather was beautiful, and there wasn't nearly as much traffic as the last time he'd come down. "I could go at my own pace," he said.

"What kind of pace is that?" she asked, trying to sound interested.

"I'm a meanderer. Smell-the-roses type of guy."

She picked up a touch of a New England accent with the broad vowels and tried to remember from his profile information where he was from. *Ask. Make conversation. Be charming.*

"Remind me where you're from," she said. I can't recall because I've gone on a stupid number of dates.

"Just outside of Boston. Go Red Sox."

She gave him another smile, feigning interest. "Do you like sports?"

"Sure. Doesn't everyone?" he asked.

Not really.

Zane arrived with their drinks. After initial sips, they fell into an awkward silence.

"What about you?" Troy asked finally. He wiped the condensation from the pint glass with a napkin.

"I'm sorry?"

"Do you like sports?"

"Oh, sure, yes. My brothers love football." *I love watching football with Trey.*

He tugged on his ear. "Is it true Brody Mullen lives here?"

She tilted her head, watching his buttered-toast face carefully. Was he making conversation or fishing to see if she knew Brody Mullen? Brody had once been the best quarterback in professional football until an injury a few years ago took him out of the game. Now he was a color commentator for one of the sports channels. She did in fact know him. He was one of Kyle's best friends. The Mullens were fiercely private about their personal life. Kara was never photographed with her famous husband. She made sure their baby boy was kept from the public as well. Kara was currently pregnant with their second child—a girl they would name Ruby Sloan Mullen. Autumn thought that was about the cutest name she'd ever heard. She'd struggled not to feel jealous when Kara had told her, but she had been. Terrible and ugly jealousy had burned her stomach. She disliked herself for it, but really, how much could a girl endure? Everyone was getting married and having babies. Meanwhile, she was on yet another online date, praying to God that he might be the one.

Autumn was sometimes invited to the Mullens' house for parties or dinner because of Kyle's close friendship with Brody. She'd been there just last night with Trey. Celebrating his latest beautiful design.

Do not think about Trey.

"Who's that now?" she asked, pretending she hadn't heard him right.

"Brody Mullen. You don't know who he is?"

"Football, right?" she asked.

"Yes, football." A note of ridicule edged his voice. "I'm pretty sure he lives here."

Once again, she studied her companion carefully. Most likely he was simply curious if the rumors were true and wondered if she had any inside scoop on the famous athlete. Yet her instinct told her to stay away from this topic. "I don't think so. It's just a rumor as far as I know."

He looked disappointed. "That's too bad. I was hoping to run into him. Huge fan."

"This is a small town. The people here are very private. So even if he did live here, no one would tell you."

He lifted his eyebrows. "So maybe he does live here, and you just don't know it."

"Could be. I haven't lived here that long. The natives are protective of their own. They hate that it's become such a popular vacation destination." Thanks to Kyle's lodge and spa, the town was busier with tourists than it had ever been. "Tell me about your work." Anything to get off the subject of Brody Mullen.

They chatted for another fifteen minutes. The conversation grew easier as time passed. However, the more he talked, the more confused she became about his profession, until it finally occurred to her that he was not an attorney, but a legal secretary. Had he out-and-out lied about that on the profile, or had she just assumed it by something she read? How subtle wording could be.

"What's up with your leg?" he asked as he finished the last of his beer. "You mentioned in your profile that you walk with a limp and there's some scarring. Did you say it was because of an accident?"

"That's right. A car accident when I was fourteen." She sat on her hand to keep from touching the scar on her cheekbone.

"Sorry to hear that. It sure isn't obvious with what you've got on."

"No, but I like to be up-front about it on the dating sites. It's a deterrent to some."

"Well, they must be pretty shallow."

She'd love to test this guy right here and now. She imagined lifting her pant leg to show him. No one had ever brought it up on a first date.

"I mean, like, how bad is it?" he asked as he motioned to Stephanie for another round.

No one had ever asked her that question, either. "Bad enough that I don't wear short skirts." The shame crept up her neck and heated her cheeks. Who did this guy think he was to ask her such intimate questions on a first date?

A muscle in his neck twitched. "We could go back to your place and you could show me. You're super pretty. I wouldn't care much about a little scar on a leg, trust me."

Stephanie brought their drinks, giving her an opportunity to think through her escape. When the girl left, Autumn took a long drag of her wine, then set it down and fixed her eyes upon him. His earnest face didn't match his heart. He was a man hoping to get laid by the woman with the lame leg, figuring it was a sure bet. He'd probably ask her to turn off the lights. It was a good thing there was no silverware on the table. She'd love to stab him with a fork.

Instead, she reached for her purse and pulled out enough cash to cover her own drinks. She set it on the table and turned back to Troy. "When I was a kid, we lived near a pig farm. If you haven't ever seen a pig close up, you might be surprised to know they're cute, with their dumb pink faces and fuzzy ears. But nothing could disguise the foul smell that hovered over that farm. You can be outwardly nice-looking, but nothing can hide the stench that comes from being a pig. And you, my friend, are a pig." She stood and clutched her purse to her chest. "I'll be going. Don't bother to call."

* * *

LATER, she let herself into her cottage and slipped out of her sandals. She should make something to eat but didn't know if she had the energy. She thought about calling Sara to see if she wanted to come over with Harper Reese, but she was probably in the middle of dinner and bath time. They'd always been so close, but lately, the divide between them seemed large. Sara was a mother. She had a little person who needed most of what she had to give. Sara didn't have time for Autumn.

Autumn had time. Way too much time.

She wandered around the cottage, turning on a few lamps and adjusting throw pillows that didn't need attention. Built in the forties when Cliffside Bay had been a small fishing town, her cottage was nestled at the foot of the southern hill. Back then, the style had been small, enclosed rooms. Trey had suggested they knock down the walls and make one great room. She'd agreed to that as well as installing a set of French doors out to the patio. Doing so had given it an open, airy feel, despite its fairly small footprint.

There was not a day that she didn't stop for a moment and take in the beauty of her cottage. Her home. Trey had been so instrumental in helping her decide what they should keep and what they should change. Not much had stayed.

She'd made sure he knew from the beginning that any hint of dark or dingy was unwelcome. Nothing that would remind her of the trailer they lived in as children. During their initial meeting, he'd nodded and taken notes without comment. When they met a week later, he had an entire proposal drawn out with paint and color swatches. His suggestions for the furniture were done in pencil drawings.

They'd gone with simple decor, since the space could easily look cluttered. The walls were a pale green with cream trim. The same cream had been used on the cabinets in the kitchen. Counters and the island were covered with white granite. Sea-glass green and black were used for accent colors. Flooring had been cut into wide planks salvaged from an old barn. A restored farmhouse table just off the kitchen looked out to the view. Soft, comfortable couches and chairs were arranged around a gas fireplace in the sitting area.

The small square footage was of no consequence to her. She was only one person, and compared to the house she'd grown up in, this was her own version of a mansion. Also, there was the view of the sandy beach and ocean from her back windows. From almost everywhere in the great room, she could see the cement walking path that ran the length of the beach. Some might not like being so close to so much activity, but she found it comforting. She loved to sit on her wood patio and watch the runners and walkers go by or surfers catching waves. Being here made her feel part of something instead of the isolation she'd experienced for so much of her life.

Her stomach growled, reminding her that she was hungry. She changed into sweats and a T-shirt, then heated a frozen dinner in the microwave. She sat at the table to eat and watched the sunset in her sliver of the world. Some nights, mother sun painted the sky in pink and orange as she played with the clouds. Tonight, though, she was a round golden globe of polished glass hovering between the blue sky and sea.

In her peripheral vision, she noticed a movement in the sliver of space between two of her tall flowerpots. She turned toward the far left corner of her patio, hoping to catch a glimpse of one of the little boys from next door. A family with four boys stayed in the house during the summer months. Autumn knew the mother only by sight and a wave here or there, but she seemed nice and definitely kept to herself. Given the Range Rover and Mercedes in their driveway, she assumed they were a wealthy family from San Francisco. The husband stayed only on weekends, most likely working in the city during the week.

City ordinances made fences illegal for the houses built so close to the boardwalk and beach. A four-foot patch of grass separated her patio and the cement boardwalk. Her neighbors' yards began where her patio ended. To give herself a little privacy on either side, Nico had suggested tall blue planters. Filled with annuals, the splashes of pink, purple, and yellow flowers contrasted nicely with the sand, grass, and sea. Although they didn't provide privacy from the people who strolled along the boardwalk, they helped to give a sense of some separation from her neighbors while she enjoyed her outdoor seating.

She rose from the table and went upstairs to investigate further from her bedroom windows, which overlooked the small yard. Several times from this vantage point, she'd seen the little boys crouched in the shade of the planters playing with their cars. She fully expected to see them in the same patch of grass now. But instead of seeing one of the boys behind the pots, she saw a man crouched there. Had he dropped something?

He stood and looked around, as if making sure no one had spotted him. A baseball cap and dark glasses hid most of his face. He wore long shorts and a T-shirt, like most of the beach-combers. Nothing unusual there. He was tall enough to see over the planters. He looked toward her house and squinted. Alarmed, she brought a hand to her throat. Why was he looking at her house? A second later, he dropped to his knees and started feeling around in the grass. He must have dropped his keys. That was all. He brushed his hands on his shorts and then walked toward the boardwalk. Once there he strode away at a pace just under a run.

She shrugged it off and went back downstairs.

She ate the rest of her dinner, enjoying her view. Many evenings were like this. This was her life. Simple and without fuss, surrounded by beauty. She had more than most: a good job, lovely house, great friends, her brothers and nieces and nephews. Complaining, even to just herself, seemed wrong. Yet she was lonely. Perhaps admitting that wasn't a crime even if she should be only grateful, without further requests from God.

But if she had someone to share her blessed life with, everything would be that much sweeter.

Months before, she'd made it a goal to at least try to meet someone. Thus, the online dating site.

She'd gone on at least a dozen first dates over the last few months. Most of them were with decent men, but there was no chemistry. A few had asked her out again, but she'd declined. This one tonight was one of the worst. She had to ask herself, was it worth it to try to meet someone? Maybe there weren't any decent guys left. All the good ones were taken. At least in Cliffside Bay. Had it been a mistake to move here from Denver?

No. She was with her brothers. After all the time they'd lost, being near them was a priority.

She finished the dinner and pushed aside the plastic container. The sun slipped beneath the horizon, and the sky shed an orange glow over the beach.

Tonight, she would delete her dating site profile. There was no reason to keep doing this, especially given the odds stacked against her. She moved her hand down her left leg until she reached the cuff of her sweatpants and pulled the fabric up to her knee. In the dim light, the red scars weren't as noticeable, but the dent in her calf was. After what happened with Darren, it would take a special man for her to trust again.

Her thoughts drifted to her mother, as they so often did these days. Valerie Hickman had disappeared from their lives when Autumn was four years old. Her brothers had been six and eight. Their mother had suddenly shown up in town last fall, begging forgiveness and confessing to the murders of the boys who'd tortured Kyle and caused the accident that almost killed them both. She'd set fire to their house with them inside.

Their mother was back in their lives. And she was a murderer. Kyle and Stone had forgiven their mother with such rapidity that it left Autumn reeling. She found forgiveness difficult, especially since she had no memories of Valerie Hickman ever being in her life.

Maybe it was the setting sun that made her think of her mother. The sun was gone. It was as if it had never been here at all and had not showered the trees and plants with its glorious power that caused the new spring growth on the pines and the buds of the apple trees and the tulips that rose out of the earth in their jaunty splendor. This was like her mother. She made them, and then she left. Leaving Autumn to wonder, had she ever existed at all?

Growing up, she always told people she had no mother. The Hickman kids had raised themselves with little help from her drunk but harmless father. When she thought about her mother now it was like trying to remember something you once knew, some fact that you'd memorized but was now gone. Void of all emotion. Not love or hate or disdain or grief, because how could you feel anything for someone you'd never known?

A *ping* from her laptop drew her attention away from the windows. She'd left it on the coffee table, having had it open before she left for the date. That *ping* was the particular sound of the dating site, letting her know she had a new message. Great. One more temptation.

She disposed of her plastic dinner container and drank a glass of water before sitting on the couch with the computer on her lap. With her legs spread out on the coffee table, she brought up the dating app and clicked on the message from Artyboy34. His profile picture was of a cubist painting, perhaps a self-portrait. Given his name and profile photo, she assumed he was an artist. Kind of interesting. Maybe. Probably not.

DEAR AUTUMN007,

Your profile crossed my path and although I'm not sure this online thing is for me, I felt compelled to write to you. I'm currently on an extended job in Paris working on a commis-sioned series of paintings for a bored countess and her fleet of dogs. I'll be here for some time, so I won't be able to meet you in person. So why write, you ask? Good question. I'm writing because, despite the miles between us, I felt a kinship with you.

As you can see from my profile photograph, I have a rather unconventional picture. The reason for this is because one side of my face is scarred from an accident. The cubist self-portrait painting captures a little of what I look like, at least to myself. I don't go out much. When I do, I always wear a low-brimmed hat and sunglasses, but still, people stare. I can almost hear them asking—what happened to you?

I'm sure your friends will warn you against someone without a real photo. I don't blame them. If I were your friend, I would do the same. But I'm a real person, not one of those catfish people. I think that's what you call them, right? Anyway, I just wondered if you'd like to write back and forth and maybe be a support system of sorts? Recently, I met a woman who I really like but we're only friends. I have no idea if she'd be open to more, but I'm too scared to ask. If she rejected me because of my appearance, it would crush me.

I'll close now. I don't expect to hear from you because this is such a weird letter. I'll just have to hope you're the one-in-a-million type who might respond to a man trapped behind his face.

If you do answer, tell me why you chose 007 for the end of your name.

Art

SHE SAT STARING at the screen, stunned. What a strange letter. What an odd request. Yet it called to her in a way both familiar and exciting, like this was a person she already knew and cared for.

Sara had told her recently she was considering attending a grief support group to help cope with the loss of her husband. Could this be the same, only made up of a group of two, formed by people who lived a continent apart? He'd reached out to her, obviously thinking she would understand in ways no one else could. This was true. She understood perfectly. Why not write him back? No harm could come from a correspondence. If he asked for money, she'd know he was a con artist and not a real artist. She would write back to him, once, and hope her instincts were right. This was a real person on the other side of the computer.

DEAR ART,

I've never had this kind of message waiting for me on this site. Thank you for writing to me. I hope my inclinations are correct and you're not some con artist trying to get my money. If so, you'll be sorry to know I don't have much. All my savings has been poured into the renovation of my cottage, so if your plan is to bilk me of money, then you're out of luck.

If not, and I'm assuming so, I'll start with saying how sorry I am about your accident. I was fourteen when my brother and I were chased in our car by two bullies in a truck. Essentially, they caused a terrible accident. My brother was fine, thank goodness, but my legs were crushed. The doctors were able to save them, but my left leg is badly scarred and misshapen and the other terribly scarred. I'm sure you can understand when I say I keep them hidden—all very sad since I live close to the beach. I can see the stretch of sand from my front windows.

I often watch the young people playing on the beach, so free and happy with the sun on their skin, and I wish I had the courage to do so. It's like you said, though, the stares and averted eyes are too much to bear. For me, at least. I'm weak that way. Growing up, we were poor. I wore thrift-store specials that never quite fit. If they were decent to begin with, I'd grow out of them quicker than they could be replaced. The mean girls sneered at me and talked behind their hands to one another. Their whispers were loud. *She wears the same pants every day. Is that a boy's jacket? Her shirt is practically see-through it's so thin.*

If only capris had been popular when I was a child. Instead my pants were called *high-waters*. I don't know why children are so cruel sometimes. Do you?

There was a swimming pool in our town. It cost one dollar to swim for the afternoon, or one hundred for a summer pass. We could afford neither. Isn't it strange I still remember the exact costs? My brother Stone and I used to stand outside the fence that surrounded the pool, keeping out the riffraff like us, sweating in the heat of the day. We'd watch the other kids go in, wearing bathing suits and carrying towels, and I swear my mouth would water like I was hungry. I would think, *someday that will be me.*

I used to dream of the day I could break out of the little town that trapped my brothers and me. I'd get a degree and a job and buy nice clothes and live in a house made of lumber instead of tin and I'd swim at the beach or river or swimming pool any time I could. All those things have come true except one. I have yet to feel cool water splashed on hot skin other than in my own tub. When I moved here, I promised myself I'd put on a bathing suit and go to the beach. But I can't seem to bring myself to do it. There are so many beautiful people in California, and they all seem to be in my little town at the moment, wearing nothing but a few strands of cloth.

Well, that was a bit of a mind dump. I don't know why I just told you all that. It would probably be best if I deleted the entire passage, but I probably won't. If you're a con artist, it'll probably scare you away, which would be for the best.

To answer your question, the 007 was suggested by my best

guy friend. He thought the whole spy reference would be amusing to men. He also thought it was fitting, as he thinks I'm clever and brave like a spy. His words. He's a friend who thinks a little too much of me. Do you have anyone like that in your life? One who sees you as better than you really are?

I'll close with a question for you. This woman you have romantic feelings for—are you good friends? If you are and you want to remain so, it's probably best to keep it to yourself. Friends are more important than romance. Friendship isn't based on appearance or sexual attraction, only the connection of two souls. Which is much more important, in my opinion.

When you answer, please send it to my email address: autumnhickman@xmail.net. It's less cumbersome than the private messaging on here.

All best,

Autumn007

AFTER SHE FINISHED, she hit send and then shut down the computer for the night. She'd wait until morning to see if he'd written back. If not, she wouldn't think of it again.

She ambled into the kitchen and poured herself a glass of wine, then went back to the couch and turned on the television. As she scrolled through the offerings, her phone buzzed. *Trey Wattson* appeared on the screen. She'd expected his call. He always called after one of her "dates" to check on her.

She swiped her phone to answer. "Hey. I'm home safe."

"Good. Just checking."

"What're you doing?" she asked as she stretched her legs out on the coffee table.

"Not much. Just finished eating a frozen dinner. Chicken potpie. Not terrible."

"Me too. Lasagna. Not terrible."

"How'd your date go?" he asked.

"Completely terrible." She gave him the rundown, ending with her rant about the pig.

By the time she finished, he was laughing. "I can't believe you called him a pig."

"I've entered some new phase on the douche meter. I have zero tolerance. Online dating will do that to you."

"I can imagine it would," he said.

"I'm exhausted with the idea of even one more date."

"Maybe take a break?" Even through the phone there was no mistaking the kind and supportive tone of his voice. He was that way with her. Always. She could see him on his own couch with his feet propped up and a soccer game playing on the television.

His sympathy brought tears to her eyes. "Don't be nice. It just makes me feel sorry for myself."

"Dating makes everyone feel sorry for themselves."

She held her breath until the threat of more tears subsided.

"Autumn, are you all right?"

"Yes, I'm fine. It's just been a long day."

"Well, it's over now. You can relax with a glass of wine and watch one of your shows."

"You know me too well," she said before taking a sip of her wine. "I'm doing just that. What teams are playing tonight?"

"Portland and Seattle. You know me too well."

She settled deeper into her couch. "Did you just call to make sure I hadn't been murdered and chopped up into a hundred pieces?"

His voice sharpened. "Don't even joke about that. You know how dangerous online dating is."

"It's not, really. I'm careful. You know that."

"I'm still going to check up on you."

"I already have two brothers, you know," she said.

She heard him let out a sigh. "I'm aware of that. But do they call you after one of these so-called dates?"

"No, they're too busy with their own lives. Everyone's left me behind these days. Even Sara. She's so busy with the baby, and everyone else is blissfully in love."

"Not everyone. You still have me," he said.

She flushed, shy to say how grateful she was but feeling that it was important she do so. "I'm glad for you every day." Her words came out husky. Why was it so hard to tell people how much they meant to you?

"Back at you." A slight pause. "Do you want to go up to Stowaway with me tomorrow? We could spend the day antiquing. I'm looking for a few more items for Sara's house."

Her mood brightened at the thought of a day with Trey. "Sure. That sounds fun."

"We can grab some lunch somewhere outside. It's supposed to be nice."

"I'm in," she said.

"I'll pick you up around nine."

"I'll be ready."

"You know you won't be, but that's okay," he said, teasing. "I'll wait for you. Like I always do."

She laughed. "I'm sorry, but I can never decide what to wear."

"I've seen your bed covered with all the rejects. I know." There was a short pause before he continued. "Listen to me. The right man's going to show up. Maybe in the least likely place. Hang in there. Don't let your heart close up."

"Are you speaking from experience?"

"Something like that," he said, drily. "Sleep well. I'll see you tomorrow."

"You too. Night."

"Night."

After they hung up, she pulled up the photo section on her phone and flipped through until she found the snapshot she'd taken of Trey last week. She'd meant to send it to him, thinking he might like to put it on the social media profiles he used to help promote his work. The one he had now was a stiff-looking photo he had done at a studio.

She looked at the photo. Last week, from her patio, she'd spotted Trey and Nico surfing. She knew it was them because Nico always wore a wetsuit with bright purple sleeves. Taking her coffee and phone, she'd walked down to the bench that overlooked the northern stretch of beach where the waves were the biggest, thus attracting surfers. She'd sat on the bench, located on a grassy knoll above the sand, to watch. Trey and Nico had caught wave after wave. They'd been surfing since they were kids, making it look easy.

After another fifteen minutes, they'd traipsed out of the surf and stripped to the waist. She'd stood to wave. Spotting her, they'd returned the greeting. Trey had run across the sand with his perfect, muscular legs. To her surprise, her breath had caught at the sheer beauty of the man. She'd also wondered what it felt like to have the strength in your legs to run over sand as if it were nothing.

He'd stopped just under the knoll. Shielding his eyes with his hand, he grinned up at her. "What're you doing here?" The sea air had caught his words so that she could barely make out what he said.

"I could see you from my house. I came out to watch," she yelled down to him. "Stay right there. I want to take your photo."

The sun was behind her, still inching its way up from the east. He squinted and yelled up to her, "I'm blinded by the light."

"Smile anyway."

He did so despite his complaint, opening his eyes long enough for her to take the photo.

Now she looked at the photo closely. His hair, normally so neatly combed, was laden with salt water and looked coarse and unruly and almost blond. The arms and bodice of his wetsuit hung over his hips, leaving his muscular shoulders and chest and trim waist bare. Eyes as blue as the ocean sparkled in the sunlight.

She sent the photo to him via a text.

I forgot to send you this. You should use this on your Instagram profile. You look great!

A second later, a text came back.

I look like a tool.

She wrote back.

Don't be ridiculous. You look hot.

Almost immediately another one came back.

Hot? Like "swipe to the right" hot?

She texted back, smiling into the phone.

If you ever sank low enough to join the desperate masses, you would definitely be a right swipe for any girl who saw this photo.

He didn't reply. She figured the soccer game he was watching must have drawn his attention away from the phone. Maybe someone actually scored a goal. Mostly, it seemed to her, soccer players just ran up and down the field passing the ball back and forth. She yawned just thinking about the games she'd watched with Trey.

She looked back at the photograph one more time, tracing the contours of his face with the tip of her fingernail. What would it feel like to touch him that way in real life? What if she actually did see him on a dating site? She would definitely be interested but would never reach out to him. He was way out of her league. Not that he had any plans to join one. He didn't need one, as far as she could tell. Women were always hitting on him when they were out. She supposed he hooked up with some of the women who threw themselves at him, but he never let on to her. He might think she'd disapprove of casual sex.

Her stomach turned over.

Did she disapprove?

The thought of him with someone else, some random woman, didn't feel right. In fact, it felt the opposite. His entire vow to remain detached from any romantic entanglements felt wrong. Trey Wattson was the type of man who should be married and have a family. With the right woman, of course. Not a cheater like his first wife.

What kind of woman would be right for him? Nothing came to her, just a blank spot where a picture of the woman good enough for Trey would be. She couldn't imagine anyone. Maybe, just maybe, a woman like Lisa Perry: kind, beautiful, successful. However, Lisa was already taken. Sara? No, she wasn't quite right, either. Or was she? They both liked the arts and had sophisticated taste. Sara was beautiful—very symmetrical.

No, no, no. The thought of Trey with Sara made her want to throw her wineglass at the television.

What was that about?

Her phone buzzed with a message from Trey.

Hypothetically, if YOU saw my photo and profile and didn't know anything about me, would you swipe yes?

How did she answer this one? She typed a message back to him.

I don't think so.

The next series of texts were exchanged rapidly.

Why?

You're not my type.

What is your type, then?

Men who are a little less perfect than you.

That doesn't even make sense. You know me. I'm not perfect.

To me, you are. Why this line of questioning? Are you thinking about getting into the game?

Maybe.

No way. Are you finally ready to move past your divorce?

Several seconds went by before an answer popped up on her phone.

For the right woman, yes.

She stared at her phone, shocked. Where had this come from? Since the first day she met him, he'd said he would never get seriously involved again. Now he was ready? Out of the blue like this? She didn't like it. Not at all. She preferred his resolution to never marry again. That way he would always be her best friend. Once he met someone, she'd be ousted from best friend status.

How selfish could she be? If she were really his friend, she should be glad for him, not thinking only of herself.

She would text him back with words of encouragement, even if it was only a platitude.

I'm glad for you. Moving on after betrayal is never easy. Putting yourself out there might feel excruciating, but I feel sure there's a woman looking for you right now. Swiping no after no and wondering where you are.

I doubt it, but thanks. You should get some rest. Big day of shopping tomorrow.

They exchanged good-nights for the second time. Then she tossed her phone to the other side of the couch and picked up her wine. She took two long slugs. Trey dating. An image of him and Sara laughing together by the Mullens' pool came to her. Did he like her? Was that why the sudden interest in dating? *God, please, just don't let it be Sara.*

Autumn just knew she was going to be struck down by the Lord himself for being a selfish, awful friend. *Please, God, help me let go.*

She drank more wine and shivered as a memory came to her. She'd been around eight and had wakened from her bed on the couch to the sound of howling outside their trailer.

Drifting back in time, the scene played out in her mind.

"Kyle, what is it?" she called down to her brother, who shared a small room with Stone.

"A coyote," Kyle said, sounding sleepy. "He's outside. He can't get us."

She turned toward the window, cold in her thin nightgown. A full moon shone through their uncovered windows and filled the room with an eerie silvery sheen. Another howl caused her to jump. She needed to be with her brothers. Otherwise, the coyote might jump right through the window. Her heart pounded as she dashed from her bed on the sofa and down the narrow hallway.

"Kyle," she whispered to the form curled up in the narrow cot. "Kyle, can I sleep in here?"

He sat up, rubbing his eyes. She just made out his disheveled hair and the faded plaid of his pajamas. "Come on, then." With a yawn, he crawled out of bed and motioned for her to take his place. She climbed in and snuggled under the blanket he placed over her, still warm from his body. Kyle took the other blanket and lay on the floor.

"Take the pillow," she said.

He lifted his head, and she placed it under him. Seconds later, his even breathing told her he was asleep.

The howling continued. It was such a lonesome, dreadful sound that made her feel as if her insides were numb from cold.

Back in the present, she ran her hands through her hair. She was an adult with a good job and a house. There was nothing to be afraid of now.

She moved from the couch to the French doors. Occasionally, lovers walked along the boardwalk in front of her cottage. Even with the windows open, the rumbling waves stole their voices, but she imagined they whispered secrets, desires, and wishes they could not share with anyone but each other.

She went outside and stood on the edge of her patio. In the darkness, she could not distinguish where sky met sea. Lights from the houses along the beach illuminated the white water of breaking waves and clusters of sea bubbles that accumulated at water's edge. The old lighthouse built on a rock island north of the beach was a faint yellow glow on the horizon. Out at sea, the lights from a cruise ship hung suspended in all that blackness, as if they were floating candles. Sirius, the first star visible from the northern hemisphere, winked to her, as if to remind her she was not alone.

Was this her fate? Forever looking out to the life that played before her and never really living herself?

"Will I always be alone?" she whispered into the night.

The only answer was the sea, crashing and crashing onto the shore.

* * *

SHE WOKE around seven the next morning. Despite it being her day off, she was as awake as the sun poking through the eastern windows of her bedroom. She sat up in bed and looked over at the empty side of the bed, where she'd left her laptop open the night before. A pop-up window indicated she had an email message. Would it be from her friend across the ocean? Strangely, she hoped it was. She opened her mailbox, and it was indeed from Artyboy34@hmail.com.

She decided to save it for a leisurely read while having her coffee. After brushing her teeth, she went to the kitchen to rustle up a cup of caffeine. A few minutes later, she returned to her bed with the steaming mug and opened the message.

DEAR 007,

Thanks for your private email. However, I must advise you, hoping I don't sound overly didactic, but don't give this out to men you don't know. Now I know your last name and could easily stalk you. Not that I would, but there are tons of predators out there, so it's best to be careful.

To answer your question, yes, the woman I have feelings for is a good friend of mine. We spend a lot of time together and enjoy the same activities. I've been thinking about your advice and perhaps you're right. If I told her how I feel and she rejected me or in any way showed repulsion, it would kill me. I hold her in such esteem; if she proved to be anything other than what I believe her to be, it would change everything for me. Not just about her, but about the world. I've been hurt before. Several women I trusted showed their true colors when tested. It's left me thinking there is no one out there who would be able to look past my scars and love me.

Your email made me wonder about the friend who suggested the 007 handle. Is there anything between you? I mean, of a romantic nature? Does he know about your scars? If he cares so deeply for you as a friend, might there be more? How do you feel about him? Strictly platonic?

Tell me about your work. I see you're a pharmacist. What's that like? Why did you choose it as a profession? What about your family? Are you close with them? Siblings?

Best,

Art

She hit the reply button before she could think better of it.

Dear Art,

I'm sorry the women in your past hurt you in that way. Similar things have happened on my end as well. Before I moved to this little beach town in California, I lived in Denver. I met a man through my physical therapist and fell for him pretty quickly. I kept him from the truth about my legs for as long as I could. When I finally told him, he said he didn't care. I undressed before him. I'd never felt so vulnerable in my life. I had no idea what he thought. He didn't say a word. I let him into my bed, but only after he asked me to shut off the lights. I pretended that it was for other reasons, not because he could only be with me if he couldn't see me. But the next morning, he was gone without so much as a note on the bedside table. After that, he completely ghosted me. If it hadn't been for my brother Stone, I might have curled into a ball and stayed that way.

So, yes, I have brothers. As most things in my life, family is complicated. Kyle, my older brother, disappeared from our lives after he graduated from high school. He felt responsible for my accident, and the guilt drove him away. Stone and I were devastated to lose him because he was the only parental figure we had. My mother left when I was only four years old and never returned. Kyle basically raised us, even though he was only eight when she left. My father was harmless, albeit a drunk, and unable to keep a job for any length of time. The three of us were all we had. When Kyle left that way, it was like being abandoned all over again.

Just two years ago, we found him and were able to reconcile. Now the three of us live in the same town and spend a lot of time together. Kyle and his wife have four little ones, whom I adore. They'll probably be the closest thing to having children of my own, given everything.

Last year, my mother showed up out of the blue. It's a long story, but we're slowly building a relationship. My brothers have had an easier time accepting her back into their lives than I have. This fact surprised me. I thought it would be Kyle, not me, who would hold on to the past. I can't seem to unfreeze. Stone, who is in the middle between Kyle and me, is a big teddy bear. I knew he wouldn't be able to stay angry with her, especially as she shows so much remorse and contrition. She suffers from depression, which is what caused her to leave us. Or so she says, anyway. I thought it was a man in a black car who offered her a way out of poverty that did it.

Her life was bleak with my father. I'll give her that. Imagine a leaky trailer on property next to a pig farm. The smell of pig excrement clung to everything, even after a good, hard rain, which happened frequently in Oregon. My father couldn't keep a job, so our mother made ends meet by cleaning rich people's houses. She'd come home at night and have to put supper together out of a can of beans and stale bread or whatever else she could find in the cupboard in back of my father's cheap whiskey. I can understand how she must have wondered how to get through another day.

All that said, I can't understand how she could leave us. I love my nieces and nephews so much. I'd do anything for them, and they're not even my own children. How could she leave three little children with him? Kyle had to become an adult at eight years old. Anyway, now she's back and I'm trying to soften to her, but it's not working. My resentments are thick and steadfast. Stone says to give it time, that there's no pressure to forgive overnight. I just don't understand why it's so easy for Stone and Kyle to forgive and not me.

Regarding my 007 friend—his name is Trey. He knows I have scars but has never seen them. No one has but my brothers and my best girlfriend, Sara. Trey's my best friend, other than Sara. Like you, he's an artist. He works as an interior designer, but his drawings and paintings are wonderful too. Talent oozes from him. I adore him, but it's a strictly platonic relationship. I don't think he would ever see me as anything more than Stone's little sister, thus his sister by proxy. We have such a good time together that I would never want to muddy the waters with anything as fickle as romance. We're great as best pals.

You asked about my work. Of anything in my life, it's the simplest to explain. I was drawn to it because I liked science, particularly chemistry, when I was young. After I was hurt and reliant upon painkillers and antibiotics for such a long period of time, I became fascinated with how drugs could change lives. It seemed like the obvious choice for me. Kyle, although absent physically in our lives, provided money for college tuition. I didn't hesitate to make a better life for myself. I've never regretted the decision. I love my work, even though it requires long hours on my feet, which can be problematic. Over the years, I've learned how to pace myself, alternating between sitting and standing. I love the precision of the profession, the lack of guessing or subjectivity.

I hope this isn't overstepping, but how did your face become scarred? What drew you to art? And please share how you discovered such a niche in portrait painting. I love dogs as much as the next person, but I don't think I'd have a painting done of a pet and me.

Best,

007

* * *

BY THE TIME she'd showered and dressed, there was an email waiting from Art.

Dear 007,

The dog thing came about because of my parents. I grew up wealthy, with people who have the luxury of designer everything, including dogs. One of my mother's friends asked me to paint her and Muffy together and it kind of went from there. The niche makes a good living, and I enjoy meeting the people and learning about their lives and their dogs. I suppose it sounds weird, but do you know how often a mistress or master and their dog look alike? I mean, there should be some kind of scientific experiment to try to figure out why this happens. I read once that people often choose best friends who are similar to them in height, weight, and level of attractiveness. Perhaps this happens with dogs as well?

Regarding your friend Trey. The relationship you two have sounds similar to the one I have with my friend Michelle. As I said before, I'm secretly in love with her. Has it ever occurred to you that Trey might be in love with you? Are you sure he sees you only as a little sister? If so, I'd be greatly surprised. Here's a dirty little secret about men. We're not really interested in having women friends unless we want the relationship to develop into something else.

My scars were caused by my ex-wife. She threw acid on me after I discovered her affair.

I should close for now. Countess Malinda and her dog Priscilla await.

Best,

Art

She stared at the screen, sick to her stomach. Acid on his face? How horrid. It was worse than what happened to her. The Miller brothers, who caused the accident, were not people she loved. But a wife? That kind of betrayal wounded both the inside and the outside.

She shut the laptop before the urge to write back made her late for Trey. He'd said nine, and he was always on time. For once, she wanted to be ready and not make him wait.

3

T rey

TREY DROVE his Mini Cooper with caution around the turns as they headed north toward Stowaway. Autumn had been her usual serene self, commenting occasionally on the scenery before falling asleep with her chin tucked into her neck. As the highway turned inland to loop around a high, impassable peak, she let out a faint squeak before settling back into position.

This wasn't unusual. Like a happy kitten in a splash of sunlight, she often fell asleep in the car. She had explained once that the warmth combined with sitting in one place relaxed her. He'd often wondered about her propensity to fall asleep when she rode with him, given her past. It would seem that she'd be frightened to ride in a car after almost dying in a car accident. She never mentioned it to him, though, and always seemed quite calm during their trips together.

He had to physically keep himself from reaching for her

hand as she twitched in her sleep. *Keep your hands on the wheel and off the girl.*

They traveled through a heavily forested area before the road led them west once more. When they reached the sign for Stowaway, he turned left onto the two-lane road that would take them to the heart of the seaside town. The highway ran through flat land with strawberry fields on either side. Several farms had signs that read Self-Pick. Dozens of people knelt over the neat rows, plucking the juicy red fruit that grew close to the ground.

Another mile down the road, a large red barn right before the sign for Stowaway hosted a local farmers' market. If Autumn hadn't been asleep, he would have suggested they stop for fresh vegetables to make for dinner.

Soon, he spotted the city limit sign of Stowaway, population 13,691.

Stowaway, like Cliffside Bay, was also a tourist destination, but bigger and busier. There were antiques shops on either side of one of his favorite furniture stores, Sayer's. Started by Henry Sayer back in the forties, it was now run by the grandson, who created pristine wood pieces like father and grandfather before him. Trey had bought many pieces from him over the years, including Autumn's sleigh bed.

He found a parking spot in front of the building, backing into it with ease in his short car. Since they'd started the business, Trey often borrowed Stone's big truck when he went shopping for furniture for their clients. Today, however, he'd have any big pieces delivered to Sara's directly.

Autumn woke when he turned off the engine. She blinked, then smiled. "Sorry. I didn't get much sleep last night."

"It's fine."

"I didn't snore, did I?" she asked. "Or drool?"

"You did neither," he said. "Thankfully. Or you'd be looking for a ride home."

"Very funny." She smacked his arm.

"Hang on. I'll get your door." He sprinted around the front to help her out of his low car. If he'd known Autumn would so often be his passenger, he would have gotten a car that was easier to get in and out of. "Do you want your cane from the back?" he asked.

"No, not yet."

As he did whenever they strolled or shopped together, he offered his arm for support. She took it, and they ambled down the sidewalk. They'd been to Stowaway together at least a dozen times and knew it well. Although once a modest town, it was now slick and rich with high-end stores, restaurants, and art galleries. They passed by the kitchen shop, a gallery that featured blown glasswork, then their favorite bistro.

"They opened the outdoor seating," he said, pointing toward the bistro.

"Last time we were here, it was pouring rain, remember?"

He did. They'd gotten soaked running from the bistro to the car. Autumn had looked completely adorable with wet hair. Her clothes had stuck to her breasts and hips, leaving little to his imagination. All the way home he'd cursed the car heater for working so well.

Today, however, round tables with red-and-white-checkered cloths were arranged under blue umbrellas. Servers in crisp white aprons scurried among the tables, laying silverware down for an anticipated lunch crowd.

All along the street, overhead sprinklers soaked the potted flower containers that hung from the awnings of every business. Water spilled onto the sidewalks, creating a patchwork of light and dark gray cement.

When they reached the antique shop, the owner, Frankie, greeted them like old friends as they entered. Trey was in at least twice a month. He liked to think his stunning personality caused Frankie's affection. However, it was more likely the thousands of dollars he spent a month on his clients' behalf. Frankie joked he had Trey on speed dial.

Frankie got up from his desk, where he'd been working on the computer. He was wide-shouldered with a broad face and a nose that looked as if it had been broken several times. Other than his peach suit jacket paired with cropped white jeans, he looked like a character from a Mafia movie. The outfit told a different story, as did the photograph of his wedding day with his husband, George.

Frankie swept up beside them, planting air kisses on both sides of Autumn's face, then did the same to Trey. "What are you two kids up to?" He had the male version of a voice like Marilyn Monroe's, all breathy and innocent.

"I'm looking for a few more pieces for Sara's formal living room," Trey said. "It needs an armoire and a few end tables."

Frankie made a heart using his index fingers and thumbs. "You've absolutely, one hundred percent made my day." He motioned dramatically toward the back room. "I have a new piece not even cataloged or tagged yet. You're going to die when you see it. I mean, totally and completely die."

They followed him back to the room behind the main floor where Frankie kept inventory coming in or going out. He whipped a blanket off a tall piece with the flair of a magician sweeping a tablecloth out from under a set of dishes. "Ta-da."

"What a beauty." Autumn let out a breath and clapped her hands over her mouth. Frankie wasn't the only dramatic one.

The armoire was made of walnut, probably in the latter part of the 1800's.

"George stripped it and then put a stain on it to capture the beauty of the original wood," Frankie said.

Not overly adorned with etchings or carvings, the refinished wood had a timeless feel. Frankie explained that it had been in storage somewhere, wrapped in plastic and kept dry. "For God only knows how long. George sanded and refinished the wood into the texture of a silk handkerchief. You know how he is."

Trey didn't, actually, having never met the elusive George. Frankie said he preferred to work away from people, content to bring antiques back to life in the workshop out back.

Trey spent the next few minutes examining the piece more closely, including opening and closing drawers and doors. The finish was indeed as smooth as silk. "It's a gem," Trey said.

"I want it," Autumn said, still staring at it with the eyes of the besotted. If only she looked at him that way. "I mean, if I had room."

They talked about a few more details, including price and delivery options. Trey took a few photos to text to Sara for her approval. "I think she'll want it," Trey said to Frankie. "We'll come back later and let you know."

After Frankie agreed and they looked at a few other items, he led Autumn out to the bright morning. The sun hung high and shot blinding rays of light onto the sidewalk and streets. He put his sunglasses on, as did Autumn, and they continued their stroll, turning right into a side street where another antiques shop was tucked into one of the older buildings.

"One more and then lunch," he said.

She smiled up at him. "You had me at lunch."

* * *

AN HOUR LATER, they sat at an outside table just inside the gate. Perfect for people watching, they'd agreed.

"We can pretend we're in Paris," she said.

"Paris? What made you think of that?"

She smiled. "I'll tell you later."

The server took their drink orders and delivered a basket of warm bread. Trey and Autumn watched people as they passed by in various states of summer attire. Like their own town, Stowaway was crawling with vacationers and tourists here to enjoy the beach, quaint businesses, and eating establishments.

"I have an idea," Trey said as he tore a piece of bread from the loaf.

She squinted at him and took the basket of bread from his outstretched hand. "An idea? Should I be worried?"

"Yes. Did you know tonight is a full moon?"

"I didn't, no."

"I called Kara this morning about something else and she reminded me they're leaving for a short trip up north before Ruby Sloan comes. She offered up the pool to the guys and me to use while they're away."

Autumn dipped a piece of bread into the olive oil and balsamic vinaigrette. "That's nice of her."

"It was. I'm wondering if you might like to go swimming tonight?"

"I don't swim." A flush climbed up the side of her neck and settled in her cheeks. He'd angered her with his suggestion. No going back now. He'd decided the minute he read her sad email to Art that he was going to get her in the swimming pool. The ocean would be next.

"You don't swim because you're self-conscious of your legs, right?" he asked.

She nodded and took a bite of her bread, then chewed as she watched him with big green eyes. Wary eyes. He shoved aside the hurt it caused to see her look at him like that and focused on his goal. She yearned to feel the water against her skin when she was a kid. He would give it to her.

"What if no one was there but me and it was dark?" he asked.

"Trey, no."

"What if I promise not to look? You could slip into the pool without me looking. It'll be dark. I'll turn around."

Her mouth twitched. Was it caused by irritation or humor? He couldn't be sure.

"You sound like a thirteen-year-old boy promising not to look at a girl when she's changing clothes," she said.

He laughed. "I promise I have no other agenda other than I want you to enjoy the water." He almost said *on your skin*, but stopped himself at the last second. If he was going to use her emails, he had to be careful.

"What's gotten into you? Why the sudden interest in me swimming?"

"I want you to have more fun, that's all," he said. Could she read right through him?

"Swimming is not my idea of fun," she said.

"Okay. Never mind then. It was just an idea." He bit into his piece of bread. The fruity olive oil tasted divine, but he couldn't enjoy it. Why did she have to be so stubborn? Now that he had more insight into the inner workings of her mind, he suspected she often glossed over her own feelings or needs. How long had she acted as if everything were fine while living an internal life of longing?

They both added one sweetener packet and a squeeze of lemon to their tea. He pretended to be interested in the menu, even though he couldn't care less what he ate. His mother used to say he was like a dog with a bone when an idea struck him. His current bone? He had to get Autumn into that swimming pool. The thought of her and Stone standing outside the fence of the public swimming pool was too much. If he could, he'd provide her a lifetime of swimming dates.

She'd opened up to Art so easily. Was it that she felt safe because she thought Art was as scarred as she? Sharing the dark, shadowed secrets of the past or the longings of the present was not easy. For both of them, writing them down was clearly easier than speaking them out loud.

Looking at Autumn from across the table, he saw a woman

who from the outside appeared to have it all. With her pretty face and slender figure, she was probably the envy of every woman in the restaurant. Most men probably wished they could trade places with him.

So many tried to convince everyone that they were better than fine with Christmas cards and social media posts that portrayed lives of esteem and perfection. People could construct an image with photos and selfies that had no real similarities to reality. If one were to scratch just beneath the surface of those photos, what would be revealed? Loneliness? Insecurity? Debt? Failing careers? Take him, for instance. Not only had he created a fake profile to try to win the heart of the woman he loved, his real life wasn't as he presented it, either.

For years, he'd used social media as a marketing tool to promote his business. Capturing photos of his work was the best way to show his talent. Those photos told a story of a successful business, even when it wasn't. The years after his divorce were lean. Before he met Honor Sullivan, he'd had only a handful of clients in Cliffside Bay. In fact, business was so scarce he'd considered returning to San Francisco. But the job with Honor, decorating her remodeled house, had changed everything. She'd introduced him to Brody Mullen and subsequently his wife Kara, who fed him job after job. In partnership with the other Wolves, his finances were finally back on track.

Before that, his photographs had told a false story. Surely he wasn't the only one. He wondered what it would be like if everyone told the truth instead of presenting perfect pictures. *I'm hurting. I'm broke. I'm afraid no one will ever love me.*

I want to feel salt water on my skin.

"What if we went to the beach?" he asked. "At night when no one else would be there."

"My legs aren't strong. The current could pull me to China."

"I'll hold you."

"Trey." She glared at him, then made a face. "Seriously. Let it go. I have no interest in swimming. I don't even know what gave you that idea."

He put up his hands as if she were about to hurl a piece of bread at him. "Fine. I'm done." He pretended to zip his mouth, then did his best ventriloquist imitation by speaking with his teeth clenched and barely moving his lips. "Not another word."

She laughed. His heart pulsed with joy at the sound.

"Can I ask you something?" he asked.

"I have a feeling I can't stop you." She raised one eyebrow and set her mouth in a firm line, as if waiting for an attack.

"Why are you dating if you're not ready to share your whole self with someone?"

She stared down at the half-eaten piece of bread, limp from its bath of oil and vinegar. "I guess I always hope there'll be someone out there who won't mind about...everything." She looked up at him. "I told you that when I set up my profile."

"I know you did. Yet you don't ever have a second date with any of these guys. Have you so quickly disqualified them?"

"Yes. Not because of that but because none of them have been right for me. Like you said, there is someone out there. I just haven't found him yet."

I'm right here.

He swallowed and ducked his chin, pretending to be interested in the menu to hide the pain her words caused him. How could she not see it was him?

She reached across the narrow table to take hold of his wrist. "What's gotten into you today? You're so intense."

Trey kept his attention on the menu, going so far as to trail his finger down the list of entrées to prove just how fine he was. "Nothing. I'm not intense, just in a curious mood, that's all. I'm trying to understand you better."

"Why?"

He moved his menu to look at her. "Because you're my friend and I care about you."

Her expression softened. "You're sweet. Like really sweet."

"It seems like even the closest friends don't talk about stuff beyond the surface."

She tilted her head and squinted her eyes. "That's because you're a man. Women do. All the time."

"I suppose that's true." He set aside the menu and picked up his iced tea. Slippery from condensation, the glass nearly fell from his fingers. "I'm here if you ever want to talk about anything. Even though I'm a guy."

"I'll keep that in mind," she said softly. "Right now, I'm just glad to be here with you on such a pretty day. I can't think of a thing wrong."

He could. But he'd keep that to himself.

"I think I'll get the quail," he said.

"The quail?" She raised both eyebrows, clearly surprised. "I thought you'd pick the pasta special."

"Is that what you're having?"

"Yes. I thought you'd want it too."

The pasta dish was exactly what he'd wanted, but for some reason he'd said the quail. "You don't know everything about me," he said, keeping his voice blithe. "I might surprise you once in a while."

"Oh, really?" she asked, teasing. "What else do you have up your sleeve?"

He couldn't answer, because the server came back to take their orders. Although he wanted the pasta, he ordered the quail. Now that he'd made a point about it, he couldn't back down. All those silly bird bones were sure to be a punishment for his petulance.

After the server left, she returned to the earlier theme. "Tell me something I don't know about you."

He thought for a moment. What was there he could share with her that he hadn't before? "All through high school and college, my father thought I was gay. Really, until I met Malia and brought her home, he was under the impression that I was in the closet."

"Why would he think that?"

"Because I liked art and design—things he thought were for women or gay men. Totally ridiculous."

"Did it bother you?" she asked.

Had it bothered him? When he thought about his father, his body became heavy with a dull ache, like an internal injury that never quite healed. "Not because there's anything wrong with being gay. If I had been, I certainly wouldn't have been ashamed. I have a few good friends who came out to us in high school, and it changed exactly nothing between us. Sex and sexuality are such a small part of life, if you think about it. Most of life is about the other things. But to him, homosexuality is shameful, like so much else. He wanted to shame me by criticizing the way I dressed and my interest in art. Even when my firm in San Francisco was getting so much press after we were hired to decorate Ty Hughes's house, it never impressed him." Ty Hughes was a Silicon Valley high-tech mogul. They'd had a five-page spread and article in one of the major architectural magazines. Even that hadn't impressed his father. He barely acknowledged his success. "My dad continues to call it my 'little hobby.'"

Autumn was shaking her head. "That's terrible. I'm so sorry. What about your mom? Were you close with her?"

"I was when I was younger. Since I moved away, we've drifted apart. My fault. I don't call as much as I should. They're in San Diego, but I hardly ever visit. I don't want to deal with my dad. Being around him makes me feel like a failure."

The server arrived with their entrées. They ate in silence for a few minutes. The quail, doused in a cherry reduction, was better than anticipated and had very few bones. He didn't want to think too closely about how they removed them or the poor soul who had to perform that task.

Across from him, Autumn twirled angel-hair pasta into a spoon, then brought it to her mouth and made an appreciative murmur. How was it possible to love the way someone chewed?

He let her eat in peace for a few minutes before he launched into his second agenda item of the day. "Your mom lives just outside of town, right? We could go by and see her on the way home."

"You mean Valerie?" She gave him a sweet, sad smile. "I don't call her Mom."

"Valerie, then. Would you like to visit her on the way home?"

"How come you've never asked me that before? We've come here a bunch of times."

He shrugged and placed his hand on the back of his neck, suddenly warm. Was she seeing through his act? Would she pick up on the fact that he'd narrowed in on two of the subjects she'd brought up in her emails? "I don't know. It just occurred to me today that you might like to say hello since we're here."

She seemed to consider this as she sipped from her glass of iced tea. "I haven't seen her since Mother's Day. She came down to Kyle and Violet's for brunch."

"I remember." He'd spent the day at the beach with Nico enjoying one of the first warm days after their obligatory phone calls to their mothers. His sister, Jamie, who'd just finished graduate school, had been at the house, cooking lunch for Mom. Jamie was always there to pick up the slack. In his defense, she lived in San Diego not far from their parents. It was easier for her to pop in to see them occasionally. "How was Mother's Day? Less awkward than Easter?"

"I guess. She spent most of the time with the little ones. My mom and I don't know what to say to each other most of the time." Autumn pushed her plate aside. A twinge of guilt flickered in her eyes. "We should stop by, since we're here. You're right. I'll call her. Just to make sure she's home. I'll meet you out front."

He watched her walk toward the entrance, then motioned for the check.

When he exited the restaurant a few minutes later, Autumn stood waiting under the shade of an oak.

"Was she home?"

The slight crease between her eyebrows deepened as she looked up at him. "Yes, she said to come by."

"What has you worried?"

"She sounded kind of embarrassed about her apartment. 'Don't expect too much,' I think she said." She paused and looked down the street, as if she expected someone to pull up beside them. "Maybe we shouldn't go. I don't want her to feel bad."

"It'll be fine," he said. "I think she'd like to see you more than she's hesitant about the apartment."

"She did sound excited that I called."

He walked over to her and put his arm around her shoulders. "Let's go find some pretty flowers."

VALERIE HICKMAN LIVED in a run-down apartment complex on the edge of town. Given the flat, ugly architecture, Trey guessed it was built in the late sixties. Battered by sea air, the once-blue paint had faded to a dull gray. Small dirty windows looked like square eyes of a monster.

They walked up a set of creaky stairs to the second floor. "She said 2B," Autumn said. "So this must be it."

Mold and mildew made the landing slick. There was no way this place was up to code, given the loose boards. An ashtray with two butts sat on the railing. Valerie smoked. He remembered smelling it on her at the New Year's Eve party at Kyle and Violet's.

Valerie must have heard them coming, because the door to 2B swung open and she appeared in the doorway, smiling tentatively. "This is such a nice surprise." Despite her pleasant expression, a slight shake to her voice told him she was nervous to see them.

Autumn gave her a quick hug before motioning toward Trey. "You remember my friend Trey?"

"Yes, of course. Come in." She gestured for them both to come inside.

The apartment was about the same as the outside, dreary and shabby. The front room was overly warm and stuffy, even with the windows open. An orange-and-brown-plaid couch, an old rocking chair, and a stand with a television took up the entirety of the small living room. The kitchen was an extension of the front room with orange countertops and a squatty refrigerator.

"I have some store-bought cookies, and I made coffee," Valerie said.

"No, thanks. We just ate at our favorite French bistro in town," Autumn said.

"Oh, yes." Valerie gripped a hand over her opposite wrist and nodded. "I've never eaten there, but I hear it's very good."

"We go there every time we come up," Autumn said.

"You come up often?" Valerie asked with just a slight elevation to her pitch.

Autumn flushed. "Not recently. When we were decorating my cottage."

"There's some nice furniture shops in town." Valerie released her grip on her wrist and glanced at her couch. "I bet you decorated your place real pretty."

"I love it," Autumn said. "Trey has a wonderful eye and understood what I wanted right away."

"It was a fun project," Trey said. "She has great taste, in my opinion."

"What does she like?" Valerie asked with such poignant curiosity that Trey's chest ached. She didn't know her daughter but so obviously wanted to.

He could tell her that Autumn's favorite color was sea-glass green. She favored simple designs and pale walls and rustic, farmhouse-style furniture. "Nothing too modern," she'd told him. She'd picked out prints for the walls of people in ordinary life doing conventional activities: a family bicycling down a country lane; another of three little girls holding on to one another on the edge of the surf; one of a family dining alfresco around a long table, with a house in the background. Her choices had touched him. He assumed they were all pictures of events she hadn't had as a child yet so desperately wished for. She wanted them now, too. He wanted to give them to her.

"Trey describes my taste as beachy meets chic farmhouse," Autumn said.

"I'd love to see your cottage sometime," Valerie said.

"Sure. Next time you come down, you should swing by," Autumn said.

"Please, sit. Are you sure I can't get you some coffee?" Valerie asked.

They both declined again and settled into the couch. Valerie took the rocking chair. Like the first time he'd met her, Trey had been struck by how much older she looked than his own mother, who fought the inevitable effects of aging with fancy creams, expensive dye jobs, and Botox injections. Trey remembered Autumn saying Valerie had Kyle when she was only a teenager, which meant she'd be close to fifty, but she looked at least a decade older. She wore her white hair in an unflattering ponytail. Her face was lined with fine wrinkles and marred with sunspots.

"What brings you two up here today?" Valerie smoothed the

front of her faded sweatshirt and tucked one ankle behind the other.

"I had an appointment with an antiques broker," Trey said. "To look at a piece of furniture for a client. Autumn agreed to keep me company."

"Was it nice?" Valerie asked. "The piece?"

"Very much so," Trey said. "Hopefully Sara will like it."

"Sara?" Valerie turned her gaze on Autumn. "Your Sara? From college, isn't that right?"

"That's right," Autumn said, sounding guarded, as if she wanted to protect her friend's privacy.

"Wolf Enterprises built her house," Trey said.

"Her mansion," Autumn said, laughing. "You could fit eight of my cottages in there."

"It's a stunner for sure," Trey said.

"She seemed like a nice girl," Valerie said. "I talked with her for a few minutes at the New Year's brunch. Terrible thing what happened with her husband."

"Yes, it was," Autumn said.

"I always figured rich people like that didn't have problems like the rest of us," Valerie said.

"No one's exempt from heartbreak," Trey said. "No matter how much money you have."

"How's your new job?" Autumn asked her mother. Valerie had moved down from Oregon to be closer to her children. She refused any kind of financial help, even though Kyle had begged her to let him buy her a place in Cliffside Bay. Instead, she'd moved to Stowaway, where apartments were easier to find and less expensive.

"It's fine. I miss my friends from my job back home, but that's to be expected," Valerie said. "I'm glad for the work." She'd been hired as a clerk at one of the local drugstores, which is what she'd done back in Oregon. "It's a nice store. Much fancier than the one I was used to. Just last month, I got a twenty-cent raise over minimum wage, plus an employee discount." She said the last part with pride. "Fifteen percent off most items." She touched her dangling earrings with her fingers. "Bought these for myself on my birthday."

"It was your birthday?" Autumn asked. "When?"

"Last week," Valerie said.

"I'm sorry. I didn't know." Autumn fidgeted, then clasped her hands together over her thighs.

Valerie shook her head. "No big deal. When you get to be my age, it's not really important to celebrate."

"Still, I should know the date," Autumn said.

"I wouldn't expect you to know. It's not like I was around for any of them." Valerie looked down at her hands. "What you don't know about me is not your fault."

Silence settled in the room under the weight of the terrible truth of that statement.

"You should come down next weekend," Autumn said, too brightly. "We can take you to dinner for your birthday."

Valerie smiled. "Well, only if you and your brothers aren't too busy. I'd sure love to see you."

Trey was distracted by a movement near Valerie's foot. A cockroach, without a care in the world, crawled across the worn carpet. He grimaced. If there was one, there were a million.

"Mrs. Hickman, there's a roach, I think," he said, pointing.

Valerie started and squeaked a note of alarm, then leaped from her chair and stomped the insect with her shoe. The unmistakable sound of the roach's shell crunched under the weight of her foot. "Darn things. It's the warm weather. They're everywhere. I have to keep all my food in the refrigerator." She moved away from the carcass without looking at either of them. "I'm sorry you had to see that." She scurried into the kitchen and came back with a broom and dustpan, then scooped the dead bug from the floor.

Autumn shivered. "Oregon was rainy, but at least we didn't have roaches."

"True. I'd never seen one until I came here." Valerie pointed toward a closed door. "I'll flush him. Be right back."

"That's a good idea." Autumn had wrapped her arms around her waist.

He heard the sound of a toilet flushing on the other side of the wall.

Autumn looked at him with wide eyes and whispered, "This place is awful."

He put his fingers to his lips.

Valerie returned from the bathroom and sat back in the rocking chair. She rocked, somewhat manically. "I keep a clean house. It's just..." She trailed off, then sighed.

"We know. I mean, it's obvious you do," Autumn said.

"They were all over the dorms in San Diego," Trey said in an attempt to normalize the roach problem. "When we turned on the light at night in the kitchen, they'd all scurry under the trim boards in a wave of black."

Autumn scooted forward on the couch and stared at the spot on the rug where the roach had crawled its last crawl.

"That's awful." Valerie watched Autumn as she answered. "Especially given how expensive college is."

"My mother mentioned that once or twice," Trey said. "I think she even wrote to the college complaining. Not that it did any good."

"This isn't right," Autumn said, looking up. "Valerie, what's your landlord doing about the roaches and all the repairs that need to be done?" She waved her hand around the room. "This is not right," she repeated.

Valerie lifted one shoulder. "According to my neighbors, other than raise the rent every year, he doesn't do much."

"You need to get out of here," Autumn said.

Valerie's mouth thinned into a painful-looking smile. "I

can't afford anything nicer. Since I lost the house, it's been one place like this after another." She looked over at Trey. "My husband died of cancer, and all his medical bills wiped me out. Not that I had much before, but I did have a house."

"If Kyle saw this place, he would insist," Autumn said. "He wouldn't want his mother living in a place like this when he owns half of California."

"He's already offered, but no," Valerie said. "I take care of myself."

"But why?" Autumn asked. "He wants to help."

Valerie stiffened, and her narrow shoulders rose to meet her dangling earrings. "It would be different if I'd raised you kids. But I didn't. I don't deserve his help."

Autumn glanced at Trey, as if for help. He widened his eyes slightly to let her know he was at a loss.

"I'd love to come for dinner next weekend, though," Valerie said in a small voice.

"That would be nice," Autumn said. "I'll talk with the boys and see what night works best." Unsteadily, she rose from the couch. "We should probably get going."

"Oh, sure, sure. You two probably have other things to do today," Valerie said as she stood so quickly from the rocking chair that it bounced against the wall.

"See you soon." Autumn gave her mother a hug by the door and slipped outside.

Trey lingered for a moment, touched and saddened by Valerie's crestfallen expression. "It was nice to see you again."

"Thank you for bringing her by," Valerie said.

"Next time, we'll swing by and get you for lunch."

Valerie's mouth twitched into a half-hearted smile. "If it's my day off, sure."

Impulsively, he leaned over and embraced her quickly before turning toward the door. "Bye for now."

He walked out to the landing and looked down to the

parking lot. Autumn was already waiting by the car. He pressed the button to unlock it as he bounded down the stairs two at a time. She was already inside by the time he slid into the driver's side.

Autumn turned to him. "Does it make me a bad person that spending time with my mother depresses me?"

"Not at all." He gave her hand a quick squeeze. "It's a depressing situation."

"Thanks for being here with me. I don't think I could've done that alone." She pressed her fingers into her temples. "I have a headache."

"Would you like me to stop for some water?"

"No, I'll be fine. Just turn on the air conditioner. Her place was so warm."

He turned on the engine and blasted the air-conditioning. "Let's get you home." He backed out of the lot and onto the street. They drove several miles without speaking.

"Do you want to talk about it?" he asked.

She stretched her legs out as far as they would go and crouched lower in the seat. "Her life is so bleak, Trey."

"You don't have to take on her problems," Trey said.

"She's my mother."

"You can't force a relationship just because you're biologically related."

"Is that how you feel about your dad?" she asked.

"Pretty much."

"I'm sorry." She touched his shoulder.

He patted her knee as he turned onto the freeway. "It's okay. I came to peace with it a long time ago."

She turned away from him to look out her window, quiet for a few minutes. Without moving from her position, she said, "Valerie Hickman never stood a chance, did she?"

"Not really, no."

"Why is that?" Autumn asked, turning now to look at him.

"Because she was poor."

"That's it? I thought this was America, where everyone has a chance to make a better life."

"That's the idea but not the reality," he said.

"Kyle did it. He made it so Stone and I could have a future out of the trailer."

"He's the exception, I guess." Trey scratched a spot on his forearm. "Once in a while someone makes it out."

She turned back to the window. A few minutes later, she let out a long sigh. "The boys and I have to help her. That's all there is to it."

He smiled over at her. "Talk to your brothers. Come up with a plan. I'm here if you guys need anything."

"You're a good friend, Trey Wattson."

I could be so much more.

He bit his tongue and kept on driving.

AFTER HE DROPPED AUTUMN, Trey went home to the apartment. Stone and Pepper were out somewhere. The place was too quiet without them. He went into the bedroom and kicked off his shoes, then sprawled on the bed and closed his eyes. He might have drifted off to sleep had he not startled to alertness when he remembered he hadn't checked his email. He sprang from the bed and over to his desk. Jackpot. There was a message from Autumn.

DEAR ART,

I'm sorry for taking such a long time to return your message. I was out with my friend today. The one I told you about. He needed to check on a piece of furniture for his work and asked if I wanted to accompany him up to Stowaway. We had a nice day, for the most part. He suggested we visit my mother after lunch, since she lives there. My first reaction was to say no. Being with her exhausts me. Not that she does anything wrong. She's sweet, actually. I guess it's the guilt and residual anger that weighs on me. That and this feeling like I'm clenching my teeth the entire visit. I leave with a headache after every encounter. I find myself holding back from being kind or warm, which is not like me. My good intentions feel stuck inside, unwilling to yield or soften enough to let her into my life in any meaningful way.

Trey, on the other hand, was his usual thoughtful self. We saw a roach on my mother's carpet, and he was so kind about it, telling some story about how they were all over the college dorms, obviously hoping to lessen Valerie's embarrassment. That's a great example of the type of man he is—compassionate, thoughtful, and so very observant. Almost every day, my heart turns over from the sheer beauty of his soul. I've decided the small gestures of kindness tell the true story of a person's character. Especially when they're done for no reason whatsoever other than easing another's burden.

Her place was awful. If my brothers see it, they'll have a fit, given what they both do for a living. Valerie's stubborn, though. She refuses help. I can't blame her for it. If I were her, I wouldn't either. Taking a gift from someone you've robbed doesn't feel right.

Enough about me. Goodness, I do go on, don't I? This style of correspondence seems to lend itself well to speaking frankly. If we met in person, I'd be way too shy to tell you all this.

I was absolutely stricken to learn of the origin of your scarring. I'm so very sorry that happened to you. How have you gotten past the bitterness? Or have you? I carried my hatred for the young men who did this to me around for a long time. It wasn't until recently that I've been able to let it go. The reasons for which have something to do with retribution but that's not my story to tell.

I should close. My friend Sara is picking me up for dinner soon. We're taking her baby to the park for a swing and then to The Oar for dinner. That's our local bar and grill and a hangout for my friends and me. During the summertime, it's always packed with happy, tanned people who smell of sunscreen and salt water.

Tell me what you're doing. Have you seen your friend much? Do you think she knows how you feel about her?

Best,

007

HE READ her words through once more before getting up from the desk and going to the window. His bedroom faced east toward town and the hills beyond. The afternoon sun had lowered, drenching the town in warmth and soft yellow light. The windows in the houses built on the northeast slope of town gleamed like mirrors.

He smiled to himself. Autumn spoke so highly of him. Could she love him one day?

He went back to the desk and hit reply.

DEAR 007,

Thanks for your message. Don't feel worried if you can't write back right away. I understand you have a life out there in California with your Trey and friends. The more you tell me about him, the more I like him. Are you sure there isn't more between you? The two of you seem like the perfect match.

I spent the day with my friend as well. Today we spent the afternoon at a café watching people. To answer your question, I don't know if Michelle suspects my feelings or not. I can't imagine she wouldn't as I do nothing but stare at her when we're together. Regarding your other inquiry, being with her has decreased my bitterness over what happened. I suppose falling in love with Michelle has reminded me I'm still alive. I'm not my scars. I'm still me. Even though my wife didn't love me, maybe someone could, even with my imperfections. Sometimes she looks at me and I can feel her seeing beyond the scar tissue into my soul. She peers into my eyes, like she might love me back. And I think then, I'll tell her. Soon. I'll be courageous and give her the chance to return my feelings. I've been thinking it's not really fair to her that I keep them to myself. Who am I to assume she sees only my imperfections? If I love her and think so much of her, I am certainly not demonstrating that with my actions. Or lack thereof, as the case may be.

Speaking of love. The way you feel about Trey is becoming more obvious with every exchange. I wonder, again, if he might be the one who sees beyond the scar tissue to your soul?

With that, I'll close. Be well, 007. Write when you can.

Art

THE MOMENT HE HIT SEND, a surge of guilt washed over him. This exchange was beyond manipulative on his part. He was encouraging her to trust him and yet he was being completely dishonest. Yet even as those thoughts came, the others came too. This was the only way he could know her true feelings and thoughts. The more they wrote, the more obvious it became that there were so many aspects of her life she kept to herself. Getting to know her better only gave him more insight into how to win her heart. He would stay the course for now.

He knelt by the side of the bed and said a silent prayer. Please God, help her to see we're meant to be together and to forgive me once she knows what I've done.

4

A utumn

AUTUMN'S MONDAY at work was one of the busiest she could remember. A batch of nasty summer colds had brought many people into the pharmacy for antibiotics and cold medicine, along with the usual elderly customers picking up their regular prescriptions. The heat had spiked to the midnineties, and the heat pump in their old building could not keep up. By three that afternoon, it was in the upper seventies behind the counter. Driving home, she blasted the cold air onto her face. She was still hot and sweaty when she pulled into her driveway.

Her cottage was stifling, too. Not realizing how hot it would get, she'd left early that morning without turning the air conditioner on. Normally, it was cool enough by the beach that she only turned it on when the temperatures spiked over eighty-five.

She closed all the open windows and turned the air on

high. While she waited for the rooms to cool, she poured herself a tall glass of ice water and went out to the patio. She drank and stared longingly at the beach. There was hardly a grain of sand without a person or an umbrella. Many people were in the water. She wished she was one of them.

She thought about Trey's offer of the Mullens' pool. Was she foolish to have said no?

Her doorbell rang. She walked through the house to the front. It was Trey. He carried a shopping bag with the Phil's Swimwear logo on the side.

"I've brought you a present," he said as he handed her the bag.

She shook her head, laughing. "You're pushy, you know that, Wattson?"

"It's ninety-five degrees and the Mullens' pool is waiting. For you and me."

She opened the bag and peered inside to see a blue suit with white polka dots. "You bought me a suit?" She held it up for better inspection. The suit was a one-piece with a halter strap and looked to be around the right size. "How did you know what size to get?"

He shrugged. "It's not that hard to figure out. Plus, the lady helped me."

"You drove all the way to Stowaway to get this for me?"

"I had to go up there to pick up something for another client. When I saw the swimwear shop, I was struck with inspiration."

"You're crazy. I'm not going swimming."

"You are." He spread his hands out in front of him as if he feared she might bolt for the door. "I'm going to take you, but I'll stay in the pool house the whole time. You can swim to your heart's content. I won't look. I promise."

She stared at him, then back at the swimsuit. The water would feel so good. It was just Trey. She could trust him to give her the space she needed. Could she do it? "I haven't been swimming since I was a kid. We had a creek nearby we used to splash around in."

"It'll feel good. Come on. Let me do this for you."

He looked so pathetic she couldn't bring herself to reject the idea. "Fine. I'll go. But just for a few minutes."

He grinned and swooped her into his arms for a hug. "You won't regret it."

* * *

An hour later, she stood in front of the full-length mirror in the changing room at the Mullens' pool house. The suit fit well, even though it emphasized her flat chest and lack of curves or muscles. And God, her skin was blindingly white. She shifted her gaze to her legs. From the thighs to her knees, they were normal, although more stick-like than shapely. The trouble started just below her knees and ended at her ankles. Her right leg was streaked with surgery scars; the left was misshapen and twisted with the angry dent in her calf.

She reminded herself of how much worse it could be than cosmetic.

Be thankful they carry you around. You could have lost them both.

She grabbed the oversize beach towel and wrapped it around her waist.

"Are you out there?" she asked from behind the door.

"Yes," Trey said. "Is everything okay? You've been in there forever."

"I'm fine." She came out from behind the changing room door.

His hair wet and unkempt, Trey stood near the pool table holding a stick in one hand. He wore a pair of shorts but nothing else. "I cooled off while I was waiting." He set aside the pool stick. "I'll just stay in here while you swim."

She nodded, flushed and overly hot. This was stupid. She was an idiot to have agreed to this. Now Trey had to hide in the pool house while she swam?

"Go ahead," he said. "The water felt great."

She held her towel in place with clenched fingers and walked to the French doors that led out to the pool deck. With her hand on the knob, she turned back to look at him. "Come with me?"

"What?" He looked like someone who'd just been surprise punched.

"I'll slip in first. You can come in afterward."

"I'm not sure..." He trailed off, obviously unsure what to say or do.

"Give me a minute and then come out." She spoke with more assurance than she felt, then tumbled out the door. Why had she done that? Would the water obscure her legs? It didn't matter, she told herself. *He's Trey. You trust him with your life.*

At the edge of the shallow end of the pool, she halted and stared into the water, now with both hands clutching the towel. The sun hovered above the sea, still owning the day with her powerful rays. Below the surface of the water, blue tiles mimicked the sky. She glanced at the beach house, half expecting Trey to be standing there watching. But no, he'd kept his promise. She took off the towel and set it on the warm stone. Holding on to the railing, she inched into the water, taking one stair at a time until she was fully submerged. The delight of the cool water on her overheated skin quenched her very soul. Her breath caught. Using mostly arm strength, as her legs were weak, she swam toward the deep end, then dived under the surface with her eyes open until she reached the bottom. The salt water buoyed her, making her movements light and effortless. Her legs no longer ached from the endless shift she'd spent on her feet. She broke through the surface of the water, sputtering with joy. Then she swam to the end of the pool and back again, remembering.

She hadn't swum since the summer before the accident. During those hot months, she and Stone had cooled off almost every afternoon in the creek on the far end of their neighbor's property. The pig farmer's wife was a generous woman and had made sure they knew it was available to them any time. The swimming hole was a five-foot-deep section of the creek with bracing cold water even through August. They didn't care. Nothing felt better than jumping in after their chores were completed and before she had to start dinner. She and Stone would splash and swim and look for crawdads under rocks. They never found any, but their enthusiasm and hope never waned.

Their search for crawdads was a great metaphor for the way she and Stone thought about their life. Even with their circum-stances, they always assumed everything would be fine. The three of them would escape poverty one day. Kyle would make sure of it. He was clever and driven and grown-up before his time. Plus, the three of them had one another. Life would not keep them down forever.

Kyle was already working every shift he could down at the diner, so most afternoons he couldn't join them. But she and Stone talked and talked with their toes in the water every day of that long, perfect summer. The plans they made on the bank of that creek would not have seemed ambitious to those who dreamed of fame and wealth. Theirs were simple wishes. A home of their own. Made from wood, not tin, Stone would always add. A great love to share a life with. One who loved them and would never leave. Children who didn't have to wear clothes from the thrift store. Enough to eat throughout the whole month instead of running out several days before the next paycheck.

She remembered those afternoons as the last time she was free. Before the accident, she had no pain. She was strong and vital with limbs that could run nimbly through a forest, avoiding roots and fallen branches like the deer they often spotted. Her whole life had been ahead of her. Sure, their home life wasn't ideal, but Kyle took care of them. To her, life was as good as it had ever been. In the fall, cheerleading would begin. After she'd been accepted onto the team, Kyle had worked extra shifts to make sure she could participate. She was so grateful to him, yet he'd already lulled her into a sense of security and self-centeredness. Like all good parents, he made sure she had everything she truly wanted. Cheer had been one of those things.

She knew in that way that young people do—she would be the star of the team. Even the others, who had taken dance classes and cheerleading camps all their lives, couldn't outdo her innate talent. She was graceful and flexible. Her body memorized the routines without much effort, as if she was born to do exactly this.

Once he worked at the diner, Kyle made sure the hot water stayed turned on, and they made a weekly trip to the Laundromat. They could bathe daily and always had clean clothes to wear. Her hair smelled of flowers, and her dewy skin glowed with health. When she looked at herself in the mirror, the green eyes that peered back at her shone with promise.

The boys in town looked at her then, not like before, when she'd been invisible because of her shabby clothes and unwashed hair. Her beauty couldn't be diminished, even by poverty. Despite faded clothes, her long, muscular legs and curvy hips caught their attention. They forgot they'd ever called her brother pig or her disgusting and dirty. Now these same boys ogled her when she walked by them. She hadn't forgotten the truth, though. She remembered which children had shown kindness to her. And perhaps more so, she remembered who had been cruel. Those slights stayed with her, despite the shallow admiration from lustful boys. She held her head as high as she always had. Proud, sure, and without any apology for the scarcity in her life, knowing that what resided inside her was more than she needed to rise above. Someday she would thrive in a world that had set her up to fail. She would not fail. Not her. Not with her light.

Kyle had called her their lighthouse. He said she shone bright enough for all three of them. With her glow, they could always find their way. But that was before the accident. In the excruciating months afterward, through the surgeries and the pain and then the awful realization that Kyle, like their mother, had left for good, her light went out.

Being in the water reminded her of the girl she used to be. She felt the lighthouse version of herself deep inside, trying to get back out to the world. If she swam every day, would her vitality return, despite her damaged legs? Could she grow strong and confident? Was it possible to live without apology or shame?

Now she draped her arms over the edge of the pool and looked toward the glass doors, wanting Trey. "Trey, you can come out now."

She watched as he tentatively opened the door and came out to stand at the edge of the pool. He wasn't a big man, but his legs and torso were tanned and muscular. Compact and just right.

Wouldn't it be wonderful if she could join him at the beach? Maybe her fair skin would turn slightly golden if she weren't too shy to wear a bathing suit. If she weren't insecure, could they stand in the ocean together and let the salt water wash over them? Could she hold his hand and ignore the stares of children, too young to know their curiosity was impolite? Would he look at her as he was right now, smiling down at her as if she were spectacular?

"Hey, there, little mermaid." His eyes burned through her as he knelt by the edge of the pool. "Does it feel as good as you hoped?"

What was the message in his gaze? Did he find her beautiful? Did he see her the way she used to see herself? She'd caught him many times over the last few months, watching her with that same look in his eyes. She hadn't recognized the expression of admiration because she hadn't remembered what it felt like to know your own beauty from the gleam in a man's eyes. But here in the water, this older, less hopeful version of Autumn recalled how it felt to steal a man's gaze, to have power over him because of her loveliness.

Her legs dangled under her, hidden from his eyes. If she imagined them as a mermaid's tail, could she swim next to Trey? "Come in?" she asked.

Like an excited kid, he plunged into the water just feet from where she clung to the side. As he sank to the bottom, bubbles rose to the surface. She held her breath, irrationally frightened that he might not return. Seconds later, he erupted out of the water with the force of a sea titan. Of course he came back up. He could swim. And so far, he'd always returned to her. "God, this feels good, doesn't it?" He grinned at her, again reminding her of an excited boy.

"Yes, yes it does."

His sinewy arms moved through the water in a practiced breaststroke toward her. When he reached her, he stopped and rested one arm on the edge of the pool. "This is the life, right?" He shook the water from his hair.

She squealed as a few droplets dotted her face. "You're like a puppy. Don't you know it's bad manners to shake your wet fur on a lady?"

He shook his head once more. "They're very loyal, you know. Puppies."

"Is that right?" She laughed and splashed water at him.

"You should get a puppy. I wouldn't worry about you living alone if you had a dog."

"I don't have time for a dog," she said. "And I wouldn't be able to walk one. They pull too hard on the leash." She splashed him again. "You worry about me living alone? I didn't know that."

"Sure I do. I wish you'd gotten the security system Rafael suggested."

She'd thought about it, but the cost seemed outrageous considering how safe the community of Cliffside Bay was. "I don't need one. Who would want to harm me?"

"You never know," Trey said. "There are all kinds of scary people out there. Especially now that you're dating so much. You don't ever tell them where you live, do you?"

"No. I know better." She thought of Art. He'd said the same thing. Why did men seem to think women needed help figuring out something so simple? "Not before the first date. So far, there have been no second dates."

Trey's eyes glimmered as he looked away from her. "It's best to have high standards."

"I do. I guess." That was just the problem. No one compared to Trey.

He gestured toward the house. "Is this the kind of man you're looking for? A Brody Mullen type?"

"You mean rich or athletic?"

Trey laughed. "I meant the rich part."

"A pool would be nice, given my shyness about showing my body in public. But I never think about money that way. I'd rather have a good man than a rich one." She turned to rest both arms on the pool. He matched her pose. They hung there, like two kids on the side of a dock. Again, the feeling of the old Autumn washed over her. The water made her young. "Why'd you ask me about that?"

"I don't know. I guess I've been wondering what you're looking for."

I'm looking for a guy like you. That thought came before she could push it away. "Someone decent, smart, and who makes me laugh. Someone not so good-looking that he needs his wife to match him. A few scars might help. That way we'd match."

Trey's shoulders rose and fell. Air whistled between his teeth as he let out a long sigh. "People are scarred in ways that can't be seen on the outside, you know."

"It's not the same."

"It is. Wounds of the heart can be deeper than any physical one."

"I suppose that's true." When Kyle had left, she'd wanted to curl up in her bed and go to sleep until he came home, realizing his mistake.

She sucked in a shallow breath as a memory came, one she didn't even know she had.

It was of Kyle. He had held on to their mother's leg as she crossed the muddy driveway to the man's car. He'd begged her not to go. How had he known she would not return?

Valerie had stopped and knelt down to speak to him. Then she got into the car. He'd stood in the driveway in mud up to his ankles and watched the back of the car barreling down the dirt road. Where had Autumn been? Where had she been standing? She remembered then. Stone had been beside her. They'd stood at the dirty front window of the trailer. He'd held her hand as sobs racked his body. "Mommy. Don't go," Stone had wailed as the car drove away, mud spraying from the tires.

She inhaled a quick, sharp breath as pain shot through her. At four years old she'd watched her mother leave them. Ten years later, Kyle had done the same. And what about the man next to her? Would he leave, too? It seemed everyone she loved the most did. Not Stone, a voice whispered to her. He never left. Maybe Trey wouldn't either.

"What's wrong?" Trey's brow furrowed. "Do your legs hurt?"

"No. I just remembered the day my mom left us. I didn't think I remembered her leaving." She touched fingertips to her chest. "And it hurts."

"Tell me of your heart's pain and I'll tell you mine." Trey gave her a sad smile, then rested his right cheek on his forearms that draped over the side of the pool. "What did you remember?"

Still hanging from the side of the pool, she rested her chin on her hands and spoke softly. "I remembered the day my mom left. I hadn't thought the memory was there at all. For years I've told Stone I remember nothing of that day—nothing, really, of my mother." She told him how she and Stone had watched from the window. "Stone was only six, but he told me we'd been instructed to stay inside. So we just stood and watched as Kyle held on to her leg, begging her to stay." Her voice cracked, and she paused to control her breathing. "She said something to him before she got in the car." Without realizing what she was doing, she inched closer to Trey until their shoulders, warm from the lingering sun, touched. Under the water, her legs swayed as gently as a mermaid's tail, had there been such a thing. "I wonder what she said to him?"

"You could ask him." Trey lifted his head and turned to face her.

"Or her. I wonder if she would remember?"

"She might not remember any of it. Maybe all she could do or think was to escape. To save herself before she could save you guys."

"That's what she says. But still, I don't understand." Autumn lifted her head to look above Trey to the awning that hung over the pool house. An empty bird's nest was nestled in the corner rafters. Where had the birds gone? Or were there eggs inside, abandoned by their mother? Could eggs hatch if their mother left? Would the lack of their mother's warmth kill them before they emerged from their shells? Or would they hatch, only to find themselves alone with only their brothers and sisters to keep them company? Would they look at one another as she and her brothers had, and wonder if they would starve without fully formed wings with which to save themselves? "After she left, Kyle had to become a grown-up. Or, at least, partially. Our dad was like half a person—there but not. Every time I soften toward her, I remember what she did, and the anger floods through me the color and temperature of a hot poker. I don't know if I can ever forgive her."

Trey was quiet for a moment, perhaps thinking carefully about how to respond to such a statement. "I thought that same thing about Malia for a long time. Not that a wife's betrayal is the same as a mother's. I understand that. Having a spouse cheat on you is bad, but nothing could ever come close to the kind of abandonment you experienced. I'm not trying to diminish your feelings."

"I know you're not," she said softly. "Pain is pain."

"Her affair cut me to the core. I truly hated her. Do you know I wished she'd died instead of *decided* to leave? That way my grief could have just been loss instead of rage. I could have just been sad. Betrayal and abandonment are a whole different breed of loss."

"Yes," she whispered.

"But after a time, my rage lessened, and I started to see that her decision had nothing to do with me. I'd loved her. I'd been faithful and wanted nothing more than to grow old with her. That wasn't what she wanted. And ultimately, we can't get anyone to do something they don't want to do." He paused as he turned around and pressed his back against the side of the pool. "Not forgiving her was only hurting me. She was having sex with the tadpole in my bed and running the business I built and having a grand old time. I bet she didn't give one thought to me. She was too busy living. On the other hand, I was miserable. So I had to let it go."

"Yes, but you don't have to see her. You don't have to have her in your life. There's no choice about whether or not you let her back in."

"Like your choice about whether to let your mom back in?"

"Yes."

He turned back to her. His blue eyes ensnared her gaze. She couldn't look away from their beauty. "If you could forgive her, a lot of things in your life might change for the better."

"Like what?"

"Maybe coming to an understanding that her leaving had nothing to do with you and all to do with her mental illness. Really understanding that none of it had to do with you might allow you to let others in without so much fear of abandonment."

"Oh, I see." Dumbfounded by this startling insight, she stared into his unblinking eyes. "Do you think if I came to terms with this, the right man might suddenly appear? Like maybe I would recognize him when he came?"

"It could be."

She turned and lowered herself into the water until it reached her neck. The bottom of the pool felt rough against her tender feet. "I've been corresponding with a guy in Paris. He's scarred, like me. Maybe I should fly to Paris and see if he's the one." She meant it as a joke but given Trey's reaction, he didn't take it that way.

Trey's eyebrows knit together, and his expression darkened. "You're not going to Paris alone." He spoke slowly, emphasizing each word.

"Why not?" She poked his chest, enjoying teasing him for being so overprotective.

"For one thing, the bathrooms are terrible. They're mostly

up or down skinny, rickety stairs. I wouldn't be there to lean on when you tired at the end of the day."

She blinked, then laughed. "I got along just fine for twenty-eight years before I met you. I'd be fine."

"Who would carry your suitcases?" He was practically glowering at her.

"I'd travel light."

"That doesn't sound like you."

She laughed again. Since their trip to Colorado for Lisa and Rafael's wedding, he knew she had a serious overpacking problem. "Well, if you're so worried, you can come with me to Paris. You can lurk around the corner when I meet him. If he's creepy, you can rescue me."

His eyes dulled even further. "Sure. Good idea."

Was she a burden to him? Did he feel responsible for her? Was that what friendship with her gave him? A sense of responsibility? Was that what the swimming was all about? Did he feel compelled to help her even if he didn't want to? "Anyway, I have Stone and Kyle on creep patrol. God knows those two are paranoid and suspicious enough for all of us."

"That's what brothers are for," he said.

She smiled, thinking of her brothers and their big bodies and even larger hearts. "They wouldn't think it was a good idea to go to Paris without one of them. You're all overprotective."

He let out a long sigh, his gaze directed just left of her face. "We all care about you."

"I know," she said quietly. "But I hope you don't feel like you have to take care of me at the expense of your own needs."

His eyes widened. "What? Of course I don't."

"It would kill me to think you felt sorry for me or that I was a burden." She gave him a small smile, hoping to alleviate the tension in his face.

"Trust me. You're anything but a burden. You're the best thing in my life."

She jerked in surprise. "I am?"

"Totally. You're all light and goodness." His lips turned up in a smile, but his eyes glittered.

"Kyle used to call me our lighthouse. He said I glowed enough for the three of us."

"It's true," he said.

Without warning, he dipped under the water and swam toward the other side. She watched his sleek body pummel through the water, then surface. He hurled himself up and out of the pool and stood at the edge, peering at her with narrowed eyes. Water dripped from his hair and shorts.

"Trey?" A sliver of cold fear slipped under her skin. What was the matter with him? He slumped, as though a heavy cloak weighed down his shoulders. "Did I say something?" She pushed away from the side of the pool and swam over to him.

He sat on the edge of the pool with his arms crossed over his lean chest. "Are you serious about going to meet this guy?"

She draped one arm over the side of the pool and watched him, searching for clues to understand this strange mood that had suddenly overtaken him. Threads of sun glinted through the trees, obscuring half his face in shadows, while the other gleamed in the orange glow. "I was just kidding. It's just a romantic fancy. I don't even know the guy. Plus, he's in love with his best friend." She lowered her voice. "I'm lonely, that's all. The idea of meeting a man in Paris is nothing but a fantasy for someone like me. It's been such a long time since I was with anyone. Seems my whole life is spent waiting for someone who never comes."

"You hide away. No one can find you. Not the way you live, all closed up and hidden under clothes."

She smacked his calf. "I've been on five thousand coffee dates. I'm hardly hiding."

"But you don't really show yourself to them, do you? Not like with me?"

"You're my friend," she said. "It's different. I know you're not going anywhere. Right?"

"Right."

"It's different when people get romantically involved," she said.

A heaviness settled in the air between them. She glanced upward, almost expecting storm clouds to have gathered overhead.

He slid into the water next to her and spoke softly near her ear. "You should show me your legs. Right now. Swim over to the steps and walk out of here. Let me see you."

Was he insane? "What good would that do?"

"Practice. For when you meet a man you want to be with. The more you show up as the real you, the easier it will be."

She stared down through the water at her dangling legs, measuring his request. He'd pushed her into swimming. He'd been right to do so. Was he right about this, too? Would showing herself to him make it easier to imagine doing so with someone else? What if he flinched? What if she saw disgust in his eyes? She would not be able to forgive him. Losing him would be worse than all the rejection from other men by a hundredfold. Could she take the risk? Bare it all and see if he was like the others? If he reacted as her former boyfriend had, she would be devastated. The pedestal she put Trey on would crash to the ground.

"What if you don't look nearly as bad as you think?" he asked. "Women are harder on themselves than any man would ever be."

She rolled her eyes. "Men always think they know more about women than they really do."

He frowned. "That's not true. I know everything about you."

"Oh really?"

"I know how you like your coffee—two shots of espresso, nonfat milk, no foam, and one squirt of sugar-free caramel syrup. You always say a prayer before you set out in your car. You read old Agatha Christie mysteries over and over and never remember who the killer is. When you have a salad, you eat everything but the lettuce. Shall I go on?"

"Those are things any best friend would know."

He winced. "I don't know if you've noticed, but I'm a man, not a girlfriend."

Taken aback, she turned away, examining the tile on the edge of the pool.

She knew he was a man every single minute she was with him. He smelled of soap and leather. His full mouth seemed made for kissing. The corners of his eyes crinkled like crepe paper when he laughed. He moved with lithe efficiency she felt sure continued in the bedroom. She'd imagined at least a thousand times how his sensitive hands would explore every inch of her.

And that's when the fantasy ended. Because eventually he would come to her legs. She could not go further in her imagination. All fantasies stopped just below her knees.

Without warning, he took off for the shallow end of the pool. When he reached the steps, he sat on the top one and called out to her. "Swim over to me."

She hesitated, watching him, unsure what to do.

He scooted to the second step and held out his arms. Lightly, he said, "Show me your scars and I'll show you mine."

"You have none." She grimaced as she started to swim toward him. This was a dream. That's all. Soon she would wake. For now, she followed the path to Trey, hypnotized by his open expression.

When she reached the shallow end of the pool, she knelt in the water, too shy to go farther. The sun and sky played footsie as swashes of lavender and orange colored the horizon. Pepper always said lighting was everything. Would this soft light mask her imperfections?

He motioned to her to come closer. "You're all right. It's just me." His voice was like that of a parent encouraging a child's first steps.

She inched up from the water, revealing more and more of herself, until she was standing. The water came to three feet, reaching her midthighs. She locked gazes with Trey. Time and space condensed until they were insulated in the lavender twilight. Nothing and no one else existed in this dream but the two of them. Trey waited for her with his arms outstretched. She could go to him. He was her safe place.

Their eyes locked as she took one step and then another. In five, she reached the bottom of the steps. He stood and held out his hands without losing eye contact. "All the way now."

She took his hands and walked up the remaining steps. He walked backward, drawing her with him up to the deck. Together, holding hands, they exited the pool. The stone under her feet was warm, as was the air on her wet skin. Still, she shook with fright.

He never broke eye contact. "Are you ready for me to look at you?"

She nodded.

He backed up another couple inches and dropped her hands, then knelt on the smooth stone next to her legs. Under his gaze, she shivered. Goose bumps covered her arms. She looked down just as his long, sensitive fingers brushed against the dent in her left leg. "Is this all it is? I'm quite under-whelmed," he said.

Tears welled in her eyes as he traced the red scars with his index finger, as if drawing a picture on her skin. "Each one of these marks is evidence of your journey. Your bravery. Your unwillingness to give up. How could anyone see them as anything but beautiful?"

A sob rose from her chest. "That's not true."

He leaped to his feet and pulled her into his arms. Their

bare, wet skin made them slippery. She placed her hands on his shoulders to steady herself. She watched his pulse thud under his chin.

"Listen to me now," he said. "You have to start thinking of your scars as warrior paint—something to be proud of, not hide away. You're a survivor and have the scars to prove it. And if a man looks at you and sees anything but a lovely, strong woman, he's blind."

Tears fell in hot streaks down her face. She allowed her head to tilt and rested her cheek against his collarbone.

His arms tightened around her. He kissed the top of her head.

She lifted her face to look up at him and found his eyes peering down into hers, as if he could see straight through to her soul.

"You need to hold out for a man who loves you just as you are," he said.

I wish that man were you.

That thought barreled into her consciousness like a flash of unexpected lightning. Where had it come from? This was Trey. Her friend. A man, yes. But not the man for her.

Be content with that, she told herself. Friends never leave you.

She withdrew from his embrace. "Thank you for this."

"Thank you for indulging my whim," he said.

"I don't know if I can ever be as free with anyone else as I am with you."

"I'll always be here for you. Don't forget that."

"I won't."

Again, she reminded herself how much better it was to have a loyal friend than a fickle lover. Trey grounded her, gave her confidence.

"You're the best," she said, then planted a sisterly peck on his cheek. "Let's go home. I want ice cream."

5

T rey

NIGHT HAD FALLEN by the time Trey turned onto Main Street. Since they left the Mullens', Autumn had been humming to the radio while braiding her damp hair with deft fingers. Once, she remarked how relaxed she felt and that she really should make an effort to swim for exercise. "But where?" she asked.

"I'm sure Kara would invite you to use her pool any time you wanted," he said.

She didn't respond but appeared to be contemplating this suggestion as they entered the city limits. They drove past the Cliffside Bay Resort, a massive sprawl of pillars and balconies, all lit up like a Christmas tree. The grocery store was still open, even though the flowers had all been taken in for the evening. By dawn, Clayton, the flower guy, would have arranged his day's finds in front of the glass doors. Without the colorful, fragrant flowers, the storefront seemed lonely, even bereft.

Like him without Autumn.

Internally, he chastised himself for being overdramatic even though it was true.

The Oar pulsed with life. The outside seating was overrun with sunburned tourists and somewhat annoyed, tanned locals. The residents hated the additional patrons but had accepted it as part of the town's ebb and flow, just as they did the fluctuating tides of the sea that continually morphed their strand of beach. He knew without having to see that the back patio, strung with white lights, would be filled with people enjoying adult beverages in the warm night air.

Through the windows, he caught a glimpse of a local band performing. On the dance floor, couples swayed to the music. He envied them. Perhaps a few of the couples would wake tomorrow in the bed of someone they barely knew. After his divorce, he'd had a few of those nights. That was before Autumn, during his ridiculous vow to remain forever single. How had he ever thought it smarter to engage in meaningless physical encounters than make a life with a good woman? He'd been bitter and closed up like the crabs on the beach until Autumn's sweetness had drawn him out of his shell. Now he was as exposed as a crab without a shell, all squishy and vulnerable.

As they passed by the bookstore, Lance Mullen was in the process of locking the front door. His wife, Mary, leaned over a two-seater stroller holding their toddler and infant daughters and rearranged a blanket. Their dog, Freckles, waited patiently on his haunches for his family to be ready.

Trey sensed Autumn looking at the Mullen family and glanced at her from the corner of his eye. The look of longing on her face pained him. She yearned for the dog and stroller and adoring husband. He wanted to give them to her.

"You okay?" he asked.

"Oh, sure. Just fighting off the green monster." Tendrils of hair, unwilling to be tamed by the braid, curled against her neck. Without makeup, she looked young and even more inno-cent. He loved how he could see more of her freckles without her careful makeup coverage.

He didn't say anything as he turned the car down the side street that led to her house. Cottages built in the 1940s as vaca-tion bungalows and as similar as sisters with their gray shingles and white trim hugged the shoreline. He pulled into Autumn's skinny driveway and parked next to her car. When he turned off the engine, intending to walk her to her door, she put her hand on his forearm. "Trey, wait. I need to say something to you. What you did tonight was so... I don't have the words to tell you what it meant to me. Thank you for pushing me."

His throat tightened and he was unable to do anything but nod.

She reached over and gave him a quick kiss on his cheek similar to the one earlier. "I'll talk to you tomorrow."

"I can walk you to your door."

She flashed him an indulgent smile. "It's five feet away. Just watch me from here."

He nodded in agreement and watched as she unbuckled her seat belt and slipped out of his car. She tottered up her front walkway in her flat sandals. The swim had tired her. When she reached her front door, she opened it and then turned back to give him a quick wave, then disappeared inside her house.

He drove home with an uneasy feeling in the pit of his stomach. As much progress as he'd made today, he worried about the fake Art and Paris and what would happen if she found out the truth.

* * *

LATER, after a shower, he pulled on shorts and an old T-shirt, then made himself a sandwich and grabbed a beer. Neither Stone nor Pepper was home, and the empty, quiet apartment represented everything wrong about his life. Without them, the space looked and felt like the lonely pages of a magazine spread. Soon, after Pepper and Stone moved to their new house, it would be like this all the time.

In his room, he sprawled lengthwise over his bed with the plate on his lap. He watched the second half of a soccer match on television without much enthusiasm, caring little about the outcome since his LA team wasn't playing. He finished his food and decided to check his email. Constantly checking was a bad habit but he didn't care. If there was a message from Autumn, he wanted to read it now, not later.

Setting aside his plate, he swung his legs from the bed and strode over to his desk. Instead of sitting, he took the laptop back to his bed and resumed his position before opening his email. His heart leapt at the sight of her name in his messages.

DEAR ART,

You won't believe what happened today. I went swimming with Trey. He talked me into joining him at our friend's pool after promising he wouldn't look at my legs. The strangest thing happened, though. Once I was in that water, it was like the old Autumn returned. I felt young, like I did before the accident. My legs were without the usual heaviness. Swimming felt effortless, and the water was like a balm to my achy legs.

Perhaps that explains what happened next. It was like a dream then and thinking back on it now, the experience seems even more dreamlike. This will shock you. It does me, and I'm the one who did it. Trey convinced me to show him my legs. Yes, you read that right. No one, other than my brothers and

Sara, has ever seen me without covering until tonight. I don't know what got into me, but before I knew what I was doing, I strolled out of the pool and into his outstretched hands.

He looked, Art. Really looked. He didn't flinch or grimace or look away. Then he traced my scars with his fingers and told me I should wear them proudly, as they are proof of my survival. I'd never thought of it that way. I'm not convinced to run naked down the street or anything, but his reaction gave me a little more self-confidence.

I couldn't express properly what his gift meant to me. Honestly, I don't know how or why he even thought of encouraging me to swim. I've never mentioned it to him. Lately, it's like he reads my mind. Regardless, he's the most thoughtful person in my life. I'm racking my brain to try to think of a way to repay him.

Maybe by the next time I write, I'll have gone to the beach.

How are you? Have you talked with your friend about your feelings?

Best,

007

His smiled as he read her message, though sobered at the "reads my mind" section. If she only knew that his deception was his crystal ball. He needed to put an end to Art. Soon. He would do it soon. Not tonight. First, he would write to her. He glanced at the clock, doing the math in his head. It was the early hours of the morning in Paris. If he sent one back now it might seem strange to her. He decided to write it now but set it up to send later. This fake life was complicated. Lies always were.

. . .

DEAR 007,

Swimming! I'm proud of you for being brave. What's that saying? If it doesn't scare you, it isn't worth doing. Something like that, anyway. Regardless, good for you.

You may have given Trey hints about swimming that you were unaware of at the time. Men are mostly clueless, but every once in a while, we pick up on women's clues. I'm glad he reacted the way he did. I think most people will if you give them a chance. Maybe this is just what you need to tackle that beach. I hope it is.

I wish I could say things were as good on my end as your news. I've been in a bit of a funk, feeling sorry for myself. I'm still stuck in the same place with the girl of my heart. Tonight, we went...

He lifted his fingers from the keyboard. What could he say that was a little like the intimate moments they'd spent swimming that wasn't exactly that? She'd had him over for dinner and they'd had a good talk, even though he still couldn't bring himself to confess his feelings? Yes, that would do.

He continued.

Tonight, Michelle invited me to her apartment for dinner and she talked to me in a way she doesn't usually. She spoke of her background in more detail and in general seemed more vulnerable. I wish I had the courage to say something or do something, but the fear of rejection and of ruining our friendship is strong. I know you understand.

Anyway, I should go now. I have things to do for work. Have a good day tomorrow.

Talk soon.

Art

HE HIT the send button and powered off his computer. Turning up the volume on the television, he forced himself to focus on the game. Distraction. That's all he needed. Yeah, right. It would take more than a soccer game to rid his mind of the images of Autumn Hickman in a bathing suit.

utumn

THE NEXT MORNING, Autumn woke to a thick fog outside the
windows. She padded to the patio and threw open the doors.
Cool, damp air greeted her. She breathed it in, thankful the hot
weather of yesterday was gone. A layer of fog obscured her view
of the beach. Later, the haze would roll away, but for now it
made a bed over the sea like layers of gossamer blankets. To air
out the house, she left the French doors open and went into the
kitchen to make a cup of coffee.

Feeling remarkably well rested, she stretched her arms
toward the ceiling as she waited for the coffee to brew. Swimming was the gift that kept giving. Not only had she enjoyed
her time in the water, she'd been physically spent afterward.
She'd slept the entire night through, she realized, as she
popped two pieces of wheat bread into the toaster.

With her coffee and toast, she sat at her table and looked

out to the white world of the morning. The pharmacy would be busy later, and she relished the few minutes of calm before heading to the shower.

The sound of a seagull's cry startled her. She looked over to see a particularly large bird giving her the stink eye just outside the French doors. "Shoo." She stood, almost knocking her coffee over, and ran to close the doors. "Go away." The gull fluffed his wings as if offended but didn't move. She closed the doors, smiling to herself. These gulls were awfully bold. He probably wanted a piece of her toast. She locked the doors and was about to go back to the table when something stopped her cold. Obscured by the thick fog, a figure stood on the end of her patio looking straight at her. The shape stepped closer, ghost-like in the mist. A man. He wore a red cap and a black jacket. She stifled a scream and double-checked the lock. The gull suddenly lifted from the patio and flew toward the man. Obviously frightened, he backed up and then stumbled from the side of her patio. He fell on his knees but scrambled to his feet in the next instant and took off running. On shaky legs, she went back to the table, grabbed her phone, and called Trey.

He sounded sleepy when he answered. "Good morning," he said.

"There was a man on my patio. Staring at me. I had the doors open. If it hadn't been for a seagull, he might have come in."

"Crap. And you didn't know him?"

"I couldn't see him well enough to know," she said. "Then the gull scared him off."

"Good gull."

"He's probably just some vagrant living on the beach. Maybe he wandered up to my patio on accident."

"I'm going to call today and get a security system installed," Trey said, firmly. "No arguments."

"Maybe you're right," she said. "But it's so expensive."

However, with all the tourists in the summer, Cliffside Bay might not be as safe as they thought.

"I'll pay for it," he said.

"Don't be silly. I can afford it. I'd just rather spend the money on clothes."

He made a sound between a chuckle and sigh. "Your safety's more important."

"He could've just been a drunk who woke up on the beach after a bender," she said, hoping to convince them both that she wasn't in danger.

"Drunk or on meth," he said. "You're so close to the public beach that any number of types could wander onto your patio. I'm sending my guy out there today. My schedule's flexible. I'll meet him there later while you're at work."

She agreed and they hung up. Creeped out, she double-checked the front lock, too. It was secure. "Do not think of the movie *Psycho*," she repeated to herself as she walked to the bathroom for her shower.

* * *

She worked a full and busy shift and forgot about the man on the patio. However, it all came rushing back when she pulled into her driveway. In the corner of her small patch of grass a sign read, "This house is protected by Huffman Security."

Trey, true to his word, had ordered a security system. He always did what he said he'd do. She parked and texted him a quick thank-you before heading into the house.

Her phone buzzed with a call just as she placed her bag on the kitchen island. A quick glance at the screen told her it was Valerie.

Autumn answered with a simple hello.

"Hi, Autumn." She sounded strangled and hoarse.

A jolt of alarm surged through her. "What's wrong? Are you sick?"

"No, not sick. My apartment burned. The whole building's nothing but burning embers. I came home from work and there were all these fire trucks and police cars. I can't see a thing that's recognizable. The whole place collapsed on itself. Like it melted."

Autumn's throat had constricted, making it hard to speak. "Was anyone hurt?"

"No, thank goodness. Most of us were at work. There's a single mother with two little ones, but they were out at the park when the fire started. The apartment manager made sure to get the two elderly people out. They said it burned so fast, there was barely time."

"Do the authorities know how it started?" Autumn asked.

"I don't know. If they do, they're not saying. Everyone's just standing around in the parking lot. None of us know what to do."

"You have your car? It was with you at work, right?"

"Yes, I'll have to sleep there until I figure out what to do."

"Sleep in your car?" Autumn hadn't brought it up as a suggestion for a new home. "Check into a hotel."

A long, shaky sigh came from the other end of the phone. "Hotel? Honey, people like me stay in motels."

Anxiety crawled up the back of Autumn's neck. Her tiny mother wasn't sleeping in her car. There were dangerous people out there. "Motel or hotel—whatever. You need to book a room somewhere safe."

"I used almost all my paycheck for rent. There's not enough left for a motel until I get paid again." There was a sharp intake of breath and a hiccup before she spoke again. "Work. I have to go to my job first thing in the morning." Her voice rose as the reality of her situation obviously took hold. "What will I wear? How will I shower or wash clothes? I can't lose this job."

Autumn stood, helpless, with her mouth slack as she processed this bit of information. Valerie was alone, without money or even clothes, and was panicked about losing a job that kept her fed and sheltered from paycheck to paycheck. This was how people ended up homeless.

In the background, she detected the sounds of men shouting. She could almost hear the smoldering of the boards and bricks. Was her mother close enough to feel the heat on her face?

Valerie continued in the same flat, broken tone of a person who has given up on finding a solution to their situation. "Everything I owned was in that apartment. Not much, but mine. Now there's nothing left." The resignation of the poor. Autumn knew the script. She'd said it herself a thousand times when she was young. *Things are bad and won't get better. Best not to fool yourself into thinking they will. Having hope is a dirty trick.*

The mass of seething, fiery debris was the symbol of every person living in poverty. *Whatever I build eventually burns, and I'm back to nothing.*

"I'm sorry," Autumn said, thinking of the treasures she and Trey had so carefully selected for her cottage. Yes, they were just things, merely objects, but when one had grown up with so little, physical pieces had a bigger importance. They were symbols of survival, material proof of a better life. Each like a badge that proved she was bigger than her circumstances had predicted.

"It's not the stuff so much as the photographs. They're all I had left of my husband." Valerie's voice broke, and Autumn could hear her crying. The image of her sobbing, feeling all alone, was too much. This was her mother. The person who gave her life.

"Did you call Kyle? What did he say to do?" Kyle should have talked sense into her.

"I didn't call him. You were the first one I thought to call," Valerie said.

"Me? Why me?"

"I don't know. I wanted to talk to you. My daughter."

A lump in her throat made it hard to speak, but Autumn blurted out, "Mom, come stay with me." Mom? Had she just said the most sacred of titles out loud for the first time? She hadn't intended to. This was a title that should be earned but wasn't always—the mothers who abused, the mothers who left. The most important word in the English language should never be used carelessly. *Mother, mom, mommy, mama* were words bestowed on the woman who cared for you, sacrificed parts of herself to give you what you needed.

Not for her mother.

Her mother had left.

A small, quiet voice chirped inside Autumn's head, like a sweet bird's song. *But she came back. She's here now. Isn't it time to forgive her? Let her in?*

Yes, Valerie was here with a big bushy olive branch. She was trying. Had Autumn tried? Or was she more comfortable treading water in a pool of resentment? Anger had kept her from softening into forgiveness. Maybe that's what she wanted. Now, that was a jolting thought. Perhaps this distance was a place of comfort. Removed yet outraged meant she didn't risk being hurt, being rejected. Again.

A heavy silence greeted her from the other end.

"Did you hear me?" Autumn asked. "Come stay with me."

"I can't. I need this job," Valerie said.

"You can just stay for a little while."

"I can't drive all that way every day. Too much gas."

"You can find a job here. Kyle has work at the resort."

More silence.

"What is it? Why won't you just move down here? You say you want to be near us, so why live an hour away?"

"I...I don't want to be a burden. I've caused you kids so much pain."

"It's time to move on."

"To where?" Valerie asked.

"Being a real family."

"I can't sponge off you or your brothers."

"Kyle wants to buy you a home. Why won't you let him?"

"Autumn, I've already explained this. I cannot take his money. His charity. Not after what I did."

Her temper flared. "Get over it."

"What?"

"I said, get over it. Kyle owns half of California. Let him buy you a place to live. I let him help me with the cottage. I'd never have been able to afford to have it renovated without him. And he helped Stone and the other Wolves start their business."

"I'm over fifty years old," Valerie said. "I can't live off you kids for the next twenty years."

"Twenty? How about another forty?"

"Oh, Autumn." Another silence.

"Really, this is silly. Please, come stay with me. The boys and I'll help you come up with a plan."

"*Maybe* I could find a job there. Won't I be in the way? What about Trey?"

"Trey?"

"I wouldn't want to put a damper on your romance."

"We're friends. That's all." Why was everyone so sure they were lovers? Wasn't it obvious they were the best of pals?

"I had a different impression."

"No way. We don't think of each other like that."

"Okay." Valerie drew out the vowels in a very know-it-all motherly type of way that gave Autumn a sparkly feeling in the middle of her chest.

"Get in your car and come here," Autumn said. "You can borrow some of my clothes until I can take you shopping."

"Will you tell your brothers?" A slight pause. "Do you think they'll mind?"

"What have they been asking you to do for months now?"

"When you've made as many mistakes as I have, it makes every kind gesture seem suspicious," Valerie said.

"We're your family. Mistakes happen, but we're still family."

After she hung up with Valerie, she called Kyle to tell him about the apartment building.

"For real? The whole thing burned down?"

"Yes, the entire building," Autumn said. "Think of all the people who now have no place to go."

"I'll call her and get her to move in with us."

"I invited her to live with me for a while and she said yes."

"No way. That's great. Good work, little sister."

"It took some persuading," Autumn said.

"I've been working on her for a year." He said this as if it were new information.

"I guess it took a fire to convince her."

"That's scary, if you think about it too hard. We just got her back," Kyle said.

"That place must have violated a hundred safety codes."

"This really burns my hide," Kyle said. "I should buy the property and put up something, a decent place for people to live."

"Nice idea, but people who make what they do would never be able to afford the rent. We need more affordable housing in this country."

Kyle made a growling sound in the back of his throat. "You sound like my wife."

"I'm serious. Think about the elderly on a fixed income and that single mother with two little kids. Where are they supposed to go?"

"Like we were." Kyle sighed.

"Yes, like that."

"I can't house all the poor people of Northern California." Her brother's words had a defensive edge to them.

"I know. You're a businessman, not the low-income housing authority."

"True. But still," Kyle said.

"I'll talk to you later."

After they hung up, she changed out of her work clothes into a light cotton dress. She rummaged around in her refrigerator for something to eat and settled on a salad with some leftover chicken. No sooner had she finished the last bite of field greens than her front doorbell rang. There was no way it was Valerie already. Probably a salesperson or a kid asking for donations.

She ambled somewhat wearily over to the door and peeped through the glass. Trey. She yanked open the door. He grabbed her in a hug. "Thank God," he said.

"What are we thanking God for?"

"You didn't answer my texts, so I got worried."

"I was on the phone." She laughed as she motioned for him to shut the door. "You're letting all the cool air out."

"Where have you been?" He followed her into the kitchen. "I thought maybe...someone broke in...or something. I didn't leave the alarm on because I need to show you how to use it first."

"No, no. I'm fine." She swept a plate from the kitchen table, rinsed it, and stuck it in her dishwasher. "Actually, I was on the phone with Valerie." She told him about the fire and that Valerie had agreed to come stay for a while.

He grabbed a beer from her refrigerator and leaned against the counter. "Well, well, well. This is a turn of events."

She tossed the bottle top he'd left near the sink at him. "Don't be smug."

"What? I think it's nice you're softening."

"I couldn't allow her to be homeless," she said. "That's all."

"Maybe it'll be nice. Living together will give you a chance to know her in a different way."

"The company might be nice. It's lonely sometimes."

"I get it. Speaking of which, Stone and Pepper's house is almost finished."

A surge of envy passed through Autumn. Her brothers would be neighbors. Their children would be able to run to each other's homes. "The house is already done?"

Trey nodded. "They're ready for interiors, which Pepper and I've been working on for months now. It's just time to implement."

Stone and Pepper were building a house on the back of Kyle's property. When Kyle had bought the acreage, he'd split it in half with his friend Jackson Waller. Jackson and Maggie had taken the part of the land with a house, which they'd subsequently renovated. There was another piece of land behind Kyle's that had been mostly woods. When they'd settled on that piece of land, Kyle and Stone had hired men to take down enough of the trees to make room for a house.

"How does it look?" Autumn asked.

"Gorgeous. Like one of those beach houses in a magazine."

Pepper was raised back east and favored the Cape Cod-style homes. She'd recently inherited an obscene amount of money from her deceased father. Soon thereafter, she'd been offered a tidy sum to star in a movie with Genevieve Banks and their own Lisa Perry. Autumn would love to hate her for being talented and rich, but her heart wasn't in it. Pepper was as kind as she was fun. She was the perfect spice to Stone's steadiness. Together, they were unconquerable.

Another knock on the door took her attention from Trey. She glanced at her watch. Still a little early for Valerie. She crossed through the kitchen to the front door. Stone's large frame filled the doorway, and his slender fiancée was tucked against his side. "Hey, sis. Sorry to barge in, but Kyle called and said Mom's on her way."

"Word travels fast," Autumn said as she ushered them into the small foyer. "Come on in. Trey's here."

"Is Valerie on the way?" Pepper asked, shutting the door behind her.

"Should be here any minute," Autumn said.

They went into the kitchen. Stone helped himself to a beer, then they all went out to the patio to enjoy the view.

"What's with the security system?" Stone asked.

Autumn glanced at Trey. "I had a Peeping Tom this morning, so Trey had the security guy come out and install a system for me."

Stone raised his eyebrows. "Peeping Tom?"

"Just some random guy on the deck," Autumn said. "Nothing to worry about."

That seemed to satisfy her brother, because the guys broke off into a conversation about work. Autumn and Pepper kicked off their shoes and walked to the end of the deck and across the cement boardwalk to the sand. Pepper wore shorts that barely covered her narrow rear and a tank top over small breasts. Her skin remained the color of cream because of dutiful slathering of sunscreen whenever she was outside.

The yellow ball that was the sun hovered above the skyline.

"I got a call from my mom and stepdad this morning. They sold their place in the Hamptons and made an offer for a house in town here."

"That's wonderful."

Pepper smirked. "The pressure for grandchildren will reach outrageous heights."

"You know Stone's up for it."

"I know he is. I'm not ready yet, though. My career's finally taking off. I want to spend a few more years nurturing it and not a baby."

"When the time is right, you'll know."

"My mom says there's never a right time for a baby. You just have to go for it," Pepper said.

"Spoken like a woman who wants grandchildren."

They shared a chuckle as they walked slowly across sand still warm from the afternoon sun. Discarded sandwich wrappers and a few tin cans dotted the pristine beach. Pepper pulled a plastic bag from her shorts pocket. "I like to get the trash when I can." She leaned over and picked up several candy wrappers and stuffed them inside.

"Do you always do this?" Autumn asked.

"Only when I'm on the beach. Or in town. Violet's rubbing off on me." Pepper grinned. "I still can't believe how lucky I am to be marrying into this family."

They kept walking, picking up debris along the way, until they reached the edge of the wet sand. A breeze rustled Autumn's hair. Peppers shiny curls bounced as they covered her face.

"Want to sit for a minute?" Pepper asked.

Autumn did so, careful to make sure the long skirt of her maxi dress didn't ride up over her ankles. They both stretched their legs out across the sand.

Pepper put aside her trash bag and reached inside her canvas bag. "I present rosé in a can," she said as she popped the top and handed it to Autumn.

"What else do you have in that bag?" Autumn asked.

Pepper brushed her curls away from her face. "Let's just say your brother often needs a snack. That's a lot of body to keep fueled."

They sipped from their cans of wine and watched the sun sink ever so slowly toward the sea. There was a resignation to the evening, as if the earth readied itself for bed after a sun-drenched day. As they sat there, the air cooled and brushed over her bare arms and face with the promise of a cool, clear night. The light turned from yellow to orange. Pelicans and seagulls squawked and swooped, but not with the vigor they'd displayed during the hot afternoon when they'd hovered near picnickers, vying and hoping for a piece of food dropped from a sandy hand.

Next to her, Pepper fidgeted, as if she couldn't get comfortable. A tightness around her mouth hinted at a worry of some kind. She rolled the can of wine between the palms of her hands like a potter with a piece of clay.

"Everything okay with you?" Autumn asked, hoping to get a straight answer.

"Yes. I think so anyway." Pepper drew a circle in the sand with one finger. "I didn't want to say anything in front of the guys. They're both so overprotective of us. I keep telling Stone I looked after myself for years before I met him, but he's always worried. I can't blame him when we're in LA or if I'm filming somewhere far from him. Sometimes I catch him watching me when I leave to go somewhere like he thinks I might not come back."

"That's the family abandonment thing."

"I understand, but it makes me sad," Pepper said. "I'd never leave him on purpose."

She reached over and squeezed Pepper's hand. "He knows that deep down. It's just that our subconscious acts up from time to time. We're like dogs that were abused, always waiting for a smack that our new owners would never give us."

"I'd do anything to take that away from both of you," Pepper said.

"It's strange to say, but you have. You and Violet—the way you love my brothers—it's changed us."

"Even you?"

"Yes." Her gaze drifted to the waves that broke just inches from their feet. "It's given me hope that there's someone out there who will love me that way."

Pepper drew her knees up and rested one cheek against them, looking at her. "You really don't see it, do you?"

"See what?"

"Never mind. I wanted to talk to you about something without the guys present."

"Sure thing."

"Yesterday, I was coming out of the grocery store and there was this man standing by that big oak. You know the one?"

"In front of the flower area?"

"That's right. He was leaning against it and staring at me. When I looked back at him, his gaze didn't even flinch. It was like he was fixated on me. Not to sound vain, but I thought he might be a fan. Believe it or not, that awful horror movie I'm in is killing it at the box office. There's no accounting for taste. But then, I saw him again later when I came out of the bookstore. There's something really creepy about him. However, I'm paranoid, you know, because of what happened to me."

She didn't have to explain. Pepper suffered from the trauma of being raped as a teenager. She was afraid of the dark and was easily spooked by male attention. From her own experience, Autumn understood how certain people or places could trigger a person and take you back to the cruelest moment of your life. The roar of an engine or riding with someone who drove fast or recklessly shook her in much the same way. In a second, she could return to those terrifying moments as their car spun in a circle. The night she almost died. The night she almost lost her legs. The night that changed everything.

Pepper crossed her legs at the ankles. "I dismissed it until just now. But the man on the porch, staring at you, seems too coincidental."

"Like it could be the same guy?" Autumn asked.

"Well, maybe." Pepper flushed as she tucked a bouncing curl behind one ear. "Or do I sound super paranoid?"

"Not at all." Alarm bells were echoing through Autumn's

mind. "What did he look like? I couldn't see him well because it was so foggy."

"He was a big guy. Not as large as Stone or Brody Mullen, but more barrel-chested with one of those thick necks." Pepper closed her eyes as she continued to describe him. "He had a ruddy face, like guys who drink too much, and a receding hairline. I'd say he was somewhere in his fifties."

For a second, Autumn fumbled for a memory. Why did that description feel familiar? Then she knew. The man crouching on the other side of her planters fit that description. She told Pepper about him. "I didn't connect that the figure on my patio could be the same guy, but it's certainly possible."

"Crap, yes." Pepper's fingers dented the middle of her can.

"Do you think it's the same guy? And if so, why would he be following us?"

"I had a thought. It's probably far-fetched," Pepper said. "People do accuse me of having too large an imagination."

"What is it?"

"Could it be something to do with the woman who was blackmailing your mom?"

Autumn started, surprised to hear Pepper speaking out loud about the darkest secret of their family. "You know about what our mother did?"

"There are no secrets between Stone and me. I know your mother set the fire that killed the boys who tortured Kyle and caused your accident."

She took a moment, considering the question. Last year, when their mother had shown up so unexpectedly, she'd come to tell them what she'd done and that she was preparing to turn herself in to the authorities. Someone from her past had threatened to tell the police unless Valerie went to Kyle and asked for a lump of cash in exchange for her silence. Kyle had convinced Valerie to tell the woman she was ready to confess and would take the evidence of the extortion with her when she went to the police. After that, the woman disappeared. They'd thought it was all over. Could this be another connection to that? But if so, why spy on her or Pepper?

"I don't know. It's possible," Autumn said.

"As you and I know, evil is always possible."

Autumn nodded as she brought her legs to her chest and wrapped her arms around them. Fire. A burning building. Could the fire in Valerie's building have been set to target her? A warning? Or payback?

She took in a sharp inhale of breath and froze as the possibility took hold. A fire for a fire? A death for a death. "What if the fire was set on purpose? My mom doesn't think so, but what if there were still people alive who cared about those boys? Could they have somehow been contacted by the blackmailer out of spite?"

Pepper's eyes widened. "And this is like a vengeful thing?"

"Yes," Autumn whispered. Her heart sped up. "What if they're trying to kill my mother?"

Pepper rose to her feet, dusting the sand from her bottom. "We should talk to the guys before Valerie gets here."

T rey

TREY WATCHED as Pepper and Autumn walked toward them. In the sand, Autumn's gait was slower and her injury more pronounced. That wasn't the only difference in Autumn's appearance. Her expression was one of worry and, if he wasn't mistaken, fear. He glanced at Pepper. She looked much the same way.

Stone, who'd been inside grabbing a couple of beers, came out the French doors just as they walked up the steps. Pepper flounced into a chair, her black curls bouncing like springs. Autumn rested her hands on the back of a chair next to Trey's, clearly too agitated to sit.

"What's going on?" Stone's brow furrowed as he glanced back and forth from his fiancée to his sister.

"There's something I didn't mention," Pepper said. "A

couple of times I've seen the same guy watching me. Maybe even following me."

"What the hell? Pepper Shaker?" Stone asked.

At Stone's immediate agitation, she put up her hands. "Please, don't be mad I didn't tell you, but I thought I was just being paranoid, like I am sometimes."

Autumn took the story from there. "What if this creepy guy and the fire at Valerie's apartment building are somehow connected to the fire she set all those years ago?" Her fingers gripped the back of the chair as if she were using it as a way to stand upright. "What if it was set on purpose as payback or something?"

Trey and Stone exchanged a glance. He could see in his friend's eyes that he thought the women's theory was a distinct possibility.

"But what would he want with you two?" Trey asked. He must remain calm. The thought of anyone harming Autumn or Pepper made him want to howl in fright.

"That's the part that doesn't make sense," Autumn said. "Unless he wants revenge on our whole family."

"Mom said no one from that family is even around anymore," Stone said.

"That's what she thinks. It may or may not be true," Autumn said. "I mean, why else would anyone be following us?"

"But why Pepper?" Stone asked.

"Maybe whoever it is wants our whole family to suffer. Pepper's family now." Autumn's voice shook.

Trey patted the chair seat next to him. "You should sit."

She obeyed, all the fight seeming to run out of her. He reached under the table for her hand and held it in his against his thigh. She rested her head on his shoulder.

Stone's large fists were clenched on the table. "If he comes around again, I'll bash his face in."

"No, call the police," Pepper said. "I don't want you hurt."

"More likely, Stone would hurt him," Trey said.

"*Should* we go to the police?" Autumn asked.

Trey nodded. "Tomorrow. Go in and at least tell them what you saw. Both of you."

"We'll go with you," Stone said. "And we need to let Kyle know. Violet and the kids could be in danger."

He felt Autumn shiver. "Violet will freak. After what happened with the kids, who can blame her?"

"True," Trey said.

"What do you mean?" Pepper asked.

"A few years back, before they were even married, their unhinged nanny kidnapped Mollie and Dakota," Stone said. "It ended with the nanny being killed by the police. While she was holding infant Mollie in her arms."

Pepper paled. "I didn't know that."

"Violet and Kyle don't like to talk about it. Seeing that girl die in front of him still gives Kyle nightmares. You know how he is—downplays everything—but it's obvious in how protective he is of the kids."

"He does FBI-type background checks on anyone they let near the kids," Autumn said. "Again, not that I can blame them."

"What was wrong with her?" Pepper asked. "The nanny."

"She was obsessed with Kyle," Stone said. "The poor thing had it in her mind they were soul mates and meant to be together. She took Dakota and Mollie out of their beds and ran off with them."

"That's awful," Pepper said. "Why is there so much evil in the world?"

"There's more good than bad," Autumn said. "But evil attracts more attention."

The sound of a car pulling up to the driveway interrupted their conversation.

"That's Mom," Stone said. "I recognize the old muffler."

"Baby, we have to get her a new car," Pepper said.

Stone sighed as he unfolded his tall, wide frame from the chair. "You have a heart of gold, Pepper Shaker, but it's no match for my mother's stubborn pride."

* * *

TREY HUNG BEHIND with Pepper while Stone and Autumn went out to greet their mother. Leaning against the counter, he took a slug from his beer. When he looked up, Pepper's eyes drilled into him.

"What?" He chuckled nervously. When Pepper gave him that look, he knew he was in trouble.

"I know what you guys are up to, and it's a terrible idea." She folded her arms across her chest.

"For the record, it was Stone's idea."

"I'm quite aware of that. I'll tell you what I told him. You're playing with fire. Women do not like to be lied to."

"Men don't either."

She made a face. "No one's lying to you. You better stop before she finds out."

He gestured at her with his beer, as if that would shield him from the spice of Pepper. "She opens up to me in there."

"Your job, if you want her to fall for you, is to show her yourself for real. Don't hide behind a computer screen."

He didn't have time to answer because Stone and Autumn appeared with their mother. Pepper rushed to Valerie and grabbed her in a hug. "You poor thing. What can we do?"

Valerie looked taken aback but returned the hug. Pepper didn't seem to notice Valerie's trepidation. She grabbed her hand and led her over to a chair by the kitchen table. "Let's get you a drink. White wine?"

"Sure. That's fine," Valerie said as her gaze darted to Stone. "But don't go to any trouble."

"It's no trouble." Autumn was already pouring her mother a glass.

Pepper brought Valerie's drink to the table, then took the chair across from her. "We need to talk about our plan for tomorrow."

"Plan?" Stone asked as he brushed a hand through his wavy brown hair. "Pepper, I'm not sure Mom needs us to help with a plan."

"Sure she does." Pepper flashed a reckless smile. "I've had enough of this nonsense."

"Nonsense?" Valerie asked. Her hand shook as she reached for her glass.

Autumn shot Trey a nervous but amused glance before pouring herself a glass of wine. He busied himself with his beer to keep from laughing. Stone had migrated to the opposite end of the kitchen and was now leaning his backside against the cabinetry with both hands in his cargo shorts pockets. Trey moved to stand next to him, patted his shoulder in sympathy, and then turned to watch the show. Pepper in action was a fine sight to see.

"Yes, this *total* and *complete* nonsense." Pepper gestured toward Autumn. "Could I have some of that, please?"

"Oh, yes. Where are my manners?" Autumn winked at Pepper before pouring a glass of wine.

Pepper turned back to Valerie, who had seemed to shrink since sitting at the table. She gazed at Pepper with wary eyes, like a child on the first day in front of their eccentric and unpredictable new teacher.

"Here's the thing, Mrs. Hickman." Pepper placed both hands on the tabletop. "You may not know this, Valerie, but I'm filthy rich and getting richer. I just had an offer for another film, and they're giving me a ridiculous amount of money for six weeks of work. Add that to the vast fortune my cold, absent biological father left me when he passed away—God rest his soul—and you've got one rich, spoiled kitty cat. I don't want to be a rich, spoiled kitty cat because that person is not the type of woman Stone Hickman deserves. So I'm dedicated to doing good with my money and using it for people and causes that need a little boost instead of focusing solely on me, myself, and I. Which, trust me, I could do in a hot second. I mean, we all know I'm not good enough for your son. No one in this room is impolite enough to say it, but even my own parents know the truth. He was born good, and I have to try really hard to be just decent."

"Someone make her stop," Stone mumbled as he planted his forehead in the palm of his hand. The tips of his ears were the color of beets.

Trey shook with suppressed laughter.

Pepper frowned at Stone. "I will not stop, Stone Hickman. The only reason we're together is because you never gave up on me." She shifted her attention back to Valerie. "Your son knew we were meant to be together. He has this confidence, this unshakable belief in the goodness of most people. How that's possible, given what he's seen in his life, I can't imagine."

Valerie's shoulders hunched.

Pepper's eyes narrowed, watching her future mother-in-law. "I didn't mean you."

"You should." Valerie picked up her wineglass and brought it to her mouth.

"Mom, she's talking about my time in the military." Stone glared at Pepper.

Pepper lifted her chin, completely devoid of apology.

Valerie took another sip of wine and stared down at the tabletop. Trey wished he could do something, like wave a magic wand to take her pain away. Guilt was an awful thing, the way it robbed a person of light and joy. It was a weight one could never shed, no matter how many years passed.

"Baby, what's your point here?" Stone asked.

Pepper hesitated, clearly thinking about what to say next. With a defiant lift of one eyebrow, she continued. "I'll just come right out and say it. I don't want you to drive around in that beater of a car any longer. Or live in that crap-hole of an apartment or its equivalent. I don't want you to work unless you want to. I have a proposition."

Valerie's fingers closed around the stem of her wineglass, and she gazed at Pepper with the stunned expression of a bunny facing a mountain lion. She closed her eyes for a second as if she had an enormous headache. "What did you have in mind?" she asked faintly.

"We're family, and we want to help you," Pepper said. "Right, Stone? Autumn?"

"Sure," Autumn said.

Stone remained silent but acquiesced with a slight nod of his head.

"Valerie, your place burning is a sign that it's time for you to move to Cliffside Bay. You're going to let Stone, Kyle, and me buy you a nice little house here in town so you're close to your grandchildren and your children." Pepper's eyes danced. "I'm going to have a baby one of these days, and you already have four grandchildren who adore you."

At the mention of the grandchildren, Valerie's armor seemed to soften a millimeter or two. "It would be nice to help Violet with the children."

"Exactly. She needs you," Pepper said. "Tomorrow, Autumn and I are going to take you to the city and I'm going to buy you beautiful clothes—you have such a nice figure. Then we're going to a salon to have your hair cut and colored."

Valerie placed both hands on the table. "No."

Pepper smiled and spoke in a softer, less bossy tone. "You're young and pretty, but everyone needs a little touch-up every now and then."

At the change in tone, tears gathered in Valerie's eyes and then rolled down her cheeks. Stone leaped forward to offer her a napkin from the stack on the counter. "Mom, don't cry. This is Pepper's way of wanting to help you."

"Exactly. I'm worthless at most things, but I know how to make the most of my appearance, and I can do the same for you."

"That's just it," Valerie said. "I don't deserve any of this. Or any of you."

Even though this was not his family and none of his business, Trey felt compelled to speak. "Valerie, no one is perfect. Everyone in this room is like the houses Stone and I fix up. The bones are good, but sometimes they need a little love and attention in order to reach their full potential. Pepper wants to give you this gift. It obviously makes her happy."

Autumn moved closer to him, slipping her hand into his. "Mom, he's right. Just say yes."

Valerie's eyes filled once more. She dabbed at her cheeks with the napkin.

Stone crossed over to her and knelt next to her chair. "Mom, let us love you."

"I'd like to. I would. I'm not sure I know how."

Pepper reached across the table and placed her hand around Valerie's bony wrist. "Let me take you shopping. That's all. A little shopping and a haircut."

Valerie dabbed at the corners of her eyes and gave Pepper a rueful smile. "Okay, I guess. If it makes you happy."

Autumn squeezed Trey's hand and nestled next to him. "I'll get my shift covered and come too."

Pepper clapped her hands together. "Excellent. We'll have a Hickman family girls' day. I'm so excited."

Trey had to grin at his energetic, sometimes overbearing friend. Pepper Shaker was impossible not to love. Someday, if he had anything to do about it, they would both be married to a Hickman sibling. *Please, God.*

8

A utumn

THE NEXT MORNING, Autumn woke at her usual time and sniffed the air. The scent of coffee filled the house. She rolled over to look at the clock. It was just a little after seven. Her mother must be an early riser. Pepper had said she'd be by to get them at nine for their trip into San Francisco, which left her plenty of time to get ready.

She crawled out of bed and headed to the bathroom. As the water heated in the shower, she examined herself in the full-length mirror that hung on the door. In the soft morning light that sneaked through the slats of the wooden shades, her scars weren't so obvious. Even the dent in her leg seemed less angry. Since she'd shown herself to Trey, she'd been thinking about shame. Her shame. Last night, as they talked with her mother about starting fresh, she'd thought about her own decisions to hide away, to let her shame over her appearance keep her from the pleasure of swimming. She was not physically perfect, but most people weren't. There were women of all sizes and shapes on the beach every day. They didn't deprive themselves of the glorious sun and salt water on their skin because they were physically imperfect. What was it that they had that she didn't? Were they unashamed? Did they embrace the beauty of their imperfections? Did they toss aside their fear of exposure, of being seen, in order to experience life's bounty?

She showered, lingering under the warm water for longer than she should. When she was done, she toweled dry and blew out her hair using a round brush.

The bathroom wasn't too large but had room for a glass shower and a claw tub. When they'd renovated, Trey had suggested they tear out everything and start over. She hadn't argued, quite sure there was no salvaging any of the pink decor. Even the bathtub had been pink. She hadn't known there was such a thing.

They'd gone with an eggshell-white tile with light yellow accents. Bright and sunny. Clean. They'd found prints of flowers: a white daisy, a yellow rose, a pink peony, and an orange dahlia. They hung two by two on either side of the pedestal sink.

Crossing into the bedroom, her skin prickled in the air-conditioned room. She went to her large walk-in closet and chose a pair of lacy panties and a matching bra. Why did she bother with such things? It wasn't as if anyone would see.

The closet with its drawers and shelves made for various parts of a wardrobe had been a surprise gift from Kyle. Trey had helped her hang the mirror in the closet. He'd joked about renting the space out from her. Pointing to the area where her dresses now hung, he'd said he could put his bed there.

An image of Trey from the late afternoon at the Mullens' pool flashed through her mind. His hands with those long, artistic fingers on her skin, running the length of her scars. His damp, warm body when she'd hugged him. Her legs weakened. She slumped into the chair in the corner of the walk-in closet. What would it have felt like to have his hands on every other part of her?

Then another image came. Her and Trey entwined right here in the confines of the closet. Bodies pressed together, mouths exploring, fingers tracing each other's skin.

Oh my.

She shook it off. I'm lonely, that's all.

It had been a long time since she'd had any proximity to a man.

After a few centering breaths, she rose from the chair. She chose a pair of linen pants, a light blue sleeveless blouse, and flat sandals, knowing they might walk a lot while shopping. Her cane was nestled in the corner next to her shoe rack. She would bring it, in case she tired. Lately though, with all the shopping trips and running around with Trey, her legs felt stronger than they had since before the accident. She took one last look at herself in the mirror in the closet.

Autumn turned out the lights in the closet and bedroom, then headed for the scent of coffee.

A high-pitched scream jolted through her. She froze for a split second, as her mind caught up with the origin and nature of the noise. Her mother had screamed in what sounded like terror. She ran out of her bedroom and into the main room. Valerie stood by the French doors with one of Autumn's silver candlesticks in her hand. One blind on the double doors had been lifted partway and now hung crooked.

"What is it?" Autumn asked.

"A man. He was standing right outside the doors when I lifted the blinds. I screamed and ran for the candlestick. When I turned back, he was gone."

Autumn moved closer to the doors and lifted both blinds. The morning was bright and sunny. No fog to obscure the view today. Still, there was no sign of a man, other than a few joggers passing by on the boardwalk. "What did he look like?"

"Big with a beer belly. Scruffy face. Baseball cap, pulled low over his eyes, and he had on a gray sweatshirt and jeans. Other than that, I can't remember."

"You haven't seen him before?"

"No. I'm sure of it. I usually remember faces because of my job." Valerie continued to clutch the candlestick in both hands. Her entire body visibly shook.

Should she tell her this was the second morning in a row? Her instinct was to keep it to herself. Valerie seemed so fragile. However, the need to explore the possibility of a connection to the Millers and the fire won in the end.

"He was here yesterday too. And he was following Pepper as well."

Valerie's face drained of color. She slumped into the chair. "Who could he be?"

"Do you think he could be related to the Millers somehow?"

She pressed the candlestick against her chest. "Their father died years ago. As far as I know, there were no other relatives. Like Kyle said, they were hated by most in town. I don't think it could be."

"We'll call the police and tell them what we saw. Whoever it is seems to like to look, but maybe he's harmless. Could just be an old-fashioned voyeur." Autumn reached out and took the candlestick from her mother. "Regardless, from now on, we keep the security system on, even when we're here."

* * *

PEPPER HAD HIRED a driver to take them into the city. She didn't drive, having grown up in New York. Plus, she'd told Autumn and Valerie, she wanted a day of total luxury for all three. No traffic or worrying about parking while they were in the busy shopping district of San Francisco. Normally, Autumn would have insisted on driving them, always frugal, but she knew it was no use. Pepper wanted to treat them, so why shouldn't she let her?

It took about an hour and a half to get into the city, which passed quickly. The vehicle was essentially a minivan, with four bucket seats arranged in two rows facing each other. Valerie and Autumn took up one row, with Pepper across from them. Her mother seemed surprisingly relaxed in Pepper's company, asking her all kinds of questions about Hollywood and movies. All the way along the curvy road that rose up and then came down as they neared the freeway to the city, Pepper kept them entertained with tales of movie set antics and insider gossip. Before they knew it, they'd arrived in front of a Nordstrom. Autumn and Valerie stepped out of the car and stood on the sidewalk waiting while Pepper gave instructions to the driver.

Autumn noticed that Valerie had gone suddenly quiet, and her shoulders sagged as though she wanted to disappear. Valerie tugged on the front of her shirt, pulling it over the waist of her jeans. Autumn had thrown Valerie's jeans and faded shirt into the washer and dryer the night before, but they looked shabby and worn next to the hordes of shoppers and business-people who passed by them.

Pepper joined them. Perhaps noticing Valerie's discomfort, she smiled a little too brightly. "Come on, ladies. Let's go shop until we drop."

Valerie turned toward the glass doors of Nordstrom and sighed. A refined woman laden with bags came out of the store and headed toward them, most likely to hail a cab. As she approached, Autumn caught a whiff of her French perfume in the midst of the gas fumes from cars. Valerie had gone completely still, staring at the woman. She was about Valerie's age, only she had the advantage of elegantly styled hair and designer clothes that draped exactly right. Fortunately, the woman didn't seem to notice Valerie's stare as she passed them by.

Instinctively, Pepper moved closer to Valerie, as if she wanted to protect her.

"You know, my trouble was I never had anything to start with, other than my looks," Valerie said softly. "Over time, I didn't even have that."

Pepper linked her arm through Valerie's. "My mother always says, 'It's not what you look like on the outside but the inside that counts.' Which is true, of course. But heck, there's no reason why we can't get them to match a little, right?"

"I'm not sure there's much to be done." Valerie tugged on her blouse in the same self-conscious move from earlier.

"Let me try, okay?" Pepper asked. "I'd really like to."

Autumn placed her hand on her mother's other arm. "Mom, it's the least we can do if Pepper's so keen on showing off her money." She grinned and winked at Pepper to make sure she knew she was teasing.

Pepper turned slightly to look at Valerie. "This time last year I was broke. I was basically sponging off Maggie and Lisa and feeling terrible about myself. Think of it this way. You're doing me a favor by letting me pay it forward."

For the first time since they arrived, Valerie gave them both a tremulous smile. "All right. I'm at your mercy."

Arms linked, the three of them walked toward the store, only separating when it was time to enter through the glass doors. The scent of perfume and cosmetics permeated the air. They passed by the display counters filled with expensive cosmetics promising youth and beauty at the tip of a bottle or squeeze of a tube. Clerks assisted customers, applying products using brushes they pulled from apron pockets. "We'll skip this for now," Pepper said, clearly in her element. "Let's start upstairs in one of the women's departments."

They took the escalator to the second floor and walked past

the designer and couture departments. Pepper gestured toward them and spoke in a low voice. "Lisa's stylist shops here for when she has interviews and such, but we don't need to spend two thousand dollars on a dress."

Lisa, the "it" girl of Hollywood, apparently did need two-thousand-dollar dresses. Autumn shuddered. Nothing in the world sounded worse than being on television or constantly having your photograph taken as part of your job. She loved nice clothes, but Lisa and Pepper's work took looking good to another level. Lisa's fame had risen to a level where no matter where she went, people snapped photos of her. She was often on talk shows or on the red carpet, all the while being scrutinized and judged for what she wore and said and how she fixed her hair. Autumn was just fine with her low-profile job behind the pharmacy counter.

At the corner of the second floor, they entered a section targeted to the more mature woman. Incongruently, a nubile sales assistant wearing black leggings paired with high pumps and a trendy cropped sweater swooped in on them. "Hello, ladies. Can I help you find anything?"

Pepper politely declined her offer to help. "We're just looking right now."

"Please let me know if you need anything. My name's Cello. Like the instrument." Cello, like the instrument, had black hair styled in a mushroom bob. Blunt bangs fell to the middle of her forehead. They reminded Autumn of a haircut given to a doll by a child playing hairdresser. Regardless, she had the self-assurance of a young woman who saw herself as the epitome of trendy fashion and beauty.

"Nice to meet you," Autumn said. "But we're fine on our own."

Cello's gaze floated over each of them. She was too good to let her opinion of Valerie's appearance reflect on her face. "Are you all shopping today?"

"No. Just my mom," Autumn said.

"How wonderful," Cello said, focusing on Valerie now. "Are you looking for anything in particular? A special occasion? What are you? Size six?"

"I'm...I'm not sure," Valerie said.

"I have a good eye," Cello said. "I'm almost never wrong. Shall I start to pull things for you?"

"No, thank you," Autumn said. She sensed Pepper's growing irritation. "We'd like to help her pick things out ourselves."

Undaunted, Cello snatched a peasant blouse from a nearby rack. "This would be adorable on you."

"Cello, thanks so much for your help. We'll be sure to give you the credit when we check out," Pepper said. "But really, we're fine. I used to work retail. I've got this."

"Perfect. Perfect." Cello smiled as she gestured with one long, pointy fingernail toward the dressing rooms. "How about if I take that from you and start a room?"

Pepper nodded. "Great. Thanks."

After Cello walked away, she turned to Valerie. "Should we focus on day-to-day clothes for now?"

"Sure," Valerie mumbled.

Unlike the section of the store targeted toward teens or twentysomethings, the clothes here were made for a more sophisticated woman. Skirt hems were longer; blouses covered midriffs; pants were cut wider at the hips and thighs. Prices were in the medium range, as compared to the designer departments from which Lisa's and Pepper's stylists dressed them. Still, Valerie balked the instant she saw the price tag on the first sweater Pepper chose for her.

"It's too much," Valerie said. "Is there a clearance rack?"

Pepper ignored her, stepping over to a table of jeans stacked in neat piles. "You'll need a basic denim, both faded and dark. Oh, and a pair of black jeans is a must." She grabbed several and draped them over one arm.

Autumn chose a half-dozen blouses in various styles and shades. Cello glided over and took them from her, giving Autumn the opportunity to pick out a few light sweaters and a jean jacket. Pepper had meandered over to a rack with summer clothes: shorts, T-shirts, and sundresses. She slipped a yellow sundress from a rack, squinted, then caressed the fabric. Apparently it was deemed worthy, because she handed it, along with a few other dresses, to Cello.

Valerie wandered from rack to rack, touching fabric, then looking at the price tags. They continued this routine for a few more minutes, with Cello taking their choices back to the dressing room. When they had at least thirty items Pepper suggested she start to try the clothes on. Cello met them outside the room with the initial blouse choice hanging on the outside of the door. She opened the door with the key that dangled from a coiled plastic band around her wrist.

Just outside the rooms, there was an area with a couch and a trifold mirror. Autumn and Pepper both sat and waited to hear any news from behind the door. They chatted quietly about where they should have lunch while Valerie silently tried on clothes.

After a few minutes, Valerie stepped out to them. She wore the yellow sundress with a filmy white cardigan over her shoulders. A slight, shy smile lifted the corners of her mouth. "I like this one," she said, in a breathy voice. "It reminds me of a dress I wanted when I was in high school."

Autumn stood, using the sofa arm to aid her in rising from the depth of its cushions. "You look really nice. Like a daisy."

"You do," Pepper said, eyes shiny.

"What about the others?" Autumn asked.

Valerie nodded, still smiling shyly. "A few pairs of jeans and some blouses. Summer things too."

Cello appeared and made a big fuss about how good Valerie looked and how youthful. She then helped gather all the chosen items and brought them to the register. While Cello rang up the purchases, Autumn took her mother to find bras and panties. The clerk there talked her into being formally fitted for a bra, which took a while. After that, they bought a bathing suit, a modest blue one-piece with a matching hat and cover, then went down to the shoe department. There, they bought tennis shoes, flat sandals, and a pair of wedges that Pepper insisted were a staple for any woman who lived by the beach.

They were on their way to the exit, describing to Valerie the quaint bistro they were taking her to, when she tugged on Autumn's arm. "Is it fancy? The lunch place?" Valerie's lips twitched on one side as she tugged on the front of her shirt as she had earlier.

"Not really," Autumn said.

Pepper, as usual, was way ahead of her. "Would you like to change into one of your new outfits before we go?"

Valerie ducked her head. "I don't want to go there looking like this." She waved toward them. "You two look like all the ladies in here. So put together and fancy."

Pepper, who wore a short red halter dress and jean jacket paired with wedge sandals, looked like a movie star, if truth be told. Autumn liked the way her own linen pants flowed and knew the sleeveless silky blouse gave her an air of sophistication. No wonder her mother felt out of place.

"Valerie, yes, please change," Pepper said. "You look just fine as you are, but I know how it is when you get something new."

So they traipsed off to the bathroom and Valerie changed into a pair of cropped white jeans and a flowy cotton blouse and her flat sandals. She twirled for them when she came out to the sitting area of the women's lounge. "What do you think?"

Pepper jumped to her feet and gave Valerie a hug. "I think you look fabulous. Now let's go eat. I'm starving."

They exited, each carrying bags filled with Valerie's new wardrobe. The bistro was within walking distance and close to the place where Pepper had made the hair and makeup appointment. During lunch, they discussed how Valerie would like her hair fixed.

"I've always worn it long," Valerie said, tugging at her white ponytail. "But maybe it's time to try something new. Shoulder length, maybe?"

"What color?" Pepper tore a piece of bread in half.

"It was like Autumn's when I was young. Light brown. When I first met your dad, Autumn, he said it was the color of maple syrup."

"Is that what you want?" Autumn asked, holding herself back from asking more questions. She'd never heard anything about her parents' early life together. Had they been in love? When had things changed between them? She supposed there were a hundred different answers to that. They'd been seventeen years old when they married. Children, really.

"I guess so," Valerie said in response to the question.

"You guess?" Pepper asked.

"Well, I always wanted to be a blonde." Valerie played with the edge of the tablecloth. "Now that I live in California, it seems fitting."

"Great. Easier to cover the white," Pepper said.

After lunch, the three of them walked over to the salon. When a man came out and introduced himself as Mario, it was obvious he and Pepper knew each other. They hugged, and then Mario kissed each of her cheeks. "Darling, I saw your film. You're right. Dreadful. But not a person besides me knew it. The entire theater was on the edges of their seats."

"I told you it was terrible," Pepper said.

"Everything but you," Mario said. "You were sublime. Other than your character being dumb enough to walk up the stairs."

Pepper laughed. "Toast in the first twenty minutes."

Mario turned to Autumn and Valerie, greeting them with a friendly smile and handshake. "Miss Valerie, are you ready for the Mario treatment?"

"Yes...I guess so." Valerie shot Autumn a worried grimace.

Mario asked Valerie to follow him. "We'll see you two in a few hours."

They turned to each other and grinned. "What should we do now?" Autumn asked.

Pepper bounced on her feet. "I have a surprise. Follow me."

* * *

THE DRIVER MANEUVERED them through the skinny streets of San Francisco. Autumn's stomach clenched at every sound of a horn and when the car lurched as he changed lanes or rounded corners. To distract herself, she asked Pepper, "So, what's the surprise?"

Pepper, in the bucket seat next to her, turned to face her. "Your brother and I have finally picked a date and decided where we want to have the wedding."

"Finally. I thought you'd never get a date figured out."

"Between our work commitments, it was tough."

"I'm so excited. Truly." She smiled over at her future sister-in-law. "Where and when?"

"You can't laugh," Pepper said. "It's what I've wanted since I was young."

"I won't laugh. I promise."

"It's a castle in France. Well, not really in the castle, but on the grounds. Castles aren't always what they look like from the outside. We learned that on our trip. Did you know Sleeping Beauty's castle in the movie was based on a real castle?" Stone and Pepper had taken a trip over to France after Pepper finished filming the movie with Lisa and Genevieve Banks.

"I had no idea it was a real place."

"Yes. We went there. The insides were a wreck, but the outside looked like the movie. But I digress. That's not where we're having it. Instead of a castle, we found a château. It's smaller, obviously, with beautiful grounds and gardens. We'll do it outside in a garden under a tree. And we're renting the entire place out for our guests."

"When?"

"October. We thought it would be fun to go during harvest."

Autumn's eyes misted. "I've always wanted to go to France."

"You'll love it. I promise."

Maybe she could meet her new friend in Paris. She put a pin in that thought and focused on Pepper.

"I found a dress," Pepper said. "And I have a fitting today, which is where we're headed."

Autumn clapped her hands together in excitement. "I cannot wait to see what you found."

"Also, I was wondering if you'd like to be a bridesmaid," Pepper said. "Maggie and Lisa are sharing maid of honor duties. We made a pact ages ago so that no one felt jealous if they were picked over the other." Lisa, Pepper, and Maggie had met in college and had basically spent most of their young adulthood side by side. They did everything together.

"I can't marry your brother without having you in the wedding party. We're going to be sisters, after all. Will you be my third bridesmaid?"

"I'd be honored to be in the wedding," Autumn said as she squeezed Pepper's hand. "I'm touched. This is unexpected."

"I want us to be close," Pepper said. "As you know, Stone adores you. I keep daydreaming of all the fun we'll have raising our families together in Cliffside Bay."

Autumn sighed. "I don't think you should count on that. I can't even make it to a second date with someone."

Pepper, with the same expression she'd had on the beach the night before, looked as if she wanted to say something but changed her mind. "Here we are." She pointed to a wedding shop with a pink awning over the front door and windows.

The driver pulled into the alley between two buildings. Pepper thanked him and asked that he return in two hours to take them back to the salon. They scuttled out of the vehicle and over to the shop. Four mannequins in gorgeous gowns adorned the front window. "Maggie and Lisa are inside waiting. Let's go."

"Did you have this all planned before you offered to take Valerie shopping?" Autumn asked as they walked inside the shop.

"I did. I'd planned on kidnapping you today and surprising you when we got here but decided combining it with your mother's shopping trip made perfect sense."

Lisa and Maggie were waiting for them in the lobby. Lisa, dressed in a pair of red skinny jeans and a T-shirt from Maggie's latest concert tour, wore almost no makeup. Her light blond hair was pulled into a ponytail. She looked like any normal albeit gorgeous young woman, instead of one of the most famous actresses in America.

Maggie had her copper-colored hair pulled back in a long braid. She wore a pair of cropped leggings over her long and muscular dancer legs, paired with a filmy white tunic. Like nutmeg sprinkles, freckles dotted her fair skin and made her seem young and innocent. In reality, she was the mother to a toddler and a rising star in the pop folk music world. Her sophomore album was being hailed as one of the best of the year, with hints of a Grammy nomination coming.

They squealed and rushed toward them, pulling them both into hugs.

"We're so excited," Lisa said as she smoothed her hands over Pepper's curls. "You're glowing."

Pepper pretended to be embarrassed by the praise and pushed her friend away. "Stop it. You're glowing."

Maggie turned to Autumn. "How are you? We heard your mother's moving in."

"Moved in," Autumn said. "She came last night. So far, it's been fine. But Kyle and Stone will find her a place of her own. Soon, I hope." She smiled to soften the words. "I'd gotten used to having the cottage to myself, but there's no way I couldn't ask her to stay."

"I may have a solution for you, but I'll tell you after the fitting," Lisa said.

A solution. That sounded promising.

"Have you been waiting long?" Pepper asked.

"No, we arrived five minutes ago," Lisa said.

"Jackson dropped us off on his way to meet Brody over at his condo," Maggie said. "The Dogs are meeting in the city for a weekend of poker and debauchery."

"You'd think they'd be too settled down for all that." Lisa's thin brows came together in a worried frown.

Maggie gave her braid a resigned tug. "It's a bit of harmless fun, even though Jackson will come back with a few hundred dollars less in his pocket and terribly hungover. Dogs will be Dogs."

"Are they still calling themselves that?" Pepper asked.

"Until they die." Maggie shook her head, laughing.

Autumn smiled, thinking of the ties that bound Kyle and his best friends. When they were at college together, Brody Mullen, Lance Mullen, Zane Shaw, and Maggie's husband, Jackson Waller, had nicknamed themselves the Dogs after the famous painting of five pooches playing poker.

They all accepted a glass of champagne from the attendant as Lisa commented, "Rafael and Stone used to joke about grown men naming themselves until they decided they were the mangy Wolves of Cliffside Bay."

Autumn nodded in agreement. "I hear them referring to

themselves as the Wolves all the time." They'd subsequently named their building company Wolf Enterprises.

"Men need to feel part of a pack, obviously," Pepper said.

Lisa held up her glass and lowered her voice as though she was a Supreme Court justice. "Here's to our pack. The Bobcats —the pretty to our mangy Wolves."

They all clinked glasses and grinned at one another.

Autumn buzzed with joy. She was part of a group now. A place to belong. Her tribe.

The attendant returned and introduced herself as Lacy. "Come on back. Pepper, your dress is hanging up and ready for you to try on. Once you have it on, my seamstress will take a look."

Pepper thanked her. "Did you pull the bridesmaid dresses for the girls to try on?"

Lacy nodded. "They're waiting in the dressing rooms as well."

Pepper glanced over at Autumn. "I picked a few bridesmaid dresses, but I want you three to try them on and pick which you like best."

Lacy showed them to their rooms and asked them to let her know if they needed anything.

Autumn pulled the curtain closed and surveyed the three dresses hanging on the hooks. They were all in a pale green. A good color for all three of them. Pink, red, or orange wouldn't have worked for her or Maggie and her copper hair. They were all fair, so a bright color might have washed them out. Two of the choices were full-length, but the third dress had a fitted bodice with a full, short skirt.

Her heartbeat sped up, and she broke out into a hot sweat. A short skirt? What had Pepper been thinking? Didn't she know Autumn never showed her legs?

Lisa and Maggie were sharing a larger space right next to

her. Their voices, somewhat muffled, were still easy enough to hear.

"Autumn, can you hear me?" Lisa asked.

"Yes," Autumn said.

"This short dress is not what Pepper asked for," Lisa said. "Try on one of the others first. We'll ask for a full-length third option."

"Pepper would never be this insensitive," Maggie said.

"Autumn?" Lisa asked. "Are you all right?"

"Yes, I'm fine. It's not a big deal." Autumn slumped against the wall, touched by their concern for her feelings, yet embarrassed too.

Should she care this much about her legs showing? What if this was the dress Pepper would pick out if it weren't for Autumn's insecurities?

Right then and there, she made a decision. She was tired of hiding. Trey was right. How much of her life was affected by her militant decision to keep her legs covered? Plus, these ladies would not judge her. They were too kind for that. Pepper was going to be her sister, her family. She wanted her to have exactly what she wanted on her wedding day. If it was short dresses, she would have short dresses.

She undressed and stepped into the short gown. Strapless with a straight neckline, fitted waist, and a full skirt layered with tulle, the dress brought to mind the twirling ballerina in a child's jewelry box. She'd coveted one when she was young. Last Christmas, she'd bought one for Mollie, living vicariously through her niece's delight when the plastic ballerina spun round and round.

Autumn zipped up the back as best she could and stood in front of the full-length mirror. For a second, she was that ballerina. Fighting the urge to try a twirl, she gazed at herself, averting her eyes from her legs and concentrating instead on her upper torso. She pulled her hair up and wrapped it in a knot on top of her head. The woman who gazed back at her from the mirror looked beautiful in this dress. She was a ballerina princess.

This dress was like Pepper: playful, whimsical, theatrical, and very feminine. Autumn could imagine herself and the other ladies outside a château in France, toasting her brother and his delicate bride in the shadow of a hundred-year oak.

She took a long, hard look at her legs. The red marks were stark against her white skin. Her dented calf made her wince. What would others think as she walked toward Stone and Pepper, such perfect humans, with her flawed legs? No, she would be brave. Neither this day nor the wedding day to come was about her. They were about Pepper. Good, kind, giving Pepper, who should pick the dresses she wanted, regardless of their length.

There were several pairs of shoes stacked in the corner. She slid her feet into a pair of strappy high-heeled sandals. A size too big, but they worked for this purpose.

The other ladies were already in front of the three-way mirror. Lisa and Maggie wore the mermaid-style chiffon that had also been in Autumn's room. Maggie was huddled in one corner with a stricken-looking Lacy, clearly telling her of the error. Lisa stood to the right of the bride. Pepper stood on a raised platform. The seamstress, a small white-haired lady, crouched at her feet, putting pins in the hem.

Before she drew attention to herself, Autumn took a moment to look at Pepper in her dress. The strapless dress had a delicately beaded lace bodice, wide, circular tulle skirt and chapel-length train.

"You look perfect," Autumn said, rendered almost breathless by Pepper's beauty. "Like a princess."

Lisa and Pepper turned to look at Autumn. Pepper watched her from the mirror, surprise then anger slowly working their way across her face.

"Autumn, I'm sorry," Pepper said. "That wasn't supposed to be in there."

"I know you told them no short dresses," Autumn said. "But I thought I'd try it on anyway."

"You didn't have to," Pepper said, sounding desperate and miserable.

Autumn drew closer until she was on the other side of Pepper. If anything, her legs looked worse under the bright lights—the scars redder, the misshapen calf like that of a monster under the sassy flounce of the tulle. She forced herself to look up at Pepper. "Your day is not about me. If this is the dress you want, then you shall have it." Then, to her utter dismay, she dissolved into tears. "I'm sorry," she said, wiping at her eyes. "But I'm so ugly and you're all so perfect."

Pepper looked down at the seamstress, who seemed oblivious to anything amiss. "Can you give us the room for a moment, please?"

The older lady, pins in her mouth, gave a curt, irritated nod before rising to her feet and lumbering out of the room.

"Lacy, please excuse us," Pepper said. Her eyes had turned dark and stormy, and she bit off the words. "Maybe you could pull the dresses I actually asked for while we talk for a moment?"

Lacy didn't say a word as she retraced the seamstress's steps out of the room.

A muscle in Maggie's cheek flexed as she crossed over to Autumn and took her hand. "You're not ugly. Not one bit."

Autumn let herself slump against Maggie's narrow frame. They were similar in height and body type. Once, Autumn had twirled in a cheerleading outfit like the graceful ballerina Maggie had been. If only. If only.

Pepper eased off her platform to join them. Lisa came around from the other side. They huddled around Autumn. She could feel the warmth of their bodies and smell the scents of their perfumes as their arms encircled her. She breathed, shaky and light-headed.

"Come sit," Maggie said to Autumn, leading her over to a chair. "You're white as a ghost."

Autumn sat in the chair, grateful, as her legs had started to tremble. Lisa and Pepper sat on either side of her. Maggie knelt on the floor in front of Autumn.

"I showed Trey my legs." Autumn stretched them out long. The rhinestones on the garish sandals sparkled under the lights. "He said I was beautiful, even with my imperfections. But he's wrong. Do you see why I don't wear short skirts?"

"I can understand exactly," Maggie said. "And I'll show you why."

Autumn's mouth fell open as Maggie stood and shrugged out of the dress she wore. She stepped out of the pool of chiffon at her feet and stood before them, naked other than her bra and panties. "Do you see?" She jutted one leg forward. A skinny pink scar ran above her knee. "This is from my knee surgery."

"I've never noticed it before," Autumn said.

"I usually wear skirts that cover it," Maggie said. "I hate the way it ruined my perfect legs, which I was so proud of and so vain about. They were the representation of years and years of hard work. Hours of dance classes and training. Worse, this scar is also the reminder of the day my dreams died. The day that meant I would never dance again. So I understand. And if you don't want people to see your scars, then it's your choice. Whatever you choose, you shouldn't feel ashamed. *You* get to decide what you can live with."

Lisa stood then and turned her back to Maggie. "Unzip me, please."

Maggie did so. Lisa shrugged out of the gown and tossed it onto her abandoned chair. "Do you see these?" She placed her hands on her lower stomach. Silvery stretch marks dotted the fair skin of her lower abdomen. Next, she turned around to show to show her backside in a pair of thong underwear. Her buttocks and the sides of her upper legs were streaked with bluish marks. "When I was a teenager, I was heavier." Her eyes grew misty as she continued. "When I went to a mental health facility after my suicide attempt, I lost a lot of weight. Once I was out of my mother's house, where she criticized every ounce of food I put into my mouth, I lost the extra pounds. Funny how that works. But these stretch marks? They're a symbol of all the things I went through. The depression and anxiety. They are proof that I suffered but stayed around to fight another day. I earned these. When I look at them, I see that I'm strong and brave. I'm still here. Do others see them that way? Heck no. Two months ago, while Pepper and I were filming together, they cut a scene of me in a bathing suit because of them." She squeezed a portion of her lower butt cheek. "And because of these dimples, too. I look like a real person with fat and stretch marks. God knows, no one wants to see that. According to them, anyway. Therefore, the scene must be deleted, and I was made to feel ashamed because I'm imperfect. Does it make me mad? Sure. But not as mad as I am glad that I survived."

Pepper stood. "I guess that means I'm next. I don't have to take off my gown to show you mine." She lifted her hair and leaned her neck to the left. A one-inch scar, only slightly pink, ran under her right ear. "This is where a man held a knife to my throat while his friend raped me." She ran her finger over the spot. "Even though the knife only pierced the surface, it left a scar to remind me of the worst night of my life. They stole a part of my soul that night. I'll never again be the woman I was. But I won't give those evil bastards power over my life. Not anymore. They almost cost me Stone, but his love was stronger than their hate. I won. Not them."

Autumn's eyes leaked hot tears. "I'm sorry," she whispered. "For all of it."

"As we are for what you went through," Maggie said. "But mostly, we understand."

"We all have scars," Lisa said. "They make us human."

"And remind us of our strength," Pepper said. "Our resilience."

"You almost died in that accident," Lisa said. "You didn't. It doesn't mean you have to show the world your legs, but they *are* proof of your incredible fight."

"You wanted to live," Maggie said. "And you did."

"Hell yes, you did," Pepper said. "We all did."

Autumn wondered how it was possible that she'd lucked into friendship with these women. "Thank you."

The ladies helped one another get the dresses refastened.

"Personally, I like this one the best," Lisa said about the dress she was wearing. "It's simple but elegant."

"I like it too." Maggie turned to Autumn. "That way, Autumn and I don't have to feel self-conscious about our legs."

"Plus, long dresses seem more appropriate for a castle wedding," Lisa said.

"We should keep it classy," Pepper said. "At least for one day."

"I agree," Lisa said, smiling. "You can tramp it up on your honeymoon."

"If we ever leave the room," Pepper said.

"You'll need to eat at some point," Lisa said.

Pepper laughed. "Let's call the poor seamstress in and get this fitting done, then order some bridesmaid dresses. I'm ready for some scotch and cigars."

"You're *not* smoking a cigar," Lisa said.

"I know, but it sounded badass," Pepper said.

"You don't need a cigar for that," Autumn said. "None of you do."

"And neither do you," Pepper said to Autumn. "Neither do you."

* * *

VALERIE WAS ready for them when they returned, sitting in the lobby of the salon reading a magazine. She glanced up when Autumn and Pepper drew near.

Valerie said, as she stood and did an uncharacteristic twirl, "What do you think?"

"You look incredible," Pepper said.

"Mom, honestly, you're beautiful." Autumn would not have recognized her if she'd seen her on the street. Mario had cut her hair to chin level and added layers for a tousled look, then dyed it ash blond. Her makeup was subtle, with a smoky eye in soft gray, and pink lipstick. Foundation smoothed her skin, and blush made her cheekbones pop. Combined with her new clothes, she looked stylish and posh.

"Do you like it?" Autumn asked. "Because that's what's most important."

Valerie's eyes shone. "I do. It's more than I could've expected."

"Isn't it great when life is better than we expected, instead of worse?" Pepper asked.

"It never occurred to me that life could be anything other than what it was," Valerie said.

"Let's go home and show off your new look to our boys," Pepper said.

* * *

LATER, as they traveled up the narrow, curving highway toward home, the late-afternoon sun shone brightly, and the sea and sky were complementary shades of blue. They drank water and chatted about various benign subjects. They were almost home when Pepper turned to Valerie. "Lisa had an idea she wanted me to run by you."

Valerie shifted in her seat, appearing nervous.

Pepper went on, either oblivious or undaunted. "Stone and I were talking with Rafael and Lisa about the Victorian." This was the nickname Stone and his friends had given the apartment building Rafael had bought and renovated. "As you know, Lisa bought a house at the top of the hill. They had it repainted and put new flooring in, but besides that, it was turnkey. They're going to move out of the apartment and into it next week. Lisa wants to go ahead even though it won't be furnished all the way. That's neither here nor there, really." She grinned. "I'm getting off track. Anyway, they have a proposition for you. How would you feel about moving into their vacant apartment and acting as the building manager?"

"Me? Manage a building?" Valerie asked. "I don't have any experience doing that."

"Rafael said the job is simply a liaison between him and the tenants. He needs someone to be there if anyone has a leak or whatever. He has a list of providers and you'd just have to call one of them if you need anything. Rafael said it's not hard, but he needs someone who can be there most of the time. He's gotten too busy to manage it all. Plus, when he moves out, he'll be even that much more removed." Pepper snapped her fingers. "Oh, and he said you can keep all the furniture. Trey designed it specially for the apartment, and Rafael would like to keep it that way."

"I could move in, just like that?" Valerie shook her head. "But why would they do this for me?"

"Because you're Stone's mom." Pepper chuckled. "Rafael's mother lives on the first floor, as well as her best friend, Ria. Lisa's dad is living with David and the kids now. Her parents got a divorce, and her mom's finding her artistic muses in Paris."

"Paris?" Valerie asked.

"Long story," Autumn said.

"Besides that, there will be leases that need signed and rent collected. Nothing complicated, but he needs someone reliable."

"I guess I could do that," Valerie said. "It's better than sponging off Autumn."

"You've been with me one night," Autumn said. "Not exactly sponging."

She and her mother exchanged a smile. "Better not to wear out my welcome," Valerie said.

By then, they had arrived in Cliffside Bay. The driver dropped Pepper at the Victorian first, then Autumn and her mother. When they were inside with all the packages, Valerie said she'd like to take a nap before dinner.

"Go for it. I have a few things I need to do as well," Autumn said, thinking of Art. She wanted to write to him and tell him about the latest turn of events.

Dear Art,

It's been quite a busy few days. You'll be surprised at my news. I know I was.

She went on to tell him about the fire and her mother's move to Cliffside Bay.

Somehow, Pepper, my soon-to-be sister-in-law, talked her into a makeover and shopping spree. Only Pepper would be able to do such a thing. Before we knew what was happening, Pepper had us in San Francisco. Valerie bought new clothes and had her hair fixed. She looks wonderful. It's amazing what a few new clothes and a haircut will do. She's also found a job as an apartment manager for a building here in town. The same one where Trey lives.

She went on to tell him about the fitting.

. . .

THEY JUST STOOD THERE, unveiling themselves to me. And it made me think, Art, that everyone has scars. It's what we choose to do with them that defines who we are. Is it as simple as the girls said today? Are they badges of honor, proof that we've lived through heartache and hurt only to rise again?

Regardless, I've added them to the list of people now who've seen me as I am. My brothers, Sara, Trey, and now these ladies who so generously gave of themselves to me today. They bared their scars and their souls so that I might feel less alone. Isn't that the most wonderful gift we can give another human being?

I must close now. Please write and let me know how things are going.

Love,

007

9

T rey

TREY SAT STARING at his computer screen. He couldn't think how to respond. Guilt about his deceit was starting to interrupt his work and his sleep. This whole thing was wrong. He needed a way to end this. He needed to tell her the truth about his feelings and put Art to rest.

His next thought depressed him further. What would she do if she ever found out about Art? Would he have to keep it a secret forever? What did it matter, though, if her feelings for him never changed?

What had he done? Was there a way out?

DEAR 007,

I'm proud of you for taking such a big step today with the ladies. I've noticed that women seem to fall into two categories: ones who compete with other women, thus keeping them from true friendship, and ones who see women as allies, building one another up. You seem to have found the latter. For this, I'm glad. The world can be a cold and lonely place without friends to lift you when you're down.

I'm almost finished with my commissioned work here and will move on to the next project within a week. I may not have much internet where I'm going next. I'll let you know before I leave.

I've decided I'm going to tell Michelle my feelings before I go, though. It's time. Any advice?

Art

HE HIT send and went to his closet to pull a T-shirt over his head. A moment later, his phone buzzed with a text from Autumn.

HEY. Come over for dinner? We can try that new Middle Eastern recipe I found.

Sure. What time?

Whenever. Can you stop at the store and get paprika?

Sure. See you in a bit.

ANGRY, he tossed his phone on the bed. They conversed like an old married couple, yet she still thought of him as good old Trey, like a brother to her. Damn, he was never going to make this happen unless he flat-out told her his feelings.

* * *

THE NEXT MORNING, Trey's mother called as he was about to head down to the beach to meet Nico for a swim.

"Hi, Mom."

"Trey. It's...it's about your dad. He's had a heart attack." Her usual even timbre shook as she continued. "The paramedics took him to the hospital and he's alive, but he needs surgery—an angioplasty to reroute the blood flow to the heart or something like that. It's all such a blur, and they told me so many things at once. The surgery's this afternoon."

Trey froze, caught in the web of his mother's words, unable to make sense of them. His father, so fit and active, could not have had a heart attack. It wasn't possible.

"Trey? Are you there?"

"Yes, Mom. I'm here. I'm in shock."

"I'm sorry, honey."

"Did it happen at the office?" he asked.

The sounds of his mother crying came from the other end of the phone.

"Mom?"

She answered in stops and starts, still crying. "No, he was with her. His girlfriend. At her apartment. A young woman who works for him. She's one of the reps. You know the type. Pretty. Just out of college."

"Wait. What are you talking about?" His dad was having an affair with one of his pharmaceutical salespeople? How did a person of that level even have access to his dad? As CEO of the company, there were layers of employees between him and the reps. He'd never known his father to care about anything more than work. Why would he risk such a thing?

He heard Mom take in a deep breath. When she spoke next, her voice had smoothed. "Your father has a girlfriend. He was with her when he had the heart attack."

"Mom, maybe he was just visiting her? For a work reason?"

"No, honey. They were in bed. He pays for the apartment.

He has for a year now. I saw the lease." A pause on the other end before she spoke again. "I've known for a while now. He's been planning to leave me but hasn't had the courage to do it yet." He'd never heard his composed mother so vulnerable, so shredded.

"How do you know?"

"We've been married for almost forty years. I thought he was hiding something, so I hired an investigator. He found everything. Photos. Paperwork with money trails. Two cell phone numbers assigned to him."

"Does he know you know?"

"No. I keep waiting for him to tell me, but for all his bluster, he's not a brave man. So it's just gone on and on for months. The lying. Lie after lie. I want him to admit to the girl, so I have the advantage in the divorce."

"Divorce?"

"Honey, yes. I have to divorce him. There's no recovering from this."

His stomach twisted. The toast he'd just eaten wanted to come up. He didn't know what to do.

"Trey, I need you to come down here."

"I'll come as soon as I can."

"Jamie's on her way over to the house. She's very upset. I had to tell her about the girl."

His sister was currently waitressing while living in Mission Beach with some girlfriends. His parents lived in a gated community in Del Mar about a half hour from there. "I'll be there. Tell Jamie I'll get there as soon as I can." Jamie had been his parents' surprise child, born ten years after Trey. His mother had been over forty when she found out she wasn't going through menopause but was pregnant.

After he hung up, he sat there staring at his phone. His father with another woman astounded him. They'd never been close or understood each other well, but Trey had always thought of him as a loyal husband. Work had been his mistress. A young woman? An employee? The ambitious Bradley Wattson risking it all for a girl didn't seem plausible.

He picked up the phone and called Autumn. She answered almost at once, sounding sleepy. He'd woken her. "Hey, what's up?"

"My dad had a heart attack. He's in the hospital."

"Oh, no. I'm so sorry."

"I have to fly down there." He paused, fighting tears. "Could you take a few days off? Go with me?"

"Of course I will. Martin's always looking for extra hours and I have sick days I need to burn before I lose them."

"Thanks." He paused, gathering himself. "I'm feeling totally lost."

"How bad is it?" she asked.

"I'm not sure. My mom says he's having an angioplasty surgery to reroute the blockage or whatever. I guess that means it's bad, right?"

"I'd think so, yes. But surgeons do these all the time. They'll fix him."

He tried to speak, but the lump in his throat made it impossible.

"Trey, are you there?"

"Yeah. There's more. When he had the heart attack, he was in bed with a woman who is not my mother. A woman half his age. She works for his company, no less."

She surprised him by cursing loudly. "What a total prick."

"Mom said it's gone on for at least a year. He's planning on leaving her. He pays for this girl's apartment."

"Your poor mom."

"She hired an investigator," he said. His stomach turned again. "I can't believe this."

"I'm sorry, Trey. What can I do?"

"Just come with me. Can you be ready in an hour?"

"I'll hustle."

After he hung up, he found two seats on a midmorning flight to San Diego from San Francisco, which would give them plenty of time to make the hour-and-a-half drive into the city. When he checked his email for the confirmation, there was a message from Autumn.

DEAR ART,

I'm just dashing this off quickly before I leave for a trip to San Diego. Trey's father had a heart attack. In addition, the jerk's been having an affair with some girl who works for him. Men can be such total pigs. I've never heard Trey's voice sound like that. He asked me to go with him down to San Diego. I said yes, of course. I can't let him go face all this alone. I may not be able to write for a while, depending on what Trey needs.

Love,

007

INSTEAD OF WRITING BACK, he closed the laptop. As soon as he was through with this crisis, he would put an end to Art. From then on, he would be Trey. Which meant that he had to tell Autumn the truth about everything. However, it would have to wait until after his trip home. He knew the next few days would take all the energy he had.

* * *

TREY AND AUTUMN took a taxi straight to the hospital from the airport. His mother had texted while they were in flight that they'd taken Dad back for surgery and anticipated they would be done by that afternoon.

After they were dropped off in front of the entrance to a

large new hospital, they asked the receptionist in the lobby for directions to the heart wing and were told to go up to the fifth floor. As they waited for the elevator, Autumn gave his shoulder a squeeze. "It's going to be all right," she said.

He didn't answer, comforted by her touch.

They found his mother and sister in the waiting area of the surgery wing. Jamie spotted them first and ran toward them. She threw her arms around Trey's neck and hugged him. "I'm glad you're here," Jamie said before stepping from his embrace to look at Autumn.

"This is my friend Autumn Hickman," he said. By then, his mother had joined them, and they both shook hands with Autumn.

"Hi, Autumn. It's nice to meet you." From behind Autumn, his sister raised her eyebrows at him. He could almost hear her thoughts. *Have you been holding out on me?* He pretended not to get the cue.

Jamie was dressed in her typical shorts and a tank top. Her long hair, the color of a ginger ale, was currently pulled back in a ponytail. She wore no makeup and looked the same as she had since she was sixteen, other than her skin was now clear of teenage acne. They shared the same deep blue eyes, which they'd gotten from their mother.

He hugged his mother next. Slightly over sixty, her daily walks and yoga practice gave her the physical strength of a much younger woman. She wore her blond hair in a neatly snipped shoulder-length bob that matched her impeccable attire. Even today, when she must be going through about a thousand confusing emotions, she wore a designer ensemble of white pants paired with a pink cotton sweater and kitten heels.

"Any news?" he asked.

"Not yet," Jamie said.

"We should know something in the next hour." Mom played nervously with the tennis bracelet around her wrist.

"Did you have a chance to talk to him before the surgery?" Trey asked.

"Yes, we spoke." Tears welled in Mom's eyes. "He finally told me the truth."

Jamie wrapped her arm around Mom's shoulders. "He told her he wants to marry the girl. Can you believe that?"

"He said nearly dying made it clearer than ever," Mom said. "How did he put it? 'Life is too short to pass up joy.'"

"Is that her name?" Autumn asked. When they all looked at her, she flushed bright red. "Oh, right. Joy, the concept, not the name."

For a moment, no one said anything, then Jamie, Mom, and Trey all burst out laughing.

"I'm sorry," Autumn said. "Obviously, you meant the concept." She was not laughing with them. Instead, she looked genuinely horrified. "Hospitals make me nervous. It's like my brain is all jumbled in here."

His mother stopped laughing and took Autumn's hand. "It's all right, sweetheart. Joy happens to be a common name." She gestured toward a clump of chairs. "Let's sit. You can distract us by telling us a little about yourself."

They all took seats next to a fake fig tree with a fine layer of dust covering its plastic leaves. The walls were painted a glossy wheat-hued yellow and paired with army-green chairs and a mustard carpet. He'd like to meet the designer who thought this decor would comfort those waiting and worried for their loved ones and gently suggest that next time he go with shades of blue.

He took the seat next to his mother. Across from them, Autumn and Jamie sat next to each other.

"It was so kind of you to come with Trey," Mom said to Autumn. Her hands shook as she folded them together in her lap.

"I'm glad to be here. I took a sick day from work," Autumn said. "I have a ton of them left."

Jamie turned to Autumn. "What do you do for work?"

"I'm a pharmacist," Autumn said, raising an eyebrow and lifting one side of her mouth in a crooked smile.

"No way," Jamie said, obviously seeing the irony. Their father's company made some of the most powerful and commonly prescribed drugs in the world.

"True story," Trey said. "She dispenses Dad's drugs on a daily basis."

"I'm quite familiar with the medicines your father's company makes," Autumn said. "The cholesterol one in particular. Many of our older customers are on it."

"They help people, right?" Mom asked.

"They do," Autumn said.

"I have friends who think the pharmaceutical industry is evil," Mom said as she curled and uncurled her hands. "I've defended my husband's work at more teas and book club events than I can count."

"Me too," Jamie said. "It's gotten to the point I don't even mention what my father does."

"Much of the public feels distrustful," Autumn said. "Mostly because of the prices. A lot of our elderly folks on fixed incomes have to walk away without their prescription because it costs too much, especially if the pharmaceutical company has managed to keep the drug from being made in a generic form. I hate to see that, especially if I know the drug will help them."

There was an awkward silence for a moment. The Wattson family was used to this kind of criticism. Trey had had no interest in continuing his father's legacy, believing himself that drugs were overpriced. He knew, too, that bribery and manipulation of the medical community were frequent practices. His father had bragged about it, proud of his treachery while hiding behind a public persona of the benevolent curer of illnesses. "My drugs save lives," he'd often said to his attackers, both defensively and proudly.

Would the medical community he'd manipulated be able to save him this morning? Probably. There was no such thing as justice. Good people had bad things happen. Bad people had good things happen.

Then again, his father wasn't totally bad. No one was purely one or the other. He'd always reconciled his father's work with his devotion to his wife. Now what did he have left in his arsenal of defense? His father was a cheater, sneaking around with a woman half his age. He'd told his wife that he wanted out after forty years of marriage. What kind of bastard did that?

Too many. It was a trite story, because it happened all the time. Men of a certain age, facing their own mortality, clung to youth in all its forms, including trading in their loyal wife for a sparkly trinket of a girl.

For the next half hour, his mother and Jamie lobbed questions at Autumn. He worried they were too intrusive, but the questions about where she went to school and how she'd met Trey and how long had she been in Cliffside Bay didn't appear to bother her.

He did cringe, however, when Jamie asked her about why she hated hospitals. "Did someone you love spend a lot of time in the hospital? Were you sick as a kid?"

They obviously hadn't noticed her slight limp. If they had, even Jamie knew not to ask about it outright. His sister was infamous in their family for blurting out inappropriate questions.

"I was in a car accident when I was fourteen. My legs were mangled." Autumn tapped her hands on both knees. "I had a million operations over the years to repair them."

"No wonder hospitals make you nervous," Mom said.

"Totally," Jamie said, nodding.

"I spent way too much time in ones just like this," Autumn

said. "It's impossible not to associate them with pain. I'm sure my brother Stone doesn't think of them too fondly, either. I can't tell you how many of my operations he sat through just like this, waiting for the doctors to come out and tell him how I did."

"Where was your mother in all this?" Mom asked. "Or your father?"

Autumn's expression clouded, but only for a second. "My mother left when I was four. Dad was around but mostly drunk."

"That's awful," Jamie said in her usual unfiltered manner. "How could she leave you guys like that?"

Autumn glanced at Trey, and they exchanged a knowing look between two people who knew each other's stories well. "She suffered from depression and thought we were better off without her. My older brother, Kyle, basically became a parent at eight years old."

"You poor kids," Mom said. She looked over at Trey fondly. "I can't imagine this one here taking care of anyone when he was eight years old."

"That's the truth," Trey said. "I'm grateful I didn't have to."

"You never saw your mother again?" Jamie asked. "After she left?"

"Strangely enough, she's back in our lives," Autumn said.

"After missing everything?" Jamie asked, before a pointed look from their mother made her flush from embarrassment. His sister had a tongue that moved faster than her brain.

Autumn smiled thinly and clutched her arms around her middle, as if she were clinging to an old-fashioned handbag on her lap. "She had a hard time of it. Depression and a sense that we were better off without her plagued her for a lot of years. We're in the rebuilding phase. It's been hard, but also good to connect. Our family's complicated."

"Aren't they all?" Mom asked. He'd never heard the bitter

edge in her voice before. She'd always seemed oblivious to his father's controlling and critical personality. When Dad had raged at Trey for choosing design and then Jamie for her lack of interest in anything other than having fun at the beach with her friends, cooking or curling up in her room reading books, their mother had gone mute. If she'd fought on his behalf, which he doubted, the outcome might have been different. His student loans had taken ten years to pay off. When Jamie had chosen an English literature degree over business, he'd cut her off in a similar manner.

The doctor came out then and told them that his father had come through the operation just fine. He would recover and return to everyday life soon.

If only it were that easy.

The doctor continued, oblivious to the trauma of their family. How could he know? He operated on the physical heart, not the figurative one.

They'd successfully performed the angioplasty and with a strict diet and exercise program, he would be able to resume a normal life before they knew it.

"A normal life? Does that include sex?" Mom asked.

"Most certainly." The doctor's hazel eyes looked amused for a split second before he returned to a stoic professionalism.

"Good. His girlfriend will be happy to hear that," Mom said.

The doctor's Adam's apple moved as he swallowed. "Um. Sure."

His mother slumped against Trey, as if her muscles suddenly weakened. His own mind tumbled and darted around in the dark, trying to cling to something that made sense. He knew only one thing for certain. His mother was in agony.

"When can my children see him?" Mom asked.

Children, not her.

"He's coming out of the sedative—give it an hour or so," the doctor said. "He'll be anxious to see his family, and your support will be of great assistance to his recovery."

"It won't be," Mom said. "That's the sad part."

The doctor had lost all composure at this point, his face and neck splotched with red. "I should be going. Best of luck."

After the doctor left, the three of them stood together in a clump. Autumn hovered a few feet away, a pained expression on her pretty face.

"What do you want to do, Mom?" Jamie asked.

Before she could answer, the closed doors of the waiting area opened and a young woman walked in, wearing a tight-fitting slim dress over a curvaceous figure. She hesitated for a split second in the entryway, tossing straight and shiny black hair behind her shoulders. Other than her lips, which appeared chapped and abused, as if she'd eaten off layer after layer of lipstick, her makeup was as thick and expertly applied as a reality television star.

She strode toward the reception area. Black pumps clicked on the tiled floor. She was a fast, hard walker. Halfway to the desk, she halted. Her gaze flickered to them and then fluttered away. In that swift moment, he saw recognition. She knew them. He imagined from the photo on his father's desk at work. His family. And here was the mistress in all her large-chested glory. *Could you be more of a cliché, Dad?*

Her mouth formed a circle. One foot stepped backward, making an uneven stance, as if she were about to perform a lunge. Then she lifted her chin slightly before striding over to the receptionist.

"That's her," Mom whispered. As if they didn't know. "Trinity Brown."

"How dare she come here." Jamie's eyes flamed with hatred.

Mom trembled under his arm. "We should go."

"*She* should go." Jamie spoke loudly this time. Several of the other people in the waiting area turned to stare at them. Still at the reception counter, Trinity's shoulders flinched. She didn't turn around.

"She's a child," Mom said, still in the same hushed tone. "The same age as Jamie."

"Mom, let's get out of here," Trey said. "We'll go home. Make a plan."

His mother turned her glazed eyes toward him. "A plan? I already had one."

"She should have the decency to look us in the eye," Jamie said as loudly as the first time.

The entire lobby was now watching their domestic drama unfold. It was better than television. A great distraction from their own worries.

"Do you see us here?" Jamie's voice reverberated in the now-deadly still and quiet room. "You should acknowledge the family you've ruined."

Trinity turned like a dancer in a slow-motion pirouette. She walked toward them, eyes blazing. Only the young could be so sure of their right to happiness, to taking what they wanted without regard for anything but their own needs. Trinity stopped when she was a few feet from their huddled wreck of a family. "I don't owe you anything," she said.

He was surprised by the singsong timbre of her voice. She had a fake voice practiced over the years to convey innocence and compassion. He knew the type. His ex-wife had the same kind of voice. In the beginning, he'd loved to hear her talk. About anything and everything, just to relax into the music of her. How stupid he'd been. How had he not seen that her exterior role of nice, churchgoing girl hid a darkness, a catlike arrogance and deviousness? *I will take what I want because I can.* When he'd confronted her about the affair, she'd turned it on him. He was inadequate. Too reserved, too uncommunicative, too sterile in his approach to life. As the cruel words slipped off her tongue, she spoke in that sick, sweet pitch of a voice. Those words had been worse than knowing about the affair. Her accusations had simmered inside him and risen from his body in the sickly shape of shame. They became truth to him. He'd caused her betrayal because he was not good enough.

Just as he'd caused his father's disdain. Trey was not enough.

His shame had become bitterness and had changed him. This change had kept him from Autumn. His morphing into a creature who crept in silent apology had kept him from his mother and sister. Without even realizing it, he'd become apologetic for his very existence.

Now this wild young woman stared them all down with a fierceness that he could not quite fathom. She did not cower or apologize. She came at them with her teeth bared.

"None of you have any idea of the man Bradley is. You don't appreciate him. You've all left him in one form or another. But I didn't. I was there for him when none of you could be bothered."

The three of them stood there stunned and stung, as if she'd slapped them. At the end of a terrible three seconds, Autumn stepped forward, slicing the air between them, a shield between the turbulent girl and what remained of his family.

"I'm sorry for you," Autumn said, low and quiet. "When you're older and you've lost someone or something dear to you, or when someone has betrayed you and left you to bleed alone, only then will you truly understand what it is you've done here. You can justify this to yourself as much as you want. The heart wants what it wants and all that. But no misguided justification changes the fact that you took a person who was not free for the taking. You've gobbled a meal not set at your table. You don't know this now, but a man who leaves will always be a man who leaves. Coming here as you've done was cruel. Yet you don't see it. You see only what you wanted, what you believe is your right to have. Someday, it will be you. In the end, we all reap what we sow."

Trinity backed up a few inches. Her voice became falsetto as words rushed from her chapped mouth. "No, that's not how it works. People like me aren't afraid to go for what they want. I don't swallow the conventional bullshit, believing in some false, made-up rules about how to live. It's only stupid, weak people who won't grab what they want."

"Good luck to you," Autumn said. She turned back to them and offered her arm to Jamie. "Let's go home and have pie."

Pie?

As if she'd heard his question, she smiled over at him. "Pie makes everything just a little better."

With his mother's arm tucked next to him, and Autumn and Jamie entwined in a similar fashion, the four of them walked out of the lobby.

When they were at the elevator, Mom turned to Autumn. "You, my dear, have quite the way with words."

For the second time that day, they laughed. This time, Autumn joined them.

* * *

Later, he sat with Autumn and Jamie on the patio under the shade of an umbrella. His mother had gone upstairs to nap.

His gaze swept the patio and pool area. This house was not the one he'd grown up in and still seemed strange to him. They'd moved to the spacious home in the hills of Del Mar after he'd left for college. His sister, however, had lived in this house since she was eight. He could tell it felt like home to her by the easy way she opened drawers and tossed her sweater on the countertop.

Jamie pushed her hair behind one shoulder and sat

forward, placing her elbows on the table. "What do we do about Mom?"

Trey shook his head. "I was thinking I should bring her home with me. Just for a while. Dad's probably going to send someone to get his crap, which she won't want to be here for."

"I'd love to take it all to the beach and burn it in a bonfire," Jamie said.

Autumn chuckled. "I like that idea."

"Do you think Mom would be open to staying with me for a while?" he asked his sister before explaining that Stone and Pepper were moving out. "She could even have her own bedroom."

Jamie nodded. "I think it's a great idea. Nothing like a change of scenery to get your head on straight."

He excused himself and went upstairs to use the bathroom. As he passed by his mother's room, he heard her crying. He stopped at the door, unsure if he should go inside or not. Had he wanted comfort when his marriage had blown up? Those days were fuzzy, but he recalled long phone conversations with both his mother and Jamie. For a time, he'd come to stay here at the house before he moved to Cliffside Bay. Jamie had dropped in frequently, even though she was finishing her last year at college. They'd helped him come up with the plan to move to Cliffside Bay.

He knocked softly on the door to his mother's bedroom. "Mom? Are you okay? Do you need anything?"

The sounds of sobs abruptly stopped. "I'm all right."

"Can I come in?"

"Yes."

He pushed the door open a few inches. Mom was perched on the side of the bed, still in her clothes and shoes from their hospital visit. She clutched a wad of tissues in her hands.

He crossed over to her and sat next to her. "What can I do, Mom?"

"Nothing, really. Your being here is very sweet." She patted his leg. "I miss you. Your father was often away, and this house felt so big." She sniffed and dabbed under her eyes. "I know now that it wasn't work."

"I'm sorry, Mom."

"I don't know why I'm surprised. I should have seen it coming. I'm not the first of my friends to have this happen."

"Do you know what you want to do? Have you thought about it?"

"Besides divorcing him, not really. I've been fixated suddenly on selling this house. It's too big."

"If that's what you want."

"And too full of your father," she said.

His presence was certainly reflected in the decor. The bedroom was all dark greens and mahogany furniture. Very masculine and imposing, like him. Downstairs, a large painting of him hung over the fireplace.

"I'll put it on the market and maybe find a place of my own."

"I thought you loved this house," he said.

"I've been asking your father to downsize for some time now. I thought he'd retire soon, and we'd travel together. Enjoy life. He's always worked so much, which gave us this lifestyle, but he never took time to enjoy it. From the moment I met him, he was always so ambitious. I would've been happy for a quieter, less grandiose lifestyle. Especially if it meant I would've had more time with him." She took in a jagged breath. "The truth is, he's been checked out of this marriage for a long time. I was just too stupid to see it."

"Not stupid, Mom. You trusted him. We all did." He hesitated, playing with his watch. "When it all came out about Malia and her affair, she made it seem like I'd practically forced her into cheating by being inadequate. I took that to heart, and

I've let it affect me. I've allowed her judgments to dictate too many things."

"I've seen that," she said. "You were so bitter and angry. You seem better now."

"It's been over three years. A lot of great things have happened for me since then."

"I'm proud of you—the way you've started over. I hope I can do the same."

"You could come home with me," he said, gently, as if he'd just thought of it. "Stay for a while. Just until you figure out your plan."

"No, I'd be in the way."

"Stone and Pepper are moving out next week. I've been dreading it, to tell you the truth. I'd love the company."

"What about Autumn? Will I be in the way of that?"

"We're just friends."

"Is that right?" she asked, raising one eyebrow.

"Mom."

"Don't try to fool me. I can see the way you look at her. What's the problem?"

"It's complicated." If she only knew how complex or the mess he'd gotten himself into pretending to be someone else. "But seriously, Mom. Come back with me. You can put the house up for sale from there. Let the Realtor take care of things." Everything was in perfect order and clean. No staging required for his mother's house.

"It would be good to get away."

"Let's plan on leaving tomorrow. You can decide later about the house."

"What about your father? I can't just leave him in the hospital. Someone will need to look after him when he gets out."

He stared at her, unsure he'd heard her correctly.

She laughed, a bitter, abrupt croak from the back of her throat. "Right. Force of habit. He has someone else for that now." Tears swam in her eyes. She dabbed at them, then sighed. "Oh, Trey. This just seems too much. I'm so old. How do I start over?"

"One day at a time. And you have Jamie and me. Lean on us."

"I feel like such a fool," she said.

"Betrayal has a way of making you feel that way, Mom. But this isn't your fault."

She rubbed her forehead with her fingertips. "I'm so tired. I didn't sleep at all last night."

"Take a little rest," he said. "I'll wake you up before dinner."

Mom slipped her shoes from her feet as he tossed a few pillows aside. She lay back, curled slightly with her hands under her cheek. He knelt by the side of the bed and looked into her eyes. "Do you remember what you told me when I came home after Malia and I split?"

"No," she said, smiling. "I hope it was something helpful."

"It was. You said, think of this as the beginning of a whole new life. A second chance."

"That wasn't bad advice, I guess."

"No, it's not." He looked down at the hunter-green comforter, smoothing it with his hand. In his mind's eye, he traveled the rooms of the house. Dark grays, greens, and reds were the colors of choice. He looked back at Mom. "What's your favorite color?"

"Yellow."

"There's no yellow in this house."

"Your father likes dark colors. And big, imposing houses. Everything big."

"We can find you a small house and decorate it in shades of yellow."

"And light blue, maybe?"

"Whatever you want."

She closed her eyes. "That's a good idea. Maybe it'll be a home in Cliffside Bay, near you."

He kissed his mom's cheek. Her skin was soft and warm. "We'd have fun together. Like the old days. Do you remember how we used to go the beach and art museums?"

"We had good times, didn't we? My whole life hasn't been a lie, right?"

"Of course not, Mom. He did this, not you. It's too soon for you to know this, but his cheating has nothing to do with you and everything to do with him."

"I could see it in his eyes this morning. A panic about his own mortality."

The clinging to a sense of youth. A hot rush of anger washed over him. His father had made a promise to grow old with his wife all those years ago. But now, when it came down to it and when youth with her supple skin and tight body had presented herself, he'd jumped. Not for the first time—and this time for very different reasons—he vowed to never be his father.

"How long did you know?" Trey asked. "About Trinity."

"For the last six months." She stared back at him with her pretty blue eyes. "It's odd, I know, that I didn't do anything— didn't confront him or take steps to sort out all the details of what was next."

"Why didn't you? Do you know?"

"I think I needed time to adjust to the idea—to process the fact that my life as I knew it was over." She closed her eyes. "But now I'm just so tired."

He kissed her soft cheek. "Take a rest. I'll check on you later."

He stood and walked from the room, closing the door softly behind him. At the landing, he stopped and looked down into the formal sitting room where his father's portrait hung above the fireplace. For a few minutes, he stared at his father's face, the firm, determined mouth and hard jawline. The glint in his intelligent eyes that the artist had captured in tiny brush strokes. However, the artist had failed to identify the streak of selfishness and narcissism under the classically handsome features. Perhaps, like inner beauty, cruelty could not always be detected by the human eye. One had to look carefully to see such qualities.

10

A utumn

FROM THE DOORWAY to the kitchen, Autumn watched Trey standing on the landing. She noted the squaring of his shoulders and the way his eyes hardened into dull stone as he looked at the portrait of his father. It didn't take much imagination to guess his thoughts of disappointment in equal measurement to resignation. Trey had already known the level of loyalty Bradley Wattson had toward his family. When his children hadn't done exactly as he wished, they were cut off financially. This wasn't much different, really. Bradley Wattson wanted what he wanted, and no one would stop him from taking it. Except death, of course. Which was Bradley Wattson's true fear. She suspected he would soon find out that entanglement with the girl would only make him feel older in the end. Instead of the woman upstairs who'd given him the best years of her life and expected that they would melt into the twilight years as one, he'd chosen betrayal as the answer to his fear.

Ainsley Wattson had seemed to have everything. Autumn imagined what her own mother would see if she saw this house and cars and the photographs of vacation homes. She would think: this woman has it all. In the end, wealth mattered little when the one you loved loved someone else.

What was it about love and leaving that seemed to reside so closely together? For her and Trey, it seemed the ones they loved the most were the ones who left or had never shown up at all. Her parents, then Kyle. Trey's wife, now his father. The risk was so great. Love and betrayal, like twins born from the same mother. One marked with grace and the other with darkness.

Standing here, she would give anything to snatch Trey's pain away from him. If she could, she would do anything to make him happy.

A startling thought hit her in the middle of the chest. Was it Trey she wanted? Was he the one she loved? Was she unable to admit it to herself because she was afraid to risk rejection?

She closed her eyes and gave herself strict instructions.

No, don't go there. Do not set yourself up that way.

She stumbled into the kitchen. Jamie was at the cooktop, stirring a red sauce that smelled of basil, garlic, and tomato.

"You hungry?" Jamie asked.

"Starving." She smiled, trying to get herself together.

"You look strange, like you saw a ghost," Jamie said. Trey's sister was like an open-faced sandwich. Nothing hidden. Everything delicious right out for the world to see. She seemed to expect the same from others.

"I'm fine," Autumn said in response to Jamie's question. "Maybe a little hungry." Her stomach growled, as if to back her up. "That smells delicious." Autumn sat on one of the tall stools at the island across from Jamie. The kitchen had dark wood cabinets and black granite, everything dark and classic and austere. Quite the opposite of Autumn's cozy light-filled cottage. Funny, she would have thought Mrs. Wattson would favor lighter colors. Trey certainly did. His aesthetic matched the beach and landscape of Cliffside Bay.

"This is my secret recipe for pasta sauce," Jamie said. "Someday, when I have my own restaurant, I'm going to serve it as my main course."

"You want to open a restaurant?"

Jamie looked away, as if embarrassed. Why did women always apologize for wanting something? "My father thinks it's ridiculous."

"People open restaurants all the time."

"Yes, but how many are successful?" Jamie asked. "Dear Father loves to say that restaurants are only successful at failing."

"Some people love to tell others they'll fail. It's a great way to feel better about all the dreams they were too afraid to pursue."

Jamie looked up from her pot of sauce and tilted her head slightly. "It's hard to imagine my father having any dreams other than making money." She lifted the wooden spoon from the pot and held it midair as if the next thought suddenly occurred to her. "But maybe his dream was to find a woman half his age." She set the spoon aside and moved from the cooktop to place both hands on the counter. "My poor mom."

"I'm sorry," Autumn said, unable to think of anything else to say.

"She's tougher than she looks, though."

"Women mostly are."

They exchanged a knowing smile.

"Anyway, it's not really a restaurant I want. I'd like to create entire experiences for people. I want to open a small inn with only six or so rooms. I'd serve a light breakfast of pastries and scones or whatever. Then, for dinner, I'd have four courses. One of those long dinners where people eat leisurely and don't care how much butter is in the dishes. I'd have a little library full of books, and guests could hang out in front of the fire and read or chat. Everyone would bring one of their favorite books to leave behind and take one from the library. Oh, and I'd have wine-and-cheese hour at four every day. People would come for the weekend and fall in love or come after they were already in love to spend time together. Or, maybe, coming to my inn would restore relationships or bond families or aid in healing past hurts." She let out a happy sigh. "Couples could get married in my inn. Or have honeymoons."

Autumn found herself mesmerized by this open-faced girl and her dream. "Do you have a location in mind?"

"Not exactly. I just know I want it to be by the ocean, away from noise and city life. I'd love a Victorian or an old lodge that needs renovation." She went back to her pot and brought a spoonful of sauce to her mouth for a taste. "Should we open wine?"

Autumn blinked, surprised by the swift change of subject. "Sure."

Jamie went to the wine refrigerator and pulled out a bottle of Chablis and used a server's corkscrew to open it with what looked like a practiced flick of her wrist. The cork slipped from the bottle without making a sound.

"It's going to take me forever to make my dream come true. Waitressing barely covers my rent and expenses. The way I'm going, I'll be eighty by the time I have enough to buy anything." She poured wine into both glasses.

"Don't give up," Autumn said. "I've found that once a person knows what they want, it comes to them. Eventually."

"Was that true for you?" she asked as she set the glass in front of Autumn.

She had to think for a moment before answering. "For the

most part, yes. I have a career that keeps me interested and well paid. My home is a dream. Thanks to my brother and yours, it's exactly how I wanted. Growing up, I just wanted a home no one could take from me."

Jamie waved the wooden spoon in the air. "Growing up like this, you think everyone's experience is the same. It wasn't until I went to college that I got a clue about how hard it is for some. There were these older ladies in my classes who were going back to school after raising kids. They were all so clever and had such great work ethics. I had so much admiration for them." Her round blue eyes sparkled under the pendant lights that hung over the island.

"Trey told me your parents cut you off when you changed majors. You know what it's like to pay your own way."

"I do now. When I lived here, I did not."

They both sipped from their glasses, quiet for a moment. Where had Trey gone? Was he still staring at his father's portrait?

"Come on. This can simmer," Jamie said, and gestured toward the pool. "Let's go back outside. The hummingbirds usually come this time of day for a little cocktail of their own."

Autumn followed Jamie outside, jealous of the younger woman's tanned, muscular legs. Dressed in cotton pants and a short-sleeved blouse, Autumn wasn't overly warm, but it would be fantastic to feel the air on her bare legs. When they reached the table, Autumn looked longingly at the pool. Since her swim, she only wanted more.

"Would you like to take a swim?" Jamie asked, obviously reading her desire.

"No, thank you. I don't really swim."

"Because of your legs?"

She almost laughed at the girl's forthright question. "Yes, mostly because of that."

Jamie didn't ask any follow-up questions, but simply

pointed to several lounge chairs under the beach umbrella. "Sit then?"

"Yes, thank you." Autumn had just settled in when Jamie turned to her. "So, what's going on with you and Trey?"

"Going on?"

"Are you guys just friends or what?" Jamie asked.

"We're friends."

"For now?"

Autumn laughed. "Trust me, we're just friends. Best friends."

"Really? Okay, then. Now I'll have to think of someone to fix you up with."

Autumn groaned. "I've had so many coffee dates lately, I don't know if I can take one more."

"One more could be the one. You just never know."

Why did that thought do nothing but make her feel tired?

11

T rey

THAT NIGHT, he tossed and turned, unable to sleep. He'd left the shades up, and light from around the pool stole into his room. The ceiling fan whirled above him, slow and steady, its blades just visible. The outlines of the dresser and bookshelf were shadows, their contents invisible. Not that he needed light. He had the books on the shelves memorized: Hardy Boys mysteries; all eight Dark Towers novels; all the Harry Potter novels; a history of American interior design; every *Architectural Digest* magazine published between 1998 and 2002; and various novels, mostly suspense. His mother had moved all his old books into the new house, even though he was grown by then. Now, if she sold the house, he would be forced to take the books with him.

Giving up on trying to sleep, he pushed aside the sheet and cotton blanket and got out of bed. He rubbed his eyes before shuffling over to the small desk and turning on the lamp. On the corkboard above the desk were several photographs. One of him and Nico standing with their surfboards. Another was of him and his sister. She was about nine, which would have made him nineteen. They'd been on vacation with his parents in Hawaii. He had his arm around Jamie's scrawny shoulders. She grinned at the camera. Whereas he squinted and looked uncomfortable. That had been the vacation where he told his parents he wanted to change majors. This photograph was taken before that conversation, but he could see the strain in the slump of his shoulders.

His parents' situation brought back so many feelings about the demise of his own marriage. The afternoon his divorce was final, he'd flown to San Diego. He'd arrived around cocktail hour on a Friday. He let himself into the quiet house through the kitchen door. A note on the table from his mother welcomed him and said she'd gone to the store but would be home shortly. He'd found his dad in the study, sitting at the desk with his laptop open.

The memory of the conversation between him and his father came back to him in perfect detail, playing out behind his closed eyes.

He knocked on the frame of the double doors of his dad's study. "Hey, Dad." Traditional, with dark woods and an oversize desk, the room expressed power and masculinity. Brown leather chairs with red decorative pillows and curtains. Red was a power color. No weakness in red, only aggressiveness. Like his father.

Dad looked up from whatever he was doing on the laptop. "Trey, come on in." People always remarked at how much he looked like his father. Same lean build and olive complexion. His dad's dark blond hair was tinged with silver but had once been the same color as Trey's. Their eyes were different, though. Dad's were a hazel color that changed with the light, sometimes almost brown. Trey's blue eyes were like his mother's. He'd like to think his character mimicked hers, too.

He followed directions, feeling like a kid being summoned to the principal's office.

"What brings you down?" Dad asked.

Had Mom not told him, or was he playing dumb?

"I signed final paperwork today." He left it at that. If Dad couldn't understand the layers of meaning behind that sentence, then he had nothing more to say.

Dad leaned back in his chair and put his hands behind his head. "I'm sorry you're going through this. Must be rough."

Rough? That was putting it mildly. It was more like someone had punched through his chest and seized his beating heart, then crushed it in a steel vise.

"I wouldn't have thought Malia the type to run around," Dad said. "Never saw that one coming."

"Me either." He'd thought they'd been happy. Looking back, however, he should have seen the signs. There had been many signs. So many signs. The sudden interest in meeting up with girlfriends in the evenings. Changing her pass codes on her phone and computer so he couldn't get into them. Wearing high heels to work instead of flats. "Five years of marriage and she decides to blow it all up."

"At least you found out now," Dad said. "Five years is nothing. You can write that off as a mistake and move forward."

"Sure. Forward." Trey couldn't imagine what that would be. Not another woman. No way. Never again would he put himself out there. He'd been so trusting, so sure they had the perfect marriage and partnership.

"Give it a little time, but you'll be back in the saddle," Dad said. "Maybe take some time and play around. Your mother and I got married so young, I never had time to try out a few for free."

"I'm not sure that's really me," Trey said. That was a lie. He knew for sure that wasn't him. Since the time he'd been interested in girls, he'd wanted to be in a monogamous relationship. His first crush had been Cece Moore in fourth grade. He'd asked her to go steady with him, via a passed note in class. When she said yes, it had been one of the highlights of elementary school. That is, until she wrecked him two weeks later by breaking up with him in the same manner in which they'd started.

"Take it from me, you'll be glad you experienced a little variety. Once you're married again, you'll wish you had."

He clenched his hands together on his lap. His father's suggestion to bed a bunch of women made his stomach hurt. "I don't think so."

His father angled his head to the right and narrowed his eyes. "Tell me, son. Was Malia's affair because she was lonely?"

"What are you talking about?" His nostrils flared. "Are you suggesting this was my fault?"

"Not that I condone infidelity, no matter the cause. But I've wondered if my suspicions about you are correct."

He stared at his father, dumbfounded. "Is this the gay thing again?"

His dad pushed up from his chair and came around the desk, then perched on a corner, feet from Trey. "If you are, there's nothing to be ashamed of. My head of sales is gay. Most charismatic dude you ever met."

"Dad, I'm not gay."

"You sure about that? Everything lines up that way. Decorating. Wife has an affair with some young stud. But like I said, there's nothing to be ashamed of. You should own it. This 'in the closet' stuff is no way to live."

"Malia didn't stray because I'm gay. I mean, I'm not gay. She strayed because...well, I don't know why exactly. I thought we were happy."

"Were you having sex?" Dad asked.

Not so much. Another sign. The past six months had been as dry as the Grapevine portion of Interstate 5. "It doesn't matter, Dad. The marriage is done. Like you said, time to move on."

"You're not gay, then?"

"No. I told you when I was in high school and I'm telling you now," Trey said. "I'm not gay."

"You ready to give it up, then?"

"Give what up?"

"The decorating stuff. Or whatever you call it," Dad said. "Around here, every other minute, one of your mother's friends who's never worked a day in her life decides that just because she knows how to shop for a pretty vase and some pillows, she's a decorator. I can't tell you how many of them have started their own decorating business. As far as I can tell, their little hobbies never amount to much. Mostly, it just costs their husbands money."

"I'm hardly a hobbyist or a bored housewife. I went to school. I've won awards."

As if he didn't hear Trey, Dad continued. "I have a place for you at the firm. You'd have to start at the bottom and work your way up, but I have full confidence in you."

"I'm not quitting the business," Trey said. "I love my work. Making spaces that reflect the people who live in them is my passion. You can demean it all you want. People pay me a lot of money to transform their homes."

Dad blinked and then shoved away from his desk and strode over to the window that looked out to the pool deck. He crossed his arms and fixed his gaze on Trey. "What's your plan? You gave her the business. If I'm guessing right, you didn't get much for either the business or the house."

"That's correct. But it's enough to start over somewhere else."

"Where?" His dad's voice was like a thundercloud before it

burst. The famous Bradley Wattson temper would soon unleash a downpour from which no one was safe.

He hadn't known what was going to come out of his mouth until it did. "There's a little town an hour and a half north of the city. Cliffside Bay. Nico and I go out there to surf sometimes. It's a sleepy town, but I like it. I can start small—work out of my home—until I get a few clients under my belt. Word travels fast in a small town."

They'd been interrupted then by his mother. She'd rapped on the door and held her arms out for him.

His father had shrugged and walked out of the room.

Such a symbol of his parents, really. Open arms versus a shrug.

A creak in the hallway drew him back to the present. Someone else was awake. He opened the door a crack and saw his sister making her way down the hallway on her tiptoes.

"Hey," he whispered.

She started, then turned around. "You scared the crap out of me," she hissed back.

"Sorry. What're you doing?"

She motioned for him to come closer. "I'm going down for some tea. You want some?"

He nodded as he walked the few feet to where she stood at the top of the stairs. "Not tea, but maybe a shot of scotch."

He let her take the lead down the stairs. Jamie wore cotton pajamas and a pair of cat socks with ears popping out of the front toes. As they descended the stairs, she held on to the railing, probably to keep from slipping. No socks for him in the summer months. Way too hot. The hardwood floors were pleasantly cool against the pads of his feet.

When they reached the kitchen, he grabbed a tumbler from the cupboard and helped himself to a generous pour of his dad's scotch. "You couldn't sleep?" he asked his sister.

"Nah. I just kept staring at the ceiling fan, so decided to give it up."

"Same." He sat on one of the stools at the kitchen island.

His sister moved around the kitchen, filling up the teakettle and setting it on the cooktop. She turned a knob, and one of the gas burners flamed to life.

"What's bugging you?" he asked. "Just the obvious?"

"I guess." She scooped a spoonful of sugar from the bowl his mother always left near the coffeepot into a mug. "It's just everything's so uncertain right now. I wish I knew for sure what was going to happen next." From a tin can on the counter, she pulled out a tea bag and plopped it into the mug. The tag hung down the side like a mouse's tail.

"Yeah, me too." He sipped from his scotch, enjoying the warmth on the back of his throat.

The kettle whistled. Jamie poured steaming water into the mug.

"You seeing anyone?" he asked.

"No. I was, but it wasn't going anywhere, so I broke it off."

"You're only twenty-four. Does it have to go somewhere?" he asked.

"More than a booty call, yes."

He cringed and put up his hands as if to ward off evil. "Please, don't talk like that. I can't think about my baby sister having sex."

They sipped their respective drinks for a moment. Jamie sat a few stools down from him. "What about you? Autumn told me you guys are just friends."

"That's right." The minute it was out of his mouth, he knew his forlorn tone had given up his secret.

"Wait a minute. Do you want more?" Jamie asked before blowing on her tea.

"Yeah, but it's complicated."

"Why?"

"For one, she doesn't feel the same way. And two, I did something weird." He proceeded to tell her about Art and how deep he was in now. "I don't know how to tell her."

"Maybe you shouldn't."

"I'm afraid I'll lose her if I do. Her friendship is better than nothing."

Jamie studied him from behind a waft of steam. "I think you should tell her how you feel."

"It's crossed my mind that this has gone on long enough. If I don't tell her now, I'll never do it."

"You may be surprised. I think there's more to her feelings than she's admitting. Maybe even to herself."

"Why do you say that?"

"I don't think a woman who is just a friend comes with you on this kind of family trip. You're obviously bonded."

He sighed. "I'm tired of pretending."

"Then don't. Not anymore. Tell her how you feel."

"And be ready to lose her?" he asked.

"If that's what it takes. We never get anything in this world if we don't ask for it."

He raised his glass. "Amen to that."

* * *

THE NEXT FEW days were busy ones. Trey, reluctantly, sent Autumn home to Cliffside Bay. She needed to get back to work, and in good conscience he couldn't keep her there. After she left, he and Jamie sat down with their mother and came up with a plan. They hired her a divorce attorney, who advised her that all proceedings from then on should be conducted through her. Their father had already retained counsel as well, and they began the negotiations. They agreed to put the house on the market. All other assets were to be split down the middle. To his relief, Mom wouldn't have to worry financially.

Half of his pension and stocks, plus the house, set her up nicely.

They made arrangements for her to come back to Cliffside Bay with Trey at the end of the week. This gave her time to go through the house and decide which of the furniture pieces she wanted to keep. Trey hired movers to come take them to storage, promising her that when they found a new place for her, he'd send for them. He then used his contacts in the business to find a broker to deal with the rest of the furniture. By the end of the week, most pieces were spoken for, either by consignment shops or staging companies. He helped his mother pack up what she wanted from her kitchen, which also went into storage.

During a phone call with Stone, he'd assured Trey all was well with the business. "Take whatever time you need," Stone had said to him. "We've got your back."

In more ways than one, he thought, as he enclosed his mother's good china in Bubble Wrap.

He'd called Rafael to ask if it was all right that his mother move in with him until he could get her a place of her own. Rafael didn't hesitate, as Trey knew he wouldn't. "Maybe Autumn's mother and your mother will become friends," Rafael had said. "Poor David and Lavonne are going to be surrounded by mothers."

"They could both use one," Trey had said. "And my mother needs a project, so maybe it'll work out for the best."

Trey kept a close watch on his mother but all in all, she seemed resigned to the divorce and perhaps even a little relieved to have it decided. He caught her crying by the pool one evening, but she assured him she was fine. "Crying is what I need to do for now."

Having gone through his own divorce, he couldn't agree more. Maybe he'd have handled things better if he'd done a little more grieving and a lot less raging.

Although they didn't go back to the hospital with her, Trey and Jamie went to see their father the afternoon before he left for Cliffside Bay.

Surprisingly, they'd let him go home. As it turned out, his home was an apartment on the beach with Trinity. His home of choice, anyway. That was obvious when they walked in and saw that he'd been living there for a while. Large, with light wood floors and bright blue cabinetry, the place screamed of youth. The apartment was so unlike the house that Trey was taken aback.

Dad was resting on the couch when a sour-faced Trinity let them in. When they'd called to see if they could come by, Trinity had said, "As long as that crazy woman doesn't come with you." That crazy woman happened to be the one he loved, but he bit back his words and agreed politely. He and Jamie wanted to see him and wish him well but make it clear they wouldn't be stopping by for Sunday dinners anytime soon.

Dad smiled at them when they came into the room. "Hey, guys. Good to see you."

"How're you feeling?" Jamie asked as she sat in a bright green armchair across from the couch. The entire place was decorated in circus colors.

"Much improved. Thanks. Trinity's taking great care of me." Trinity sat on the arm of the sofa next to Dad and stroked his arm.

Trey's stomach turned. His legs felt shaky and weak, so he sat in the chair next to his sister.

"We just came by to tell you we've taken care of everything for Mom," Jamie said.

"Sounds like you found her one hell of an attorney," Dad said, chuckling. "She's a real shark."

"You were married almost four decades, Dad," Trey said. "Fifty-fifty."

Dad flashed another smile that reminded Trey of a satisfied

cat. "I never had any intention of robbing her of her fifty percent. Anyway, I know how this works. Doesn't matter that she never worked a day in her life. In California, she gets half of everything."

Jamie stood with such force that she managed to scoot the rather heavy armchair back several inches. "What the hell? Never did a day's work in her life? Are you kidding me? She raised us. She was at your beck and call twenty-four hours a day."

"Come on now," Dad said. "There were a lot of tennis games and lunches with the ladies, not to mention shopping sprees every week. It's not like she was abused."

Trey's fists balled at his sides. "Jamie, we should go."

"You have someplace you need to be?" Dad asked. "Trinity made a salad for lunch."

"No, we can't stay," Trey said. "We just came by to see how you were. And to say goodbye."

Jamie started pacing behind the chairs.

"Maybe you could come back sometime?" Trinity's suggestion was paired with a triumphant smirk at the corners of her mouth.

Jamie stopped and scowled at her. "Is she kidding me right now?" she asked Trey, as if he would know.

Dad patted Trinity's knee. "Don't worry, baby. They'll come around."

Baby? They'll come around? He was talking as if they weren't right in front of him. Trey thought he might actually be sick.

"Mom's going to live with me for a while." Trey put his hand at his throat to stop the tremor, but it was of no use. He sounded shaky and squeaky, like a revisit to puberty. "Just until she can get on her feet."

"That's kind of you. She'll enjoy that," Dad said.

Jamie stopped and pointed a finger at him. "You don't get to say one thing about what she does or what she'll enjoy. You don't get to be part of our family now."

"I'll always be your father," Dad said. "My marriage has nothing to do with how I feel about you kids."

"You mean your *divorce*," Jamie shouted. "And if you were unhappy you should have done it the right way. Do you know how much worse this is because of her?" She pointed at Trinity. "Do you know how badly you've hurt Mom? She'll probably never get over this." She waved both hands, indicating the apartment. "And this whole thing—playing Barbie with this girl my age—it won't last. You, Trinity, you're a statistic. And Dad, you're a cliché."

"That's enough, young lady," Dad said in the clipped tone he used when they were young and in trouble.

"It's not enough. Not nearly enough," Jamie said. "You've never supported Trey or me in our dreams. You've hammered on us all our lives to take the responsible route, the safe route. And now you've gone and done this? Blown up your life for her? Do you even know her? Do you really think she could love a sixty-year-old man when she's twenty-four, or do you think she's quite aware of the divorce codes in the state of California?"

"You wait just a minute," Dad said. "You're a spoiled brat who has no idea how the world works. Both of you were coddled by your mother and made to think that your silly dreams were something you could actually achieve. I was the only one of the two of us who ever told you how it really is in life. How dare you waltz in here and judge me for seizing a slice of happiness."

"Screw you, Dad," Jamie said.

Trey jumped up, unsteady on his trembling legs. Trinity's face had gone completely white under her tan. He moved quickly around the chair and took his sister's arm. "This was a mistake. I wish you the best, but this is the last you'll see of us.

If you want to contact either of us, you can do so through the attorney."

Trey nodded at Trinity. "Good luck. You're going to need it." With that, he took his sister's quivering arm, her skin as hot as a skillet, and steered her toward the door. He'd only just shut it when his sister simultaneously burst into tears and started cursing. The girl could really curse with the best of them.

"All right now. Let's just get out of here." He wrapped his arm around her shoulder and walked her over to the car. Once he had her inside, she'd calmed somewhat. After a resigned hiccup, she buckled her seat belt. He sprinted around to the front of the car, aware that Trinity watched from the window, and slid into the driver's seat.

He threw the car into reverse and backed out of the skinny driveway. Minutes later, they were headed back to the house. The freeway traffic was light, and soon the exit for their parents' Del Mar neighborhood appeared. By then, Jamie had quieted and was staring out her window with a forsaken expression.

"You want to talk?" he asked.

"I'm sorry for the outburst. I know it didn't do any good."

"Did it make you feel better?"

"Not really. I thought it would," Jamie said.

"Yeah, getting that angry rarely does."

"I guess we just have to move on."

"Looks like we don't have a choice." He slowed the car as they turned off the freeway onto the thoroughfare that took them up to the house. They passed a busy shopping center and another, then a horse arena, where girls in traditional riding attire practiced jumps.

"I hate my life," Jamie said. "My job's awful. Now Mom won't even be here. Have I told you about my roommates? It's a constant party at our apartment, and they never clean up."

They turned left to go up the hill into his parents' gated

community. Large homes in various architectural styles, including Spanish, early colonial, and modern, were built on either side of the lane. Yard workers trimmed and mowed. Two women dressed in yoga pants and skimpy tank tops power-walked up the slight incline. At the gate, he punched in the code, and they drove through, past several more estates until they reached the house.

In the driveway, he shut off the engine and turned to his sister. "You know, you could move to Cliffside Bay. Change it up."

"Where would I live?"

"Mom will find a house soon enough. You could move in with me. Just for a few months. Until you figure out what you want to do next. I bet I could get you a job at the local brewery or The Oar. If you're going to wait tables, you may as well do it somewhere close to Mom and me." He snapped his fingers. "Or I could see if Kyle's manager at the lodge would hire you. What better place to learn the trade, right?"

"I don't know. How does that support my dream?"

"You can save money there just as well as here. Only with me, you can live rent-free."

Her eyes widened as the understanding of what he was offering seemed to sink into her consciousness. "Do you mean it?"

"Absolutely. We're family. You and me and Mom. We should be together right now. Mom needs us."

"She does, that's true."

"Plus, Cliffside Bay's a tourist town. The type of place where you could open an inn, for example."

"Not with a lodge already there."

"There are other spots, other little towns along the coast that might need one," he said. "We could explore together."

Jamie's eyebrows drew together. She sucked in her bottom lip and tilted her head upward. This was her contemplation face. The same one she'd had as a child when she was trying to understand something. God, he'd adored her when she was a little girl. He still did. But after his marriage to Malia, he'd drifted from both his Mom and his sister. Being with them over the last few days had reminded him of the bond they'd always had. They were his family. His home.

"Maybe I could find something to renovate," she said. "You could help me."

"Sure I will." He gave his sister's hand a squeeze. "It's time for both of us to go for what we want."

"Oprah says you have to set your intention," Jamie said. "My intention is to open an inn." She fixed her big blue eyes on him. "What's yours?"

He sat for a moment, looking out the window at the birds-of-paradise that bloomed in front of the house. "I want Autumn. I want her to be my wife."

Jamie's face lit up. "Well then, let's go get her."

He scratched behind one ear and grimaced. "I'm afraid your dream is a lot more likely to happen than mine."

"You'll never know unless you try."

She was right. He had to make his move, tell the truth. "You're right. It's time."

"Let's go tell Mom."

They grinned at each other for a few seconds and then, in tandem, opened their car doors and marched across the driveway and into the house. *Intention, here we come.*

12

AUTUMN STOOD with Pepper in Lisa's new kitchen admiring the view. Built on the highest peak of the northern hill, the house had panoramic views of the ocean from picture windows in the kitchen and living room. The house style was modern meets beachy, with tall ceilings and wide-open spaces. Without much furniture, the rooms echoed. The home was a blank canvas. Trey would love it. He would make it perfect for the newly married couple.

After Lisa gave them a tour of the upstairs, which included a generous master suite and three additional bedrooms, they settled on the front deck with cold drinks. The infinity pool mirrored the color of the ocean and truly did seem to go on forever. Autumn ached to jump in and swim. Up here, away from prying eyes, would be the perfect place for her to enjoy the water. Talk turned to Pepper's wedding shower. Autumn had offered up her cottage since the other ladies would be busy moving.

"It's weird that it's in two days," Pepper said.

"Sneaked up on me too," Lisa said. "Soon, you'll be an old married lady like me."

"If only I could cook like you," Pepper said. "Stone made such a beautiful kitchen in the new house, and I'll probably never use it other than to heat up takeout from The Oar."

They were laughing when Maggie came through the glass doors. She wore dark, wide sunglasses that covered most of her small face. Always conscious of protecting her fair skin, she was dressed in a long-sleeved linen shirt and jeans.

They greeted her cheerfully as she slumped into a chair and ripped off her sunglasses. Her eyes were clouded and red-rimmed.

"What's the matter?" Lisa asked immediately.

"Is Lily all right?" Pepper asked.

Maggie waved her hand. "Yes, everyone's fine. Jackson's at a conference in the city. Lily's with my nanny." Her face crumpled into an ugly cry.

They all stared at her for a moment.

"Did you and Jackson have a fight?" Lisa asked.

Maggie pressed her fingers against her cheekbones and breathed in and out like someone trying to circumvent a panic attack. "No, no. We never fight. Not really, anyway. He leaves his socks on the floor, but besides that he's perfect. It's just that I'm...I'm pregnant again."

"Really? That's wonderful," Autumn said, before realizing that it might not be the right response given Maggie's tears. Still, another baby for the Wallers. What could be better? Lily Mae was almost two. This was the perfect distance between children, in her opinion.

"I don't know how this keeps happening," Maggie said.

"I'm pretty sure we all know how this happens," Pepper said with a teasing yet sympathetic smile.

Maggie sent a dark look at her friend. "I mean that I'm on the pill. I was last time, too. Both times it's been a total shock."

"Why are you sad?" Lisa asked. "Lily's going to have a little brother or sister. It's wonderful news."

"I'm not sad exactly. More like terrified." Maggie sniffed and wiped her eyes with a cocktail napkin. "I'm probably going to start throwing up any day now, and I'm trying to cut another album. The record company wants me to go on tour again, but I hate being away from my family. And touring pregnant? For God's sake, I already did that once and it was not fun. Lily is suddenly in her terrible two phase. She went from my happy baby to a pint-sized monster. Seriously, everything out of her mouth is 'no.'" More tears sprang to her eyes. "I'm sorry. I *am* happy. Of course I am. I'm emotional, that's all. I haven't told Jackson yet. It's terrible timing for him, too. He's just finished opening the new office. It's been so hectic for him—moving his entire medical practice to a new building."

"Jackson's going to be thrilled," Lisa said. "He wants another, right?"

"He didn't want Lily to be an only child like him," Maggie said. "You know how he is. All about friends and family. He'll be over-the-moon happy." She dabbed at the corners of her eyes. "I don't mean to sound ungrateful. It's just that…it kills me to admit this but juggling motherhood and my career is harder than I thought it would be. There's this yearning in me to create music. I love writing songs, and I love performing. This career is everything I dreamed of for so long. I love Jackson and Lily more than anything, even my career. When I'm away from them, I miss them so much. When I am with them, and trying to write or manage the business aspects, I'm not fully present. That eats at me. I keep thinking maybe Kara's doing the right thing by staying home with her two. Honestly, I'm struggling. It seems like I can't ever be enough. There's not enough of me to go around. Taking care of my own needs is last on the list, which makes me resentful. Like today, for instance. I feel guilty for having the nanny at home with Lily while I'm here with you ladies. I should be working or with her. Not here having fun."

"Most mothers feel the same way you do," Lisa said. "I'm assuming, anyway."

"Most *women* feel this way," Pepper said. "We're always trying to be everything to everyone."

"Which is impossible," Autumn said.

"But Mags, you're doing magnificently," Lisa said. "Taking an afternoon off to spend with friends is not a crime."

"If you don't feed yourself, you have nothing to give anyone else," Autumn said.

"Very true," Lisa said. "We're here for you. I'm always happy to take Lily. You know that."

Maggie smiled as she pushed tendrils of hair away from her face. "I *do* know that. Without my village, I'd be toast. God, please, let's talk about someone besides me. I'm so embarrassed."

"Don't be," Pepper said. "That's what friends are for."

Maggie looked over at Autumn. "How are the coffee dates going?"

Autumn groaned. "I think I've retired from coffee dates."

"Dating is awful. We remember only too well," Pepper said. "I swear, Lisa and I dated every loser in New York City."

"You'll find your prince," Lisa said.

"Maybe he's right under your nose," Pepper said.

The other two froze in place as Pepper's cheeks flushed. Then Pepper and Lisa exchanged a quick look between them. A look that said, *we know something we're not supposed to know.*

"What do you mean?" Autumn drew out the words. "Right under my nose?"

"She's talking about Trey," Maggie blurted out before covering her mouth with her hand.

"Trey?" Autumn asked. "Trey isn't right under my nose."

"Isn't he, though?" Pepper crossed her arms over her chest and spoke softly but with a serious glint in her eyes. "You guys are inseparable."

"Trey's not interested in a long-term relationship with anyone," Autumn said.

"You sure about that?" Maggie asked.

"He doesn't talk about his feelings that way," Autumn said. "But I'm pretty sure his ugly divorce made him resistant to trying again. Now there's this awful split between his parents."

Lisa nodded. "My parents' divorce shook me, too. Not enough to pass up a life with Rafael, but I get what you mean."

"I keep thinking about the way he carried you inside the house that night before Lisa's wedding," Pepper said. "When the snow was so thick underfoot and he didn't want you to have to traipse through it in your good shoes."

"That's not why," Autumn said. He hadn't cared about her shoes. He'd worried because he knew how tired her legs were after the day's festivities. "He knew my legs were too fatigued to make it through all that snow." He'd lifted her in his arms without a word, knowing her the way he did, and carried her across the snowy walkway and up the stairs to the house. When they'd danced together later that night, a warm, excited feeling had settled in the pit of her stomach. She'd lifted her head from his shoulder to look up at him. His heavy lids were half closed, and his jaw set in the same firm way it always was. Nothing there. Just friendship. She'd rested her cheek on his shoulder and told herself to be grateful for what they had.

She realized now that her musings had taken her attention from the ladies around her. Pepper and Maggie had their heads close together and were whispering. Lisa stared down at her hands. When Pepper and Maggie drew away, Lisa shook her head at them. "No, don't do it. It's not your place."

Pepper's eyes flashed. "I'm telling her. She needs to know."

"Interfering in their business is not a good idea," Lisa said. "It will happen when and if they're ready."

"I call bull," Pepper said. "Cupid needs to interfere."

"You're Cupid now?" Lisa asked.

"What's going on?" Autumn asked.

"Trey's in love with you," Maggie said. "Everyone knows it."

"Except for you," Pepper said to Autumn.

Autumn looked from one of the women to the other. "No, you're mistaken."

"We're right. Think about his actions," Pepper said. "The amount of time he spends with you. Men don't spend that much time with women they're not into."

"Trey and me?" Autumn asked. She was falling down a deep hole, unable to grasp what they were telling her.

"We shouldn't have betrayed his confidence," Pepper said.

"Except that it's so hard to see him miserable," Maggie said.

"He's miserable?" Autumn asked. He hadn't *seemed* miserable.

"He's a man in love with a woman he thinks he can't have," Pepper said. "That means he's miserable."

Can't have?

Was that true?

Autumn turned to look at Lisa. "Lisa? What are they saying?"

"What they're saying—which they have no *business* saying —is that Trey's feelings for you are stronger than just best pals. He's loved you for a long time."

"And everyone knows this but me?" Autumn's eyes stung as embarrassment washed over her. "Like everyone?"

"Not everyone," Pepper said.

"His friends, yes," Lisa said.

"Only because he needed advice." Maggie twisted a handful of her hair around her index finger. "He was feeling desperate."

"All those coffee dates gave him a fright." Pepper gestured toward town.

"Coffee dates?" Autumn's thoughts careened with each new bit of information. Attempting to capture their meaning was like chasing a child's tiny rubber ball that bounced higher and faster with each object it hit. "He was the one who encouraged me to try online dating."

"Well, men don't make sense half the time, now do they?" Pepper asked.

"Why didn't he just tell me?" Autumn asked. But he had told her, hadn't he? She'd brushed it off as a joke. Now, she could see the truth in his seemingly lighthearted question. How had she not seen the sincerity behind the words? Her chest ached as she thought about how hard it must have been for him to suggest, only to have her shoot him down immediately.

"He's been too shy—too scared to tell you," Pepper said. "He was certain you didn't feel the same way."

Autumn lifted her face upward, focusing on the wooden spokes of the outdoor umbrella to steady herself. Trey in love with her? How could that be?

"*Do* you feel the same way?" Pepper asked.

"I...I don't know." Autumn stood.

"You haven't thought about him that way," Lisa suggested, softly. "Maybe because you didn't allow yourself to?"

"Maybe," Autumn said. "I never thought he would ever think of me that way. He loves beauty, symmetry."

"What does that have to do with anything?" An edge of impatience had replaced Pepper's apologetic tone.

"She doesn't think she's symmetrical enough for him," Maggie said.

"Autumn Hickman, you're gorgeous." Pepper's cheeks

flushed as she turned from Autumn to Maggie. "What's she talking about?"

"She doesn't think she's pretty enough for him," Maggie said, more emphatically than the first time. "It's not that complicated. Even if her thinking is deeply flawed. Autumn, you're no more asymmetrical than anyone else."

"Not true. You're all symmetrical." Autumn pointed at them. "You're stars. So is Trey, even though he's not in the movies. Did you see that spread of him in the interior design magazine? He looked like a model. I don't belong next to him."

"That's ridiculous," Pepper said. "You think just because you're broken in places, you can't be loved?"

"Not by someone like Trey," Autumn said.

"I adore you, but that's just screwed-up thinking," Pepper said. "You need to think a moment about what you know about Trey Wattson."

"What do you mean?" Autumn was hot now, irritated. Pepper could be so pushy sometimes.

"He has the eye of an artist," Lisa said. "Trey loves objects the way he does people. He's attracted to the unique—the special. Think about how he chooses pieces for his designs. He doesn't shop at a chain department store but from boutique shops. He buys pieces battered from time or abuse and restores them to their prime."

"I can't be restored," Autumn said.

"Maybe not physically," Maggie said. "But inside here is what needs your attention." She tapped her chest. "You can't see what's right in front of you because of the damage to your insides."

"You hide away because of your scars," Pepper said. "And you're missing out on your life because of it."

No one spoke for a moment. Autumn's throat hurt. Tough love seemed to be the special of the day.

Lisa, her voice tender, finally broke the silence. "If you

could see yourself the way he sees you, then you'd know how special you are."

"I need some time to think." Autumn shifted from one foot to the other while holding on to the back of the chair.

"We've overwhelmed you," Lisa said. "Or rather, these two and their big mouths have overwhelmed you."

Pepper looked up with sorrowful eyes. "I'm sorry, Autumn. But Trey is such a good man, and I want him to be happy."

"I know. I understand," Autumn said as she clasped her hands together. "And you guys are right. I have a freight train's worth of baggage about my appearance. Obviously, I've let my insecurity rule my thinking." And blind her to what was right in front of her all along.

"Sweetie, we get it," Lisa said. "All three of us. More than you could ever know."

"I pushed Stone away for months because of my freight train," Pepper said.

"We don't want you to pass up what could be the greatest thing that ever happened to you," Maggie said. "I had to say something."

"You were right to do so. I clearly was blind to what was happening. Please, don't tell him I know. I need time to think through all this."

The other women rose to their feet. All three wore contrite expressions.

Trey had shared something very personal, and they'd just blabbed it to the very person from whom he hoarded his secret. Maybe they shouldn't have. Yet they were nudging love along for two people they cared about. Surely there was no harm in that. He was such a reticent man. Shy and decent. Scared to love again. He'd gone to his friends for advice. About *her*. He loved *her*.

Autumn smiled at them, one by one. "It's all right. You were trying to help two people find love. There's no greater reason to betray a confidence. Don't feel bad. I need a minute to sort through all this. I'll be in touch later."

With that, she crossed the patio and through the house to her car. Her legs trembled. Not because of fatigue but from wonder and anticipation of what was to come.

Trey loved her.

* * *

WHEN SHE RETURNED HOME, she went out to the patio. The potted flowers were wilting in the sun. She turned on her hose as her mind chewed through this new, unbelievable information.

What did she feel for him? Could she imagine his hands on her, his mouth kissing her? She'd done so a thousand times before pushing away the thought. The ladies were right. She'd focused on her detriments in an unhealthy way.

She traipsed around the patio with the hose in one hand, continuing to water. He was in love with her? This was like someone suddenly switching to a new language, one you never knew they spoke.

When she was with him, the terrible loneliness lessened. Without him, it was as if there were too much space in the world. She was a lone entity floating around, looking for something, someone to fill that space. *He fills that space, you little idiot.* She thought of all the times they shared together, all the things they had in common, and how easy it was to be around him. Was that love? Romantic love?

She turned off the water and curled into one of the chaises and gazed unseeing out to the ocean, rocking back and forth. This was such a surprise. She wasn't good with the unexpected. What did she do now? The thought of going to him seemed impossible.

An image came to her from the evening at the Mullens'

pool. The way he'd looked at her. She'd been right. She'd dismissed the idea so quickly, talked herself out of what had been so obvious. Her legs might be weak and scarred, but her eyes weren't. When she'd shown him all of her, he hadn't flinched or run away. Instead, he'd been encouraging, loving. Why couldn't she see what was right in front of her?

Her mother and Kyle had left her. Her inability to recognize Trey's feelings or allow herself to love him was because of her abandonment issues. The idea was too simple, really. But there it was. People who are left by those they love the most never fully trust again. The part of them that assumes love lasts forever, breaks. That section of their heart never repairs, doesn't rejuvenate, not even when the people return. From the moment she and Trey first met, the spark and connection had been strong. However, both had been abandoned before. They could not let the strings of their hearts interweave. They'd cut them off before they could wrap together into a cohesive knot.

She had not allowed herself to love Trey. But now? Now that she knew, all the repressed emotions rose to the surface, like bubbles in a glass of champagne.

I love Trey. He's the one. Right in front of me this whole time.

The front door *ping*ed. With the new security system, a high-pitched alert sounded anytime someone entered or exited the front or back door. She looked over her shoulder to see Valerie entering the kitchen, carrying grocery bags. Autumn went inside to greet her.

"Hi there," Valerie said. "Since it's my last night here, I thought we'd celebrate. I stopped at the store and bought ingredients for spaghetti and meatballs."

"I love spaghetti and meatballs."

Valerie lifted a package of ground beef from the bag, then a package of dried spaghetti. "I know. It was your favorite when you were a little girl. You called it 'getty and balls,' which always made me smile. Back then, I didn't smile often."

Autumn leaned against the island and bowed her head. Spaghetti and meatballs *had* been her favorite when she was little. A memory came, sudden and sharp. They were seated around their Formica kitchen table. Her brothers, and Valerie, smiled as she blew out four candles on her pink birthday cake. The pink frosting had been teased into little waves. They'd had spaghetti and meatballs for dinner. She remembered red sauce boiling on the stove and the scent of stewed tomatoes and garlic. She'd stood on the footstool and watched as her mother stirred the pot with a wooden spoon. Her fourth birthday. Soon thereafter, Valerie had left with the man in the shiny car.

"You made them for my birthday," Autumn said. "Home-made sauce, too."

Valerie nodded. "That's right." She placed a loaf of bread near the cooktop, then smoothed the paper bags one on top of the other.

"Then you left."

Her mother looked up at her with pained eyes. "Yes."

"I'd forgotten about that birthday until just now." She placed her hands flat on the cool countertop. "Before you came back, I couldn't remember anything about you."

"I remembered everything about you."

Autumn bit the inside of her mouth to keep from crying out in sorrow, *Then why? Why did you leave? Why didn't you come back?* Come on now, they'd been over all that. Depression. Unmedicated depression. Valerie Hickman hadn't been able to function. She knew this, but still it hurt. Wasn't her love for them enough of an antidote against depression?

"Do you want me to tell you about that birthday?" Valerie asked.

"I guess," Autumn whispered.

"I cleaned an extra house that week, so I'd have enough for

hamburger meat and cake mix and a doll I knew you wanted. There was this little toy store in town. In the window, a baby doll with a pink dress had caught your eye. You'd stared and stared at it one afternoon. You said to me, 'I want that baby.'"

As she told the story, Valerie's gaze averted away from Autumn to the wall behind her. "And I had to say, as I always did, 'not today.' I had to tug you away from the window. You never kicked or cried or anything. Not that day or ever. Kyle and Stone sometimes would if they didn't get their way, but not you. Instead of crying, you just let out a long, sad sigh and took my hand. As we walked the block to my car, you craned your neck to look backward at that doll. We went off to my next job." She paused and dipped her head. "You used to come with me when I cleaned houses. Do you remember?" She glanced at Autumn. "No, of course you don't. You just said that.

"There were a few clients who had children's rooms, and the women whose children were at school said it was all right if you looked at books while I cleaned. I'm not sure why, but sometimes kindness makes things worse for a person like me. I let you do it, but it made me mad to be the recipient of pity. There was this one house—real fancy—the husband was a lawyer. The Morrisons. She was from the South and had this rolling accent that made her seem genteel. Mrs. Morrison was a nice person. I can see that now, looking back. At the time, I hated her for her nice manners and kind way she had toward you. She'd look at you, super sorry like, and offer you a cookie and tell you that she'd left a stack of books in Carrie's room and would you like to look at them while your mother was busy. You'd nod and smile, so sweet. Prettiest smile I'd ever seen. People commented on it all the time. I knew back then that if you'd been born to another family, you would have been able to move up in the world. Anyway, they had all these hardwood floors and she liked them to be polished by hand. I had this one rag that worked just right on them, but that's neither here nor there. I guess I mention it because I want you to know that no matter how humiliated I was by our life, I still had pride in my work." Her mouth curved up in a bitter smile for a split second before she continued.

"That day we had to walk away from the doll, I got up from polishing the hallway floor and saw you with your head bent over a book in that little rich girl's room and I...I was so bitter, so angry." Valerie paused as her words caught in her throat. Her face contorted with the effort not to cry. She waved her hand in front of her eyes. "Here was my perfect, beautiful little girl in old clothes and shoes with holes sitting in an all-pink room with fluffy pillows and everything lace this or sparkly that, looking at a picture book I was too poor to buy you. What did I have to offer you? Nothing."

You. You offered you. Before you left me.

"I vowed right then and there—I was going to get you that damn doll for your birthday. I asked Mrs. Morrison if she had anything special that needed doing so I could earn a little extra money. To this day, I'm not sure if this was true or if she took pity on me. She said she was having a party over the weekend. Would I like to clean Saturday morning, so it was perfect for her guests? I agreed, of course, even though I had three other houses that day.

"After I cleaned that Saturday, she paid me in cash like always. I came home and stashed that money in my secret hiding place and fell asleep. Next morning, it was gone. I knew right away your father had taken it and blown it at the bar. He was passed out on the couch to prove it." Valerie looked up at the ceiling, shaking her heard. "I howled with rage—woke up your hungover father with my crying. He was sorry, like always, but it didn't matter. Not this time. I couldn't get my girl the baby doll she wanted. I felt like my heart had broken in half. By that time in my life, I didn't want much. I'd already given up. But I wanted that doll for you. I wanted that."

"I remember that doll," Autumn said. "I had her forever. Her name was Hillary." She'd slept with Hillary every night. After her accident, that doll had been her only comfort during those long, desolate nights. "How did you do it?"

Valerie took in a long breath, then let it out slowly. "I washed my face and drove over to Mrs. Morrison's house. It was Sunday, and all the good people in town were coming home from church. The Morrisons were good people. Mr. Morrison took his family to church instead of curing a hangover with a few beers like my husband. I sat on the top step of their porch and waited. There was the remnant of a slug on the bottom step. Someone had put salt on him, and he'd dried up. That's how you kill them—cover them with salt and they dehydrate into nothingness."

Autumn did know this. She'd always thought it was a terrible thing to do.

"A few minutes later, they drove up in their BMW. She told the kids and her husband to go inside and sat next to me on the steps, even though she wore a pretty yellow dress the color of butter. She was the type who'd look real carefully into your face, and she must have seen I'd been crying. She said, 'Tell me what I can do.' Not a question, mind you. I told her flat out. My husband drank up the money I'd earned from cleaning her house and now I couldn't buy the doll you wanted for your birthday. I was crying by then, all slobbery and pathetic. I'd been poor all my life, but I'd never begged—never asked for something I hadn't earned. Doing so made me feel like the life was seeping out of me. I was the slug and my shame the salt. Mrs. Morrison didn't say a word, just nodded and opened her purse and took out three twenties, which was twice as much as she usually paid me to clean her house. I said, 'I'll pay you back.'

"She said, 'No need. I grew up in Mississippi without a daddy. My mother had to tell us no a whole lot more than she said yes. Birthdays and Christmas were right up there with funerals for her. Just take it. Give your little girl a nice birthday.'

"I thanked her and drove right down to the toy store and I bought that doll. I bought a cake mix and pink icing and hamburger meat. We had dinner that night, then I surprised you with the doll. I've done a lot of bad things in my life, but I did one good one. The look on your face when you opened that box has stayed with me all these years. On lonely nights, I've taken that memory out of the box and watched it over and over."

"I'm sorry I can't remember," Autumn said.

"I wouldn't expect you to."

"You left soon after that, didn't you?"

"That's right. After that day when I shriveled up like that slug, it was like something switched off in me. The demons I'd fought all my life, the ones that wanted to pull me under, they took over. I can't explain it other than to say it was a dark hole, like I'd been buried alive and didn't even care. Depression is like the devil. He whispers to you how worthless you are, how your children would be better off without you. One of the men I cleaned for had hit on me for years. Redman. Everyone called him Red. About a month after your birthday, I finally said yes. A few weeks later I left with him. We moved to Eugene, and you know the rest."

Neither spoke. Autumn stared at the uneven pattern in her granite.

"I can see you trying to forgive me," Valerie said. "But I understand why you can't."

"There's a hole inside me. I think the hole is you. Not you, but the absence of you."

"I never stopped loving you. I simply couldn't love myself. I was an unfit mother."

Autumn's eyes blurred from tears. One dropped onto the

granite. "Kyle left me, too. I had to find him, like a detective. He didn't want to be found."

"I'm sorry, honey."

"I've forgiven him, but it took a while," Autumn said.

"There's hope, then?"

Autumn smiled. "Talking like this, hearing more about what you experienced, helps. With Kyle, I was there with him. I knew how much the accident messed him up, because it did me too."

"If I'd been well, I never would have left," Valerie said. "I'm well now. I'm here now."

Autumn's vision blurred with unshed tears as she looked up at her mother. "I'm glad you're better. I'm glad you're here now."

Valerie crossed around the island and took her into her arms. Autumn was stiff at first, but after a second, she leaned into the hug and let herself be loved. "I don't deserve a second chance, but thank you for giving me one. I'll spend the rest of the time I have left making it up to you."

"Mom, it's all right. I'm all right."

"You're my beautiful baby girl, and I love you."

"I love you too," Autumn said. Tears leaked from her eyes, soaking the fabric of her mother's blouse.

After they parted, Valerie pointed at the package of ground beef. "Would you like to know the secret to my meatballs?"

"There's a secret?" Autumn sniffed.

Valerie smiled and shook her head. "Not really. There were a lot of secrets in our family, but the meatball recipe wasn't one of them."

"Secrets are overrated."

"Amen."

They smiled at each other as Valerie smoothed Autumn's hair away from her face. "I'd like to try to fill that hole."

"It feels a little smaller already," Autumn said, ducking her head, suddenly shy. "A few meatballs might help too."

* * *

LATER, after Valerie had retired to the guest room, Autumn brought her laptop into bed with her. She wanted to write to Art before she went to sleep, hoping that writing it all down would help her sort through her tumbled thoughts. Before she could start an email, her phone buzzed with a call from Trey. Her pulse raced at the sight of his name and photo flashing on the screen.

"Hi, Trey." Why did her voice sound wobbly and strange? This was Trey. She talked to him multiple times a day.

"Hey. Just checking in. Everything good?"

"Yes, fine. I had a busy day, then dinner with my mom for her last night here."

"How'd that go?"

"Good. We talked about some stuff."

"Yeah?" he asked. "Anything important?"

"Just rummaging through the past." She didn't want to get into it over the phone. "What about you?"

"Stone and I helped Rafael move the rest of their things to the new house, then we cleaned the apartment to get it ready for your mom."

"What about your place? Are you an empty nester?"

Trey chuckled. "Yes. Stone and Pepper finished moving their things out yesterday. My mom and sister arrive day after tomorrow."

"Are you excited to have them?"

"Sure. Mom told me she's going to buy a place as soon as she can. She already accepted an offer on the house in San Diego. I predict she'll buy a place here before the end of the summer. Stone thinks there are a few houses about to go on the market that might suit her. My sister, on the other hand, will probably be here for a while."

"Did you talk to Zane or Kyle about a job for her?"

"I mentioned it to Zane, and he told me to have her come by the brewery when she's ready. He thinks he can find a spot for her." There was an awkward lull in the conversation. "Are you sure everything's all right? You sound weird."

Could he really hear it in her voice?

"I'm fine. Tired, maybe."

"I'll let you get some rest. But before we hang up—I wondered if you wanted to do something tomorrow? It's Sunday. Maybe a Sunday drive somewhere? I heard about a new Mexican place with amazing fish tacos in Stowaway."

She thought for a moment. When she told him the truth about her feelings, where did she want to be? Here. Here in the home he'd helped her create. "Actually, I'm in the mood to cook. Come for dinner. We can make fish tacos here."

"Sure. Sounds great."

"Trey?"

"Yeah?"

"Never mind. It can wait until tomorrow."

"Good night. Sleep well. Is the alarm on?"

"Yes, it is. Night."

After they hung up, she scrolled through the photos on her phone. So many of them were of Trey. The entirety of their time together documented right here on her screen, from photos of their shopping excursions during her cottage decoration until last week in San Diego. It didn't take a psychic to see how she felt about him, given the dozens of photos of his face. What had she been thinking all these months? Her denial was as thick as morning fog on a Cliffside Bay summer morning.

Art. She wanted to tell Art all that had happened. He'd been right all along. She set aside the phone and pulled her computer onto her lap.

DEAR ART,

I had a strange day, one that's left me wrung out emotionally and a little uncertain as to how to proceed. My mother moves to her new apartment tomorrow. Tonight, she surprised me by coming home with the ingredients for spaghetti and meatballs, my favorite when I was a little girl. A memory came back of the birthday I turned four, right before she left us. She told me more of what it was like for her. The picture she painted of her life with my father, of her dark depression, made everything clearer for me. I've seen it only through my own eyes. The eyes of a child who missed her mother. A child who never knew what life would have been like *with* a mother.

We made meatballs together after our talk and spoke of more mundane subjects, like our favorite movies and books. Turns out, she reads a lot, just like me. She told me she's traveled all over the world in books, even though before she moved to California, she'd never been out of the state of Oregon.

The evening was strange but so very sweet. Cooking dinner with my mom was never an event I ever thought I'd experience. We have a long way to go. I mean, she's still foreign to me. But tonight, I could see how our relationship might grow strong, maybe even close.

All that got me thinking about how hard it's been for me to trust that people won't eventually leave. My abandonment issues run through me like blood itself. Which leads to the next thing I want to tell you.

I spent the afternoon with Pepper, Lisa, and Maggie. They told me Trey has feelings for me. Or rather, he's in love with me. According to them, he has been for a long time.

They wanted to know if those feelings were reciprocated. I didn't know what to say. I couldn't think straight. I came home and sat outside on my patio and watched the waves roll in and all the happy people on the beach and I finally admitted to myself that, yes, I have feelings too. Ones I've stifled and hidden, even from myself, because the idea of losing him is terrifying.

All my feelings for him are mixed up with my mom and Kyle leaving. But I have to be braver than this. I have to tell him I love him, too. The idea of it makes me want to throw up. Not kidding. But the girls assured me his feelings are strong and real. If I don't tell him how I feel, we'll never move forward. Isn't that true in all relationships, if you think about it? Even in friendships, we keep so much inside. I wonder what would happen if we all said what we felt? Not the petty stuff, but the big stuff.

I'll close now. I hope you're well. Write when you can.

007

13

T rey

THE NEXT MORNING, Trey woke to an email from 007. His hands grew wet with perspiration as he read the last two paragraphs.

He read it again, then again. After the sixth time, he pushed away from his desk and went into the living room. He paced around the room. She loved him. She loved him.

What did he do now?

The place looked the same without Pepper and Stone living here, but it was quieter without Pepper's swift energy and Stone's calming presence. At this moment, he missed them with a fierceness he hadn't expected. They would know what he should do. They would help him plot out his next move.

He needed all the Wolves. Needed their advice. They'd helped get him in this mess, and maybe they'd know what to do now. He sent a group text.

Emergency Wolves meeting at The Oar. Meet there at noon.

He sent that off and then stood at the window staring out to the parking lot below. Autumn loved him.

* * *

LATER, he entered The Oar and sauntered up to the bar. Sophie, from behind the counter, smiled at him. "What's up?"

"Can I get a large pitcher of Dog's IPA?"

"Sure. Grab a table. I'll bring it out to you."

He was happy to see that their favorite table in the back was open and grabbed an extra chair to make sure there were enough seats for all five.

Sophie, blond ponytail bouncing on top of her head, plopped the pitcher and five glasses down in front of him. "Should I bring Nico a glass of wine?"

"How'd you know it would be all the Wolves?"

"Five chairs gave you away," she said.

"Wait until he gets here," Trey said. "He might not be in the mood for wine."

She gave him a knowing smile. "He's always in the mood for wine." The way she said it made him think the word *wine* could be substituted for *me*. He'd been so preoccupied with Autumn and 007 that he'd completely neglected his friendship with Nico. What was going on between these two?

"What?" she asked. "You're looking at me weird."

"Was I?"

"You sure were." She frowned as she poured him a glass of beer from the pitcher. "I don't know why everyone thinks Nico and I are such a bad idea."

"Everyone?"

"My brother. My dad. All the Dogs."

"How do you know the Dogs think it's a bad idea?"

"Zane told me," she said.

"Well, for the record, I think you guys would be awesome together."

She pursed her full lips. "What about the other Wolves?"

He shrugged. "I'm not sure any of us is against it." Except maybe Nico himself.

"I'm *not* too young for him," she said. "I'm mature for my age. I've already carried a baby for heaven's sake."

While being a virgin.

He kept that observation to himself. "What's Nico think?" Trey asked. "That's the most important question."

"He thinks I'm too young," she said. "But that doesn't keep him from wanting me."

"So, are you guys...?" He let the question trail off, figuring she knew exactly what he was asking.

"No, we're not sleeping together. As much as I've tried, he keeps me at arm's length. Trust me, I've made a complete fool of myself over that man. To no avail." Tears swam in her eyes.

She has it bad for him. Nico was an idiot to pass this woman up over something as trivial as age.

"Sophie, you could have any man you wanted."

"Not true. I can't have the one I want."

"You're drop-dead gorgeous, sweet, smart, and fun. If Nico's too much of a dolt to look past the age thing, it's his loss."

"No, it's my loss." A lone tear leaked from one eye. "I've never felt like this about anyone in my life. And all he wants is friendship."

"Trust me. I get it." He took a sip of his beer, then wiped foam from his mouth. "Listen, no promises, but I'll talk to him. Honestly, I've been so self-obsessed lately that I haven't had a chance to spend time with him."

"Would you put a good word in for me?" she asked, so hopeful it made his gut ache.

"Of course I will." He patted her arm. "But can I give you a little advice?"

"Sure."

"It's really your brother and your father you need to talk to. I know Nico pretty well—we've been friends since we were eighteen—and if he had their blessing, he'd go for it. Word on the street, Zane kind of semi-threatened him."

"What did you say?" If he hadn't known better, he would have sworn smoke came out of her shell-like ears. "Zane did what?"

Trey cleared his throat. Had he just stepped in it or what? "He had a little talk with him one night. Right after Nico moved here and it seemed like you two might hook up."

"Oh my God. I'm going to kill him." She placed her hands on her hips. "Did he threaten him? Like physically?"

"I believe it was more of the 'I'll run you out of town if you touch my very young sister' type of thing."

"I actually might kill," Sophie said.

"Nico's an old-fashioned guy. He would never want to get in the way of family," Trey said. "Not to mention that Zane and his friends kind of rule this town. We're building a business and need their support."

"Zane Shaw has no right to threaten anyone when it comes to me. I'm a grown woman. I date whomever I please."

"In Zane's defense, he's just trying to protect you. He doesn't know Nico from Adam."

Stone and Rafael arrived then, and Sophie scampered away, her cheeks flushed bright pink.

"Sophie okay?" Rafael asked. "She looked upset."

Stone settled his long frame into a chair, dwarfing it as usual. "Let me guess. It has something to do with Nico."

Before Trey could answer, Nico and David walked into the bar and headed their way.

"What's up, bro?" Nico asked, taking the chair next to Trey.

"I have a problem." Trey laid it all out there: the ladies

telling Autumn about his true feelings; her subsequent email to him; his uncertainty about what to tell her about Art.

"Holy crap. I knew she loved you," Stone said. "I don't know whether to wring my big-mouth fiancée's neck or kiss her."

"I say you have Art tell her he can't write any longer," Rafael said. "He's going somewhere without internet or something."

"I agree," Nico said. "What she doesn't know can't hurt her. Or you, as the case may be."

David shook his head, slowly. "I'm not sure about that. Secrets and lies have a way of messing everything up."

"True," Nico said. "But this is such a harmless one."

"Totally." Stone leaned forward to pour a glass of beer from the pitcher.

"There's something bothering me," Trey said. "The way she opens up to Art in those emails is way more than she ever has to me."

"Why do you think that is?" Stone asked in a way that implied Trey knew the answer, which he didn't.

"I don't know," Trey said.

Stone closed his eyes for a moment, as if Trey were a slow, slow learner. "Am I going to have to mansplain this to you?"

"Apparently," Trey said, growing more annoyed by the second.

"The reason she opened up to you is because Art opened up to her." Stone looked around the table. "You boys need to take a chapter from the old Stone playbook. Talk to women like they do one another and you'll have their hearts."

"Wait a minute," Rafael said. "When did you get so smart about women? Weren't you the one who said they misunderstood you?"

Stone grinned and raised both eyebrows triumphantly. "That's before I tamed a wild Pepper."

"You've hardly tamed her," Nico said. "She went all rogue on us and told Autumn about Trey's secret."

"Okay, well, that's true," Stone said. "But we're losing focus here. Trey, Autumn loves you. Go get her."

"I feel super worried about the Art thing," Trey said. "If she finds out, she might lose trust in me. She's skittish. Afraid to be left."

"Then don't tell her," Stone said. "I'm her brother, and I'm telling you, forget it. She loves you, man. That's all that matters."

Trey looked around the table. The rest of the Wolves seemed to be in agreement.

"Go get the girl," Rafael said.

"Sweep her off her feet," Nico said. "Flowers and wine. Kiss her in her kitchen."

"Bring a little heat to that kitchen," David said. "And don't look back."

"Um, yeah. If you bring the heat, you better put a ring on it," Stone said. "Sooner rather than later. This is my sister we're talking about."

14

utumn

AUTUMN HAD SPENT the day helping her mother move into the Sotos' former apartment. They were done by four, and she headed to the grocery store for dinner ingredients, then showered and applied a new coat of makeup. Trey rang the bell right at six. Butterflies fluttered in her stomach as she walked to the door. *It's just Trey*, she reminded herself. *He knows you. He loves you. There's nothing that could go wrong.*

She flung open the door a little more forcefully than she intended. Apparently, nerves made her extra strong.

Trey stood there holding a bouquet of red and orange dahlias in one hand and a bottle of her favorite Chablis in the other.

"Good evening." He smiled as he handed her the wine. "Grabbed the last bottle from Sophie's personal stash for the occasion."

"Thank you. Come on in. Are those for me?" she asked, indicating the flowers. Her heart pounded hard in her chest. Of course they were for her. Who else would they be for? She was acting like an idiot already. Being his friend was as easy as eating ice cream. This was different. Now it was all loaded and weird.

"I couldn't resist. They were in front of the store and just called out to me."

Flowers. He'd never brought flowers. Like a date. It was as though he knew what she was going to tell him. Had the girls confessed?

"My favorite colors," she said, making sure to keep her voice steady even though her thoughts were anything but, tossing about in her brain like Ping-Pong balls. "My favorite flower."

"I know they're your favorite flower." He placed the flowers into the vase on the entryway table. "That's why I chose them."

"Oh." She stepped backward, tripped on the foyer rug, and stumbled.

In a flash, he reached for her, keeping her upright with his strong arm around her waist, then pulled her closer. "Easy now."

She held her breath, staring up at him.

He maintained her gaze, his blue eyes unwavering as he peered down at her. "I know your favorite flowers. I know what you like in your coffee. I know your favorite colors. Someday— it might not be today—but someday I hope to know what it feels like to kiss you."

"Kiss me?" she murmured, almost to herself.

"Yes, kiss you." He loosened his arm from her waist and stepped a few inches away but continued to look at her with the same intense expression. "I brought you flowers so that you know this is a date."

She just stared at him, a sense of panic rising. This was

really happening. She understood on a visceral level what it meant to be a deer in the headlights.

"I repeat, this is a date." His eyes flickered with what seemed like hesitation for the first time since he'd walked in the door.

"We've had dinner together so many times. You never called it a date before." Her voice felt stuck in the back of her throat.

He smiled and brushed her cheek with his free hand. "I'm not playing it safe any longer. I'm in love with you and I'm not going to pretend otherwise. Not for one minute more."

She continued to gape at him, unsteady and unsure. The chilled bottle of wine had left her fingers cold, but the rest of her sizzled with the sudden heat between them. Droplets of sweat sprang out on the end of her nose. Bright afternoon sun streamed through the glass skylight. Dust particles floated in the steady stream of air coming out of the vent. "I don't know what to do now."

"How do you feel about me?" He spoke in his same quiet manner, but the force of his words sounded different. Disconcertingly so.

She swiped at the end of her nose. Could she say the words out loud? "You're my best friend."

"Is that all?"

"That's everything. Or the foundation of everything, anyway. But as far as we go, I'm worried we're unsuited."

"How so? We like all the same things. We never get tired of talking or being together. At least, that's my take on it."

"All those things are true." The muscles in her face tensed, as if waiting for a punch. She had to ask him, even though she was scared to hear his answer. "I want to be married and have a family. You said you'd never get married again."

"That was before I met you. I'd marry you the minute you said yes." He studied her, then ran a finger along her bottom lip. "If I was lucky enough to win your heart, I'd never let you go."

They were only inches apart. Could he detect the scar on her cheekbone that she so carefully disguised with foundation? "But Trey, you could have anyone."

"There's no one but you for me," he said.

"Is this about your dad?" She blurted out her sudden fear.

He made a sound at the back of his throat, as if someone had pushed into his neck with a blunt object. "My dad?"

"Yes, like some strange reaction to his infidelity? Like you're going for the sure thing or something?"

He stepped back a few inches and stared at her open-mouthed before speaking. "Sure thing? Do you know how much courage it took to tell you this?" A vein bulged in his neck. "You're anything but a sure thing. I'm so in love with you that I've felt sick. Seriously, I'm like a lovesick fourteen-year-old boy. All I can think about is being with you. Kissing you. Taking you into my bed. Do you know what torture it was to have your almost-naked body next to me in the swimming pool? Not being able to have you hurts like hell. It's like I'm thirsty all the time and you're the well with all the cool, sweet water just out of reach."

The honesty of that statement socked her in the belly and took her breath away. "Trey, really?"

"Yes, really. You're my best friend, my favorite person, the one I want to wake up next to each morning. You're the one I want to spend every moment with. I love you. All of you. Tell me, do you feel the same way?"

The longing in his eyes shot through her, woke her own yearning. She smiled and cupped his chin with one hand. "Forgive me if I need a moment to catch up."

His expression softened. He reached for her hand and stroked it with his thumb. "Do you love me?"

"I do," she said. "I never let myself go there because I didn't think you could ever feel the same way about me."

"You didn't know? I can't believe it wasn't totally obvious."

"You're symmetrical and I'm uneven."

"To me, you're the most beautiful woman in the world."

The sunlight bounced off his thick hair. She could see the fine lines around his eyes in this bright light. Eyes that were currently ablaze with passion. Passion for her.

Dumbfounded, she stared at him again, then laughed. "Is this one of those movies where the hot guy thinks it's funny to trick the ugly girl into a date so that everyone can make fun of her?"

To her surprise, his eyes filled with tears at her dumb joke. "Don't ever call yourself ugly again."

"I'm sorry. I was just teasing."

"It's not funny to me. I'd never hurt you or mistreat you. Anyone who does won't live long."

"But you've seen me. You know what's under all this." She gestured toward her long skirt.

He tapped his temple. "They're my eyes. All I see is beauty."

"You and me, it's so strange. Everything I thought I knew is all blown to bits."

"Sometimes things have to be blown up in order for the right pieces to fit back together."

She realized she was still holding the bottle of wine. "What about that kiss? Is it going to be right here in my foyer?"

His blue eyes sparkled as he looked down at her. "I think it should be in your kitchen. All the best things in life start in the kitchen."

He took her hand, and they walked together to the kitchen. When they reached the island, he took the bottle from her and set it aside. He slid his arms around her, looking into her eyes. "I'm suddenly nervous. I've dreamed of this moment for so long."

She lifted her face to his. "If it's not perfect, that just means we need to practice more."

He laughed, then leaned down and pressed his mouth to hers and kissed her. For a split second, she thought she might fall over from the sheer pleasure of his soft mouth on hers. He tasted of mint. His skin smelled like a mixture of leather and soap. She splayed her hands in his wavy hair, delighted by its soft texture.

They fit together, she realized. Pressed together, it was obvious they were two halves of a whole.

He kissed her neck. His hands traveled down her spine to cup her backside. She nearly exploded with desire when he pushed her gently against the island with his hips. He returned to her mouth, teasing her with his tongue.

She groaned and wrapped her arms around his neck. He lifted her onto the island and tugged her long skirt up to her thighs, then drew her closer to him. With long, sensitive fingers, he brushed her skin from her ankles up to her thighs while kissing her.

Her skin mended under his touch. She imagined she was no longer scarred but flawless, as free and weightless as she'd been in the water.

"I love you," he whispered as he planted kisses from her ear to her collarbone. "I've loved you from the minute I first set eyes on you."

They kissed again, this time harder and with so much heat she thought her pretty kitchen might catch on fire.

"Would it be wrong to sleep together before we've had a real date?" she asked.

He looked into her eyes as he pulled her closer. "We've had enough time together to count as a hundred dates. I think we can head to your bedroom without guilt."

"Lead the way."

He scooted her off the island and secured her legs around

his waist. Without letting her down, he carried her across the kitchen and up to the bedroom.

* * *

THE NEXT MORNING, she woke a little later than usual to the sound of the shower running. She blinked awake and rolled over to look at the other side of the bed as the events from the night before rushed into her consciousness. The night had not been a long, luscious dream but reality. Now Trey was in her bathroom. Naked under the sheet, she shivered thinking through all of the things they'd done the night before. For a bedroom that had seen no action since she'd moved in, the walls had certainly gotten an eyeful last night. She slipped quietly out of bed and pulled on a pair of pajamas that hung over the back of the chair.

In bare feet, she padded down the stairs to the kitchen. The room was dim with the shades drawn. She lifted the edge of the shade that hung over one of the French doors to peek outside. There were no creepy lurking men in sight, so she pulled up each shade, one by one.

The gauzy morning light filtered in through the glass. A low, translucent fog hovered just above the water. Blue sky above the half-hearted blanket hinted at the warmth to come. The sun was behind the house, creeping up the eastern sky. Soon, the beach would be flooded with people. For now, the sand and walking path were empty.

She made coffee in rote movements, her eyes scratchy from lack of sleep. Not that she was complaining. Losing sleep with Trey was worth every moment.

She'd just poured a mug of steaming coffee for herself when Trey came in, dressed in the khaki pants and cotton shirt he'd worn the night before. His hair was damp and curled at his neck. Unshaven, he looked gruffer and older than usual with a whisker shadow. "I have an early meeting with a client, so I have to scoot." He leaned down to kiss her. "Sorry about the scruff. Next time, I'll bring my shaving equipment."

She averted her eyes and fussed with the collar of his shirt. "Maybe you should get an extra set. One for here and one for your house."

He lifted her chin, forcing her to look up and into his eyes. They went soft as he brushed her bottom lip with his thumb. "Leaving stuff here? Sounds serious."

"Are we?" she asked. Her old enemy insecurity cramped her stomach. "I mean, are we together now? Like exclusive?" She winced with embarrassment at the pathetic sound of her voice. *Don't be needy. You'll drive him away.*

"Is that a serious question? After last night? Is there any doubt in your mind that I love you? We've been close for a long time. I would never have told you how I felt if I wasn't serious about making you my wife. Anyway, Stone already told me I'd better put a ring on it if I did what I did to you last night. Since I plan to do it again tonight, a ring is forthcoming."

"Do you mean it?" she asked.

The corners of his mouth twitched in an uneasy smile. "I'm not playing around here. I want to give you everything you want. It took me way too long to admit to myself how I felt about you. I was so battered after my divorce that I truly believed I'd stay single for the rest of my life. Then you walked into this ratty cottage, and my heart's never been the same. If I hadn't been such an idiot, I would've acted on this sooner. I should never have let you think we were doomed to the friend zone. My ex-wife really did a number on me. Scarred me on the inside, like she'd thrown acid in my face."

Bile rose from her stomach. She swallowed. Acid? Was it a coincidence? She backed away from him a few inches, staring at his face. "Acid? That's a strange thing to say."

He seemed to freeze in place. His face blanched of color.

"Trey. Why did you say that?"

"It's a metaphor." He shrugged and gave her a half smile. "Just a bad metaphor that came to me."

She stumbled backward into the island as the truth came to her in a tidal wave. All the events of the last couple weeks stacked together, telling the story. He'd manipulated her confessions, acting on them, laying the groundwork for so many things. The swimming. Her mother moving to town. "Oh my God. Art's you."

His expression turned immediately to panic. He moved closer to her with his hands outstretched. "Let me explain."

She shook her head and tried to melt into the island. "Do *not* touch me. Why would you do such a thing?"

"I was trying to help my case." His voice had risen in pitch. "It was stupid, but I thought you'd see that your fear about your scars was just fear about getting involved with someone you cared about so much as a friend."

"And how exactly was this supposed to happen? By lying to me? By pretending to be someone else?" She stared at him in horror before turning toward the window. "I wrote so many intimate things in those emails." Her skin burned, remembering.

"Why couldn't you say them to me?" he asked.

She did a double take. Was he serious? "That's not the relevant point here. You tricked me into sharing my inner thoughts with you, and then you used that information to manipulate an outcome. Who does that?"

"I was desperate to find a way to reach you."

"Reach me? Why didn't you just tell me the truth?"

"I tried to, but you shut me down. Can't you see this was a good thing? We've learned about each other at a much deeper level. I know you better than before because for whatever reason you could talk to Art about things you couldn't talk to me about."

"Art is not a real person. You do not have a scarred face, Trey. I wasn't talking to Art. I was talking to you, only I didn't know it. You've completely breached my trust." The enormity of what he'd done engulfed her like the most forceful riptide. "I told Art how I felt about you." She clutched her throat, horrified as she remembered the last email. "You came here acting like you didn't know."

"I'd never have been able to tell you had I not known already," Trey said. "I was too scared I might lose you if I pushed it before knowing how you felt."

"So you used a false identity to get information?"

He shook his head and ran his hands through his hair. "It's not as seedy as you're making it sound. I couldn't share how I felt out loud. It was so much easier to talk about my feelings by writing them."

"How could you possibly have thought this was a way to win me over?"

"It was Stone's idea."

She drew in a deep, sharp breath that hurt her chest. "Stone?"

"And the guys...we thought this might be a way for me to get through to you. To help you see that your scars don't mean anything to me. I needed a way into your heart, because you'd shut me out."

"How could any of you think this was a good idea? It doesn't even make sensc."

"I'm sorry. I didn't mean to hurt you or make you angry. I just wanted a chance. You were going on all those coffee dates and I started to think how you might meet someone else and I'd lose you forever. I was desperate for you to understand that I could love you, scars and all, by presenting a character with the same problems. We thought you would see it differently once you got to know Art."

"I...I don't know what to think right now." Her entire body

shook. She walked over to the kitchen table and sank into a chair.

This table. She loved this table. They'd found it together at a used furniture store in Stowaway. He'd said to her, "I can sand it, make it smooth as polished stone, then paint it eggshell white. Make it good as new." They'd agreed it would be a perfect display for the sea-glass bowl he'd found for her. Was she merely a thing to restore, a way for him to feed his ego? "Am I one of your fix-it-up projects?"

"What are you taking about?" he asked.

She lifted her chin to look at him. "You can't let an object go once you decide something has potential. I'm not some vintage bargain deal you needed to restore."

His head reeled back as if she had slapped him. "Is that what you think this is? I'm rescuing you?"

"What else could it be? You come up with a fake persona to teach me how to love you?"

"You're wrong," he said. "You couldn't be more wrong. You're just finding another reason to reject the idea of us. I may have done something stupid, but that doesn't change the fact that we love each other. You're letting your abandonment issues rule your life, Autumn."

"I'm not." But even as she said it, she knew it to be true. There was a part of her she wouldn't allow to soften, because it meant she could be hurt. She imagined her heart was not made of human cells but of steel.

"I know the truth," he said. "We're meant to be together. We're soul mates. I've known it for so long now. If you're too afraid to let yourself love me, then we'll miss our chance, and that will be a damn shame."

"I need some time to think," she said.

All the air went out of him. His shoulders slumped, but he didn't argue or plead his case. "I'll give you some space. Just remember I love you. My intentions were good if misguided."

He swept by her, opened the back door, and slipped out to the patio. The door closed behind him in a gentle *thud*. Still, the sound thundered through the house as if he'd slammed it shut.

She sat there, too stunned to move. Then red-hot anger flooded through her. Once again, the person she trusted most had betrayed her.

Anger fueled her, made the pain more bearable. Wasn't that how this worked? Anger was the steel material of her heart. As long as she kept the anger close, she could not be hurt.

She got up from the chair, knowing she had to put this aside for now. Soon, all the ladies would arrive for Pepper's shower. She had to hold it together. She could cry later.

15

T rey

TREY DIDN'T HAVE time to wallow, even if he wanted to curl up in a ball and die. His client meeting kept him busy most of the morning. By the time he pulled up to the Victorian, his mother and sister had arrived. The rest of the day was spent moving them into his apartment. They'd brought little. Jamie didn't own much, other than clothes and a few books. Mom had put whatever she wanted from the house into storage, bringing only clothes.

By that evening, they'd settled into the spare room. Until Mom found a place of her own, Jamie was going to sleep on the couch and let Mom have the bed. However, they were sharing the closet.

"It's just temporary," he'd said. "We'll find you a house soon." The Wolves were on the job. They'd have her in a home of her own soon enough.

Around dinnertime, Jamie came back from the grocery store with ingredients for a chicken stir-fry. He'd sent several texts to Autumn, but she hadn't replied. He prayed it was the wedding shower that kept her from answering and not her anger. After everything, if he lost her over this, he would never forgive himself.

While he and Mom sat at the table in his kitchen, Jamie scurried around making their meal. If they'd noticed his sadness, they hadn't mentioned it to him during the day. He should have known that wouldn't last. No sooner had he opened a bottle of wine than his sister, in her usual blunt fashion, asked him what in God's name was the matter with him.

He thought about denying and just pretending that he was fine, but the need to talk outweighed his weariness. "It's about Autumn." He told them everything from the fake profile until the argument that morning. When he was finished, both his mother and sister wore an expression of pity mixed with disdain for his obvious stupidity.

"I'm with Autumn," Mom said. "In that this was the worst idea ever. And I blame myself."

"What?" Trey asked.

"I taught you by my example to keep everything inside." She nodded toward Jamie. "It seemed to have the opposite effect on this one. She, obviously, doesn't have a problem expressing herself."

"Very funny," Jamie said, good-naturedly.

"I'm afraid I've blown it for good," Trey said. "She's really angry with me."

"Give her some time to cool down," Mom said. "If she loves you, she'll move past it."

He hoped so. *Please, God, help her to forgive me.*

* * *

HIS MOTHER and sister must have contacted Nico, because later that evening, his friend showed up at his door with a six-pack and an invitation to walk down to the beach. The sun had already set as they meandered down Main Street to the stretch of sand that curved like a quarter moon around the landscape. A starless twilight-blue sky hung over the dark sea. They sat on the bench that overlooked the water. Nico opened two beers and handed one to Trey.

"What you need, brother, is a plan," Nico said.

"We had a plan. That's how I ended up in this situation."

"Plan B. Yep. We need a plan B."

"What do you suggest?" Trey took a long pull from his beer.

"Clearly, I have the worst luck with women in the entire vast universe, so I'm not really the one to help come up with a way out of the mess we made. I'm thinking honesty is the only way out."

"I'm afraid it's too late for that. You should have seen the hurt look on her face." His throat went dry, remembering the way her eyes had stared at him, like a puppy left on the side of the road by its beloved best friend. "She took this as a betrayal. The one thing she thought I'd never do."

"You want me to talk to her?" Nico asked.

"If any of us do that, it should be Stone. He's her brother. She has to love him, no matter how many stupid things he does."

"Shouldn't that be how all love is? Unconditional? Even when we make mistakes, we're still loved? If she truly loves you, she'll see this for what it is. An attempt to win her heart. I truly believe that someday she'll see this as romantic."

Trey thought about that for a moment. "That's not how it works in real life."

"Sometimes it does. We don't see it that way because our fathers made their love conditional. 'Do as I say, or I can't love you.' They made those rules, and when we didn't abide by them, they rejected us."

A sadness enveloped him, crushed his hope. Maybe he was too damaged to have the life with Autumn he so craved. He drank from his beer and watched the tide creeping ever so slightly over the sand. Soon, it would be high tide. Too late to save any of the sandcastles that had taken beach dwellers all day to make. They would be trodden under the inevitable tides of the sea.

"Come on, man. Let's take a walk," Nico said.

"I don't feel like it." He tipped his beer and took another long drink.

"Let's walk up to Autumn's house. The wedding shower is probably over. Maybe she's cooled off by now. You know you won't rest easy until you've got this worked out."

"She doesn't want to see me."

"By now, she'll have softened, maybe even forgiven you. I see the way you two are together. She loves you. This is going to be fine. I promise."

He got to his feet and accepted another beer from Nico's outstretched hand. "If you say so."

"That's the spirit." Nico slapped his back as they started down the cement pathway that ran parallel to the beach. "We're fighters, remember?"

Trey shrugged and let out a long sigh. "Right now, I feel like a loser."

"No way. You're the best guy I know. Let's go get the girl."

16

AUTUMN HAD MANAGED to get through Pepper's wedding shower without bursting into tears. Still, she'd sighed with relief when the last guest left, leaving her alone with Pepper and Violet, who had stayed behind to help clean up. The party had been a success, with many laughs, great food, and crisp California chardonnay in their glasses. The three of them put away the leftover food and cleared the table and scrubbed the kitchen. Pepper and Violet chatted away, but Autumn only half listened, responding with polite murmurs when it seemed appropriate.

All day the sky had been a vivid blue, with temperatures in the mid-seventies. Autumn had opened both French doors. As they enjoyed appetizers and wine, guests had mingled in the great room and on the patio. A breeze off the water had filled the air with the salty scent of the sea.

Pepper had asked that guests bring only white elephant

gifts. They'd sat around her in the living room as she opened each package, howling with laughter when she opened a ceramic fertility goddess, his and her throw pillows edged with pink faux fur, a pregnancy test, Twister bedsheets, and a baby doll lingerie set adorned with feathers.

When they had her house put back in order, Pepper grabbed another bottle of wine and suggested they sit outside on the patio. Violet sighed with pleasure when she sat in one of the chairs arranged under the umbrella. "This is such a treat to be out of the house. No one's asked for milk or apple juice all afternoon."

Pepper lifted the cork from the bottle. "You deserve an afternoon off."

Violet, slim and fit from teaching and practicing yoga, did not look as though she had four children. She wore her light brown hair long and fixed in loose waves. Today, she wore a white sundress that showed off her brown eyes and caramel skin.

"Kyle's a great help, but he's so busy with work that some days are challenging," Violet said. "I love my brood, but it's nice to get away, too."

"What happened with Dakota's testing?" Pepper asked, referring to Violet and Kyle's son's aptitude test. His teacher suspected he was gifted and wanted him enrolled in a special school for exceptional children.

Violet frowned. "He tested off the charts. Now they're bugging us to send him to that school in the city."

"You're not thinking of it, are you?" Pepper asked.

Violet shook her head. "There's no way we would ever send him away from us. Our home is here. We believe strongly that it's better for him to stay with his family and in regular school. I should never have had him tested. It's not like we didn't already know he's smart."

"Agreed," Autumn said. "He's much too young to be sent away."

"Right?" Violet said. "I don't care how wonderful that school is, nothing replaces family."

"True." Autumn looked out to the dark sea and sighed.

Pepper crossed her arms over her chest and looked directly at Autumn. "What gives?"

"Pardon me?"

"Something's wrong." Violet's gentle brown eyes were sympathetic as she patted her on the shoulder. "You can't hide from your sisters."

The tears she'd managed to keep inside burst from her eyes. "It's Trey." She proceeded to tell them the entire story, including their wonderful night, Trey's fake profile, and their subsequent fight. "He left this morning and I haven't talked to him all day."

Violet's had widened in obvious shock. "You poor thing."

"It was Stone's idea," Pepper blurted out.

Autumn went hot with new anger. "Pepper, you knew?"

"After the fact."

"And you didn't tell me?"

"How could I?" Pepper asked. "I mean, they'd gone all in by then. Plus, Stone begged me not to. They really thought this was a good idea."

"I'm so embarrassed," Autumn said. "I feel stupid."

"No, don't feel that way," Pepper said. "None of this is your fault. Trey meant well, but how they even thought this up, I cannot fathom." Pepper's eyes sparked with her trademark fire. "They're idiots."

"Men are so dumb sometimes," Violet said.

"Especially when they're trying to avoid speaking about their feelings," Autumn said.

"That was a huge part of this," Pepper said. "Trey didn't know how to tell you how he felt. You'd shot him down when he brought it up, which spooked him."

"That, and he and the guys thought creating a scarred man would somehow show me that my own scars didn't make me unlovable."

"They're complete fools," Violet said in her usual soft tone. "I don't suppose my husband was involved?"

"No. It was just the Wolves," Autumn said.

"Good. Now I won't have to go home and throttle him," Violet said.

They all laughed, breaking the tension.

"I'm sorry, Autumn," Pepper said.

"I know you are. You didn't do anything. None of you did, other than try and help your friends figure out what was right in front of our faces all along." Autumn gazed out to the sea. High tide was coming in, destroying sandcastles and filling holes dug by happy children earlier in the day. She turned back to Pepper and Violet. "Do you know what he said to me after he accidentally told me that he was actually Art?"

"I can't imagine," Violet said.

"He asked why it was I could tell Art my deepest feelings and not him," Autumn said.

Pepper scrunched up her face and sucked in her upper lip. "Well, it's not a terrible question."

"Really?" Autumn asked. "Because I thought the more relevant question was how he could possibly think it was a good idea to lie to me."

"Well, sure. That too," Pepper said, quietly. "But it might be worth examining the other."

Violet tilted her head one way, then the other. "Was there a quality about Art that made it easier to talk to than Trey?"

Autumn considered the question. What quality had come through in the emails that had made it so easy to be intimate with Art? Or Trey. Art *was* Trey, she reminded herself. "Like Trey, writing my feelings is easier than saying them out loud. Maybe that was the trouble between us."

"And emailing took your relationship to a more intimate place," Violet said.

"In the emails, he told me he was in love with his best friend," Autumn said. "Which was me. It's all so confusing."

"I'm the queen of screwing up my life," Pepper said. "So I'm not really one to talk. However, it seems to me that there's only one thing that truly matters. You two love each other. The rest of this is noise. Can you forgive him?" Pepper asked.

"I already have. I just had to get over my initial anger," Autumn said. "Actually, in some ways it's funny."

"Romantic too," Violet said.

A movement on the far corner of the patio startled her. A man stood at the base of the stairs that led to the grass. She gasped, realizing it was the same man she'd seen the other morning. Before she could move, he ran up the stairs and crossed over to them, then lifted one side of his windbreaker to reveal a revolver.

Pepper let out a scream, but Violet seemed to be in the same state as Autumn: mute and frozen.

"Get up, nice and easy, and go into the house." His voice, coarse and low, sounded like a smoker. He had a bulbous nose and a puffy face.

Autumn glanced at Pepper, who nodded and stood, then pulled Violet from her chair. The man motioned with his free hand. "Go ahead. I'll follow you."

Pepper, practically dragging Violet, went first. Autumn followed, but in her fright, she twisted one ankle, and the open-backed sandal on her weaker side slipped from her foot. The man shoved her forward. "Leave it. Get inside."

When they were in the house, the man waved the gun at them. "Sit on the couch."

When they were seated, side by side, so close Autumn could feel Pepper trembling, he slammed the French doors closed and locked them. He turned back to them. "Good girls."

Keeping the gun and his gaze focused on them, he twisted slightly to pull the shades down.

Autumn slipped her hand into Pepper's, who did the same to Violet's.

"What do you want?" Pepper's voice sound pinched and breathless.

The man sat in one of chairs opposite the couch. He was a big man, with skinny legs and a protruding belly. She guessed he was close to sixty, with a receding hairline and stringy gray hair that hung too long in the back, as if he thought it was still 1989. "What is it you young people say?" he asked. "It's complicated?"

The three of them were quiet, waiting.

"Do you have any whiskey?" he asked.

Autumn nodded and pointed to the cabinet where she kept the liquor. Trey had found it for her, a farmhouse cupboard from the 1800s that he'd refinished and painted white. "I have scotch, not whiskey." For Trey and the other Wolves.

Trey. What if this man killed her and she never got to say she was sorry?

They watched as he went to the cupboard and picked up the bottle of scotch and a tumbler, all with one hand. The other continued to hold the gun. Pepper's eyes were narrowed, as if contemplating jumping him. Autumn shook her head no. *Not yet. Wait until he's drunk.*

"What's your name?" Autumn asked. She knew from years with her father that it was best to ask drunks questions. Get them talking about themselves. Drinking and talking would weaken them.

The man sat back down in the chair. "Stanley Tipton." He indicated with a jut of his chin toward Violet. "You might recognize my last name. My daughter worked for you."

"Oh my God," Violet whispered. "You're Mel's father?"

"That's right. My baby girl. You and your husband killed her."

"She kidnapped our children. The police killed her, not us," Violet said, her voice stronger now.

"Who pulled the trigger is not important," Stanley said. "You and Kyle Hicks killed her. And now I've come for revenge."

An icy dread rushed through Autumn's veins. Pepper's grip on her hand tightened.

Violet made a sound between a whimper and a gasp before she exploded with a rush of words. "Revenge? Your daughter stole my three-year-old son and infant out of their beds. She took them to the middle of nowhere and threatened to hurt them if my husband didn't run away with her. What did we do that deserves revenge?"

"Your husband is a known womanizer. I did my homework on him. He seduced my baby girl and then dumped her. What was she supposed to do?"

To Autumn's surprise, Violet didn't back down. She leaned forward slightly and practically spat words at him. "The entire time she worked for us, she did nothing but hit on Kyle. He had no interest in her. The two of us were falling in love then. She was nothing to him but an employee."

Pepper shifted slightly. She must be thinking the same thing as Autumn. Maybe Violet should take it easy. They were being held by an enraged, half-drunk man with a gun.

"Wives are always the last to know," Stanley said. "Everyone with half a brain knows that men like Kyle Hicks sleep with their nannies and lie about it."

"You've got this wrong," Violet said, softer now. "I don't know what she told you, but it's all lies. She was sick, deluded."

"That's not the way I see it," he said. "And the three of you are going to pay for the pain you've caused me. My baby's gone. They killed her with a bullet. My perfect girl. I'm going to kill you three in just the same way."

"What do these two have to do with any of this?" Violet asked. "Let them go."

His gaze lingered on Autumn, then moved to Pepper. "It's simple. Your husband loves his sister and brother. Stone Hickman loves this one. When you're all three dead, Kyle suffers. In one fell swoop, all the women he loves are gone. Maybe then he'll realize what he did to me."

"You'll go to jail," Pepper said. "Stone and Kyle will make sure of that."

He took a slug of his drink. "I can't go to jail if I'm dead."

Think of something. Anything.

But nothing came. Only a dark surety that they weren't making it out of here alive.

17

T rey

TREY AND NICO walked in silence until they reached the southern end of the beach where a line of houses, including Autumn's, were built along the coastline. Lights shone from most of the houses and patios. Through open windows Trey could see people watching television or having dinner. A few were out on their patios and lifted a hand in greeting as the men passed by. As they drew nearer to Autumn's place, Trey noticed a half-empty wine bottle and three glasses on the table. The patio lights were on, but no one was in sight. The shower was probably over by now. Maybe Autumn was inside cleaning up? The shades were drawn, but the lights in the living room and kitchen were on. Strange. Why would she have closed the shades if there were still guests? It wasn't like her to leave wine and glasses outside if she and her guests had gone inside.

Trey stopped at the edge of the patio.

"Do you see that?" Trey pointed at the table.

"It looks like she had guests and they were interrupted."

Something shiny caught his eye. Upon closer look, he saw it was the rhinestone on a sandal. Autumn's sandal. He knew that pair. They were the ones with the rhinestones fixed on the top strap. Why would there be only one? It's not as though someone kicked off one shoe and left the other one on. And it was by the door, as if it had fallen off. As if someone shoved her.

Call it instinct or a premonition, but fear crawled up the back of his spine. He thought of the strange man who'd lurked outside her house and followed Pepper. "Something's not right. Call Rafael. Tell him to get down here."

Rafael, former cop, would be good backup. He peeked around to the front of the house. He lowered his voice. "That's Violet's car. I saw her earlier at the store with Pepper. They were on their way to the shower. That means they're still there."

Nico didn't answer. He was already on the phone with Rafael. After explaining the situation, he nodded in response to whatever Rafael said on the other end of the phone. "Yeah, okay. You're right. I'll do that. Right. Okay." He hung up, muttering. "He's coming but said to call 911. He and Stone were together. They're both coming."

While Nico called 911, Trey tiptoed up to the side of the house to see if he could get a glimpse into the house. What he saw chilled him. Autumn, Pepper, and Violet sat together on the couch. A man stood over them with a gun.

He ran to Nico. "Tell the cops not to turn their sirens on. He's got a gun on them."

18

 utumn

STANLEY HAD FINISHED his drink and poured himself another. This was good. *He's gathering courage. The more he drinks, the better. Or worse.*

She could see her phone in the charger on the kitchen counter. If only she could reach it. While she was thinking about how she could get it to teleport over to her, she saw a shadow move just outside the kitchen window that hung over the sink. No one walked around the side of the house except for her and Trey. That's where he'd suggested they put a hose, so she could easily water the pots on her patio. Was there someone there? She purposely took her gaze back to Stanley, not wanting him to follow her eyes.

Stanley was pacing and drinking and muttering to himself under his breath. Violet had gone completely white, and tears leaked from her eyes. Autumn knew her thoughts. She was thinking about her four children and leaving them without a mother and a devastated father. A glance at Pepper told Autumn she was in strategy mode. The muscle in her cheek pulsed, and her eyes were fixed in her own lap. That mind of hers must be tripping over itself trying to figure out how to get them out of here.

She detected further movement outside the kitchen window. This time she glimpsed a shock of light brown curls. She knew those curls. Trey. Her heart leaped with hope. He'd come for them. If he'd seen through the window, he knew the situation.

Outside on the patio, shadows moved behind the shades. Cops. Trey had called the cops. She looked at Stanley. He was over by the liquor cabinet again, filling his glass. Autumn squeezed Pepper's hand and tilted her head toward the west. Pepper moved just her eyes in that direction, then back again.

Autumn would distract him. Keep him talking so he wouldn't see that the house was most likely being surrounded. She prayed the booze would aid her efforts. "Stanley, are you going to kill us here at my house?"

He fixed crazed, beady eyes on her. "Where else?"

"I don't know. I've never killed anyone before," Autumn said. "Have you?"

"What? Of course not," Stanley said. His words were starting to slur. "Never had a reason to before now."

Autumn motioned for him to come nearer. "I understand about revenge. Really, I do. But wouldn't it make more sense to go after the police officers who killed your girl?"

"I already went over that. Kyle Hicks is responsible." He pointed the gun directly at her. "You're first." Sure she was dead, Autumn buried her face in her arms and scrunched her eyes closed and waited. Then came a terrible, deafening *boom*. Pepper and Violet screamed. Glass shattered. A sharp pain pierced her neck. She'd been shot in the neck.

Another shot blasted through the room. More screaming. She felt her neck, and her hand came away covered with sticky blood.

"Autumn," Pepper screamed. "Autumn's hurt."

She opened her eyes. Stanley was on the ground, bleeding from the head. A pool of blood seeped into her light gray rug. Four cops rushed into the room, guns raised. But they hadn't shot Stanley, she realized. The shot had come from the kitchen window. Rafael stood there with a rifle in his hands. He'd been a sharpshooter, she remembered then. The cops had arrived a split second too late. If not for him, she would be dead. Or was she dead?

Paramedics rushed in next. Two lifted Stanley onto a stretcher. Two others turned to her. One crouched down and examined her neck. "A piece of glass," she heard him say to his partner.

"That's all it is, sweetheart," he said to her.

"I'm going to pull it out and bandage you up, okay?" the other one said.

Everything went into slow motion. Stone and Kyle ran into the room. Stone lifted Pepper from the couch and carried her away from the blood and the dead man on the stretcher and into the kitchen. Kyle grabbed Violet and sat on the coffee table with her in his lap and reached out to Autumn. "I thought I lost you both," Kyle said.

"Autumn's hurt," Violet said, sounding dazed.

"Not bad," Autumn said. "Just a nick."

"It was Mel's dad. He came for revenge," Violet said.

"Oh God. No." Kyle's skin had turned green. He turned his head to look at the dead man on the stretcher. "Rafael killed him. He can't hurt us now."

Cops ushered Kyle and Violet outside, leaving Autumn alone with the paramedics.

Cops and paramedics seemed to be everywhere. They

covered Stanley with a sheet and carried him away on the stretcher. She turned away, afraid she might be sick.

The paramedics continued to work on her. She was too shocked and numb now to understand what they were doing, even though they talked her through each move. "Tugging the glass out now, sweetheart. Pressing this to the wound to stop the bleeding. Superficial cut, doll, nothing to worry over."

Autumn's gaze darted around the room, searching for Trey. Where was he? She needed him. "Trey," she whispered. "I need Trey." Her voice rose in volume and pitch. "Can you get Trey for me?"

The paramedic nodded. "You're almost fixed up." He taped a bandage to her neck. "All good. We can find your Trey now."

Suddenly, Trey was there. He knelt at her side in the blood and brains of the dead man. "I'm here. I'm here. They had questions for me. The police, that is." He wrapped his arms around her legs and dropped his head into her lap. "Thank God you're all right."

She stared at him, unable to focus. "They said it was a piece of glass."

Trey's eyes were wet. "That's right. The mirror shattered. That's all. A piece cut your neck. When he tried to shoot you, he misfired and got the mirror."

She held up her hand to show him. "But there was so much blood."

"It's a cut, but nothing serious." She'd never seen him look pale before now. "The paramedics said you're fine. You can come with me outside."

She'd started to shake violently. "I think I'm going to be sick."

"I'll take you outside." He sprang to his feet. She couldn't look away from the blood that stuck to his skin and the hairs of his shins. Bile crept up from her stomach into the back of her throat.

Trey lifted her in his arms and ran with her out to the patio and down the stairs, across the boardwalk to the sand. When they reached the edge of the incoming surf, he lowered her gently onto the sand. She knelt on her knees and vomited once, then again. All the while he held her hair and caressed her back.

When she was done, she collapsed on the sand, too tired to move. The surf came and carried the remnants of her stomach away.

She gasped for air as another wave came, splashing over her and Trey. "Are you okay?" he asked.

"Yes, yes. Fine now."

Trey stood and stumbled toward deeper water. She watched as he scrubbed his bare legs, her thoughts a tangled mess of questions. Did the blood darken the water? Were there sharks this close? Would they detect the smell of blood and come for Trey? No, they wouldn't be this close to shore. The danger was over. The human shark was under a sheet. He wouldn't be back to hurt them.

Behind them, the sounds of additional sirens and shouts of the officers doing whatever it was they did in a situation like this were muffled by the cresting waves that crashed to shore. Flashing lights from the cop cars and ambulance lit the beach like strobe lights in a disco.

Another wave washed over her bottom half. She stretched her legs out long and waited for the next rush of salt water. The sea she'd waited a lifetime to feel against her skin restored her. She'd known it would. Here in the darkness, with the first stars the only witness to her scars, she breathed in the briny scent and lifted her face to the heavens. She whispered a prayer of thanks. *Thank you for my life. For my family and my friends. And for Trey.*

She realized then, too, that she'd lived in the shadows of her own life, hidden and ashamed. Coming close to death, she understood how much she wanted to live, not in the dim dusk but in the full light of day. Hiding simply because her outside appearance was flawed made a mockery of the life God had granted her. Our bodies were simply the vessels that carried our souls.

Trey waded through the water toward her. Last night his hands and mouth had lovingly explored every inch of her. He'd asked for the light to remain on, but she'd said no. Again, shrouding herself. He loved her as she was, not how she wished to be.

Trey loved her. He wanted to spend his life with her. Joy surged through her. She would have him by her side for the rest of her life, making a family and memories. He was her dream come true.

Trey dropped beside her. The lights reflected in his eyes. "You okay?"

"I think so." She'd meant to sound strong, but traces of the earlier tremor remained.

He put his arm around her waist and gathered her close. She rested her head on his shoulder and pressed herself into him. The heat of his body warmed her despite the cool night air and the frigid waters of the Pacific. They sat, motionless for a few more cycles of the ebbing sea, until the waves had stolen the fear and adrenaline, leaving her wrung out and chilled.

"I thought I was going to die." She touched the bandage on her neck. "I truly did. How did you know we were there?"

"Nico and I were on the beach, talking about you and what a mess I'd made of everything. He talked me into walking up to your house to see if you'd cooled off so we could talk. When we got there, I saw the wine and your sandal and knew something was wrong. I think it was pure instinct that drove me to look in the window."

"I saw you. Later, Rafael."

"Nico called him, then the police. He and Stone were up at

Rafael's house. He grabbed his rifle and jumped in Stone's truck. He said they drove here like a bat out of hell. Stone's former experience driving a tank apparently paid off. I couldn't believe how fast they got here."

A sudden thought took her breath away. "Will Rafael be in trouble with the police?"

"Nah. They're questioning him now, but it'll be fine. This is a small town. It's obvious what was happening."

"He's the father of the psycho nanny," she said. "It had nothing to do with my mom. Thank God." Her voice cracked.

He made a soothing noise and held her tighter. "It's over now. You guys don't have to worry any longer about any of that ever again. It's time to move on from the past, once and for all."

"You and Nico were so quick and clever."

He chuckled. "For a couple of flaky artist types, we did pretty well. We knew Rafael and Stone were the ones to call."

"If you hadn't come, we might have... A second later and it would've been too late." She drew her legs up and wrapped her arms around her knees. He continued to hold her tightly around the waist.

"It's going to take me some time to stop thinking about that," he said. "If Nico hadn't talked me into walking over to your house, we might not be having this conversation."

"You came for me, even though you weren't sure how I would react. You've always been here for me, Trey, even when I was too scared to see it. When I think about the last year and all the times you've been right there to comfort me, encourage me. And then tonight—there you were again at just the right moment. I'm sorry it took me such a long time to realize that you could actually love me. It's so obvious now. You're the only man who ever asked me to dance."

"If I have my way, we'll dance every night in our kitchen."

"Our kitchen. I like the sound of that," she said.

"I'm sorry about everything," he said. "Please forgive me."

"Don't be. You did what you thought you had to do to win my heart."

"I shouldn't have lied to you. The whole thing spun out of control. I was torn between wanting to know more about you and doing what was right. Please tell me I haven't killed any feelings of love you have for me."

The pain in his voice moved her to tears. She swiped at her wet cheeks with her frozen fingers as she spoke. "Nothing could kill how I feel about you. Not even a ridiculous idea by the Wolves to help their guy get his girl." She laughed through her tears. "Dumb but sweet at the same time."

"No one ever said the scrappy Wolves of Cliffside Bay were the smartest guys ever born."

She laughed again. "You were smart enough to know how to save us."

"Dumb luck. Like finding you in the first place. I'm sorry I'm not the best at expressing myself." He thumped his chest. "But it's all in here. I'll work to get better. For you I'd do anything."

"When I was sitting there with a gun pointed at me, it seemed ridiculous that I'd been mad at you for trying to love me. Nothing matters but us. We're together now, like we've been from the start. The path that got us here doesn't mean anything."

"It was wrong of me to use the information that came to me through your emails to manipulate you into swimming or letting your mom into your life. But the more I learned about what hurt you or what you were afraid of and what you wanted for your life, the more I wanted to give it to you. I'm sorry. So sorry. At the same time, you need to understand I'll do whatever it takes to make your life better. I'm a guy, so sometimes how I go about things might not be exactly right. But I'll never stop trying."

She swallowed against the lump in her throat. "Taking me swimming was exactly right. If you hadn't pushed me, I'd still be hiding from you. You were right about something else, too. I did open up to Art in a way I couldn't to you. There was such safety in writing to him because I didn't think there was anything to lose. He was a stranger, or so I thought." She nudged him in the ribs, playfully.

He groaned and laid his chin on top of her head.

"Being raw and honest makes the risk of losing someone you love greater," she said. "Or so we think, anyway. I believe that's why most people keep so much inside, even from the person they love the most. I'd like us to be different. If that means we write letters to each other sometimes, then I say we do just that."

"Like love letters?" he asked.

"I guess so. Or feelings we find hard to express out loud but that we want to share with each other."

"As long as you don't think it's cheating, I'm all for it."

"We can make our own rules," she said. "Our love story is ours to write."

"We've certainly started out unconventionally."

He kissed her as a wave came, harder and closer than before. She shivered from the damp and the nearness of the man she loved.

"They're going to want your statement. But first, you need a hot shower." Trey rose to his feet, then lifted her into his arms. He walked with her across the sand to the chaos of her patio. She was oblivious to all the noise and the ugliness. Later, she would have to relive it for the police, but for now she was content. Trey was her world. He was all she needed now and forever. She nestled her head into his neck and let him lead the way.

19

T rey

A MONTH LATER, Trey finished hanging a new decorative mirror over Autumn's couch. The glass of the first one had been shattered and the brushed nickel frame dented. She'd chosen to replace it with a replica of the one she'd had. He'd picked the right one, she'd said, the first time. And she wasn't about to let a madman ruin his lovely design.

Never one to argue with his client or his girlfriend, he'd ordered the mirror from one of his favorite shops and asked for a rush delivery, then did the same for the destroyed area rug. The sooner he had her place back together the better. She didn't need a bloodstained rug and broken mirror to remind her of the horrific events of that night. Despite the rushed order, the pieces had taken weeks to arrive, finally showing up just in time for their beach party.

He stood back to make sure the mirror was straight. Satisfied, he adjusted the coffee table a few inches to the right. Autumn came in just as he placed the vase and bowl back on the table.

"They look great," she said, shifting a bag of groceries onto her other hip. "Like nothing ever happened."

They'd had a long discussion the night after it all went down about whether her love of the house had been tainted by the incident. She assured him that once everything was back to normal, she would be fine.

He took the bag from her and gave her a quick kiss. "I think most everything is ready for the party."

They were hosting a beach party that afternoon and had invited the whole gang, including both their mothers. Before everyone arrived, however, Trey had a plan. A plan that involved a ring and some champagne.

The last month together had been the best of his life. He'd basically moved in with her, spending every night here doing to her all the things he'd wanted to do since the day he met her.

He arranged the cheeses and crackers she'd brought home from the store while she filled a couple of bowls with chips. Everyone was bringing a side dish to go with burgers and dogs from the grill. Soon, the house and patio would be filled with adults and kids. Happy chaos.

After everything was ready, he took her hand and drew her outside to the patio, then asked her to walk with him down to the beach. He wanted to ask her to marry him on the spot where they'd sat that night and where they'd spent many more moments in the days following. Whether it was the near-death experience or the security that his love provided her, Autumn, like a butterfly, had decided she would no longer deny herself the pleasure of the beach. The very next day, she came downstairs dressed only in her bathing suit and asked him to join her for a swim in the ocean. After that, she'd asked Lisa if she could swim in her pool for exercise once in a while. Being Lisa, she'd given Autumn a key to their gate and said to come over anytime. Almost every morning, Autumn had woken early to swim laps in the Sotos' pool.

When she came home one afternoon with a pile of shorts and short skirts, he knew the transformation was complete.

Today, she wore a short cover-up over her bathing suit. Her skin had tanned and the muscles in her thighs and arms had tightened from her daily swims. She looked hotter than ever. Yes, her scars were still visible, as well as her misshapen calf. However, she now moved with self-confidence and ease.

She'd suggested the party as a way to show everyone her legs at once. "Get it over with, so it no longer has power over me," she'd said. They'd since started calling it the "big reveal."

Holding hands, they walked together to their favorite spot on the beach. Swimming had given her more strength and stamina as well, which meant she no longer used her cane. The biggest difference, however, was how she could maneuver on even dry sand now. He still slowed his pace some, but not much.

She smiled at him as they walked. "I used to be jealous of people doing this. Look at me now." She tapped her temple. "So much of it was mental. I missed out on so much."

"You're making the most of it now."

When they reached the edge of wet sand, he stopped. "Sit with me?"

"Sure."

They sat side by side, looking out to the ocean. The weather was somewhere in the midseventies and the air still. Around them, people sunbathed and children dug in the sand. A couple of teenage boys tossed a football back and forth. A mother, pushed by the small hands of her children, shrieked as a wave broke over her.

He turned slightly to look at his beautiful Autumn. She

wore a straw hat, with a long braid down her back. Sparkly green stones the same color as her eyes hung from her ears. He kissed her neck just under her ear. "You're beautiful today."

She cupped his cheek with her hand. "You're not so bad yourself."

He reached into his cargo pants and pulled out the box where a princess-cut solitaire waited.

Her eyes flew open and stayed that way, as if invisible toothpicks held them open. "Trey. What is this?"

He smiled and lifted the box. The diamond sparkled under the sun. "This is a ring. One I'm hoping you'll accept."

She stared at the ring for a second before her gaze swung back to his face. "Oh my gosh. This is really happening?"

He shifted onto his knees, then to only one. "From the first lamp we chose together, I've been in love with you. Will you marry me?"

She tilted her hat up to look him in the eyes. "Yes, I'll be your wife."

He took her hand and slipped the diamond over her ring finger. They kissed and the tears that dampened their cheeks ran together like the rivers did with the sea.

* * *

THAT NIGHT, after he'd loved her thoroughly, she fell asleep. A three-quarter moon shone in through the window, lighting his way as Trey slid from the bed and into the living room, where his laptop waited on the coffee table. He opened it and leaned into the corner of the couch. Then, he typed his first love note to the woman who'd agreed to be his wife.

Dear Autumn,

You're sleeping in the bedroom. I've slipped away to write you a note on the night of our engagement. This is the first of many love letters I'll write to you. There'll be many other occasions as special as tonight. The births of our children; family gatherings; weddings; graduations. But perhaps none of them will be as meaningful as tonight, because this is the start of everything. The beginning of our life as partners. You've been my best friend and confidante, my playmate, and now my lover. All those together are the meaning of the word *wife*.

When you said yes to my proposal earlier today, my heart was so full and yet, as you know, I can't seem to express my emotions in the moment. I wish I could. Maybe someday I'll be able to. For now, I'll say them here, in this first love letter. What started out as friendship, based on mutual respect and shared interests, grew into an epic love. You've given my life joy and hope. You inspire me with your goodness and intelligence. You came to me when I'd closed off all ideas of finding love. Yet there you were. My perfect match. My soul mate.

The moon hovers over the sea as I write this, illuminating the waves we both love so much. Each ebb and flow of the surf reminds me that time moves forward. Each precious moment with you is over the second it arrives. I wish I could catch each one to enjoy again and again. Instead, we'll store them in our memories and in our love letters. Someday, we'll tell our children and their children of our love story. The one we wrote together.

The best love story of all. You and me.

Love,

Trey

HE CLOSED the computer and went back upstairs to his girl. Autumn murmured his name as he curled up next to her. He closed his eyes and breathed in the scent of her hair and listened to her easy breathing that seemed in harmony with the waves that crashed outside the cottage. Ebbs and flows, high tides and low, he would be wherever she was.

THE END

ABOUT THE AUTHOR

HOMETOWNS
and HEARTSTRINGS

USA Today Bestselling author Tess Thompson writes small-town romances and historical fiction. She started her writing career in fourth grade when she wrote a story about an orphan who opened a pizza restaurant. Oddly enough, her first novel, "Riversong" is about an adult orphan who opens a restaurant. Clearly, she's been obsessed with food and words for a long time now.

With a degree from the University of Southern California in theatre, she's spent her adult life studying story, word craft, and character. Since 2011, she's published 20 novels and 3 novellas. Most days she spends at her desk chasing her daily word count or rewriting a terrible first draft.

She currently lives in a suburb of Seattle, Washington with her husband, the hero of her own love story, and their Brady Bunch clan of two sons, two daughters and five cats. Yes, that's four kids and five cats.

Tess loves to hear from you. Drop her a line at tess@tthompsonwrites.com or visit her website at https://tesswrites.com/

ALSO BY TESS THOMPSON

Cliffside Bay Series

Traded: Brody and Kara

Deleted: Jackson and Maggie

Jaded: Zane and Honor

Marred: Kyle and Violet

Tainted: Lance and Mary

The Christmas of Cats and Babies, A Cliffside Bay Novella

Missed: Rafael and Lisa

A Christmas Wedding, A Cliffside Bay Novella

Healed: Stone and Pepper

Scarred: Trey and Autumn

Jilted: Nico and Sophie (coming November 2019)

Departed: David and Sara (coming early 2020)

Blue Mountain Series

Blue Midnight

Blue Moon

Blue Ink

Blue Thread (coming early 2020)

River Valley Series

Riversong

Riverbend

Riverstar

Riversnow

Riverstorm

Historical Fiction

Duet for Three Hands

Miller's Secret

Legley Bay Series

Caramel and Magnolias

Tea and Primroses

Novellas

The Santa Trial

Made in the USA
San Bernardino,
CA